# LIFE
## AND OTHER
## NEAR-DEATH
## EXPERIENCES

# ALSO BY CAMILLE PAGÁN

*The Art of Forgetting*

# LIFE

## AND OTHER
## NEAR-DEATH
## EXPERIENCES

*A Novel*

# CAMILLE PAGÁN

LAKE UNION
PUBLISHING

Text copyright © 2015 Camille Pagán

Published by Lake Union Publishing, Seattle

www.apub.com

Amazon, the Amazon logo, and Lake Union Publishing are trademarks of Amazon.com, Inc., or its affiliates.

ISBN-13: 9781503946002 (hardcover)
ISBN-10: 1503946002 (hardcover)
ISBN-13: 9781503945623 (paperback)
ISBN-10: 1503945626 (paperback)

Cover design by David Drummond

Printed in the United States of America

*For Laurel*

# ONE

It was all supposed to be very *Eat, Pray, Die*, but I promise I'm not spoiling anything when I say it didn't quite work out that way. Take my diagnosis, for example; Dr. Sanders couldn't even bring himself to say the word.

"I'm afraid it's malignant," he said from behind his desk.

"Malignant?" I asked blankly. It had been a long day and I'd had trouble convincing my boss to let me out of work early, even though the nurse who called said it was absolutely necessary that I see Dr. Sanders today.

"Cancerous," he said, his thin lips all but disappearing into his mouth.

"You're not saying *I have cancer*, are you?" I asked, attempting to help him clarify—as surely this was not what he meant. After all, just before he cut the golf ball–size lump out of my stomach, he said he was certain it was a fatty tumor. The surgery was just a precaution.

"Um. I'm afraid so." He peered cautiously at the paper in his hand, as though he didn't deliver bad news for a living.

"I don't understand," I said.

"Elizabeth," he said, reaching forward to take my hand—which I quickly jerked back, as I'm not big into people invading my personal space, not to mention he had more or less just told me via body language that I was a goner. "You have subcutaneous panniculitis-like T-cell lymphoma. This type of cancer is extremely rare, but when it does come up, we see it most often in individuals in their thirties, such as yourself. I'm afraid it tends to be aggressive. You'll have to—"

This was around the point at which I stopped listening and started going through a rapid-fire version of the Kübler-Ross model of grief. *Denial*: No one calls me Elizabeth; my name is Libby. Dr. Sanders is obviously talking about someone else. *Anger*: He said he was sure the lump was nothing! I'm going to give him a reason to be grateful he's been paying through the nose for malpractice insurance. *Bargaining*: If I run a marathon to raise money for cancer orphans, not only will I live, I'll become such a raging success that Oprah herself will promote my memoir. I'll start a movement, complete with races for the cure and rubber awareness-raising wristbands in turquoise, which will become the national color of—what the heck was my cancer called again? *Depression*: I can't race for a cure because I don't run. I don't even exercise, which is probably why my body is riddled with overproducing disease spores. I'm going to bite it before I see forty. *Acceptance*—

Unfortunately, *acceptance* was essentially identical to *depression*.

I was going to die. Just like my mother.

Dr. Sanders kept yammering, oblivious to the fact that I was looking right through him. "So, chemo. I'd like you to—"

"No," I said.

"What do you mean, no? Elizabeth, your best chance for survival is to try to zap this thing as fast and hard as possible. I am sure you've seen the worst-case scenarios for chemo, but today, particularly for lymphomas, treatment is manageable. And, if I may say so, the difficulty of treatment is preferable to . . . well, not getting treated."

"I'm not going to do it," I said. "I don't want chemo, or radiation, or any of it. How long will I live without it?"

"I'm sorry?"

"You should be; you just handed me a death sentence. Now, how long will I live without treatment?"

He looked befuddled. "I'd like to run a CT scan to see if the cancer has spread to other areas, but given the cellular activity in your tumor . . . well, prognosis can range from six months to . . . um, it's difficult to say. Although certainly there have been some successful cases . . ."

"Okay then," I said, grabbing my bag off the back of the chair. "I'll be in touch."

"Elizabeth! I'd really like you to meet with a counselor—"

I left before he had a chance to finish, the taste of cold pennies on my tongue, as though I'd consented to chemo and already started injecting liquid poison into my bloodstream. Oncologists, nurses, radiologists, palliative care specialists: I was all too familiar with the cancer routine, and I wasn't interested. Not one bit.

My twin brother, Paul, once told me that there's healthy denial, and then there's LibbyLand. His theory is that in order to function, most people have to ignore reality, or at least most of it. Otherwise, all of the horrible things in life—child slavery, acts of war, the pesticides jam-packed into every other bite of food you put in your mouth, knowing that you're a day closer to dying when you open your eyes each morning—would be so overwhelming that no one would ever get out of bed. "But for you, Libby," said Paul, "the whole world is filled with kittens and rainbows and happy endings. It's very cute and probably helps you sleep at night. I just worry about you sometimes."

I would be insulted if it weren't Paul, who knew me better than anyone else—better than Tom, my husband, probably better than I knew myself. And I knew Paul better than anyone, too, including the fact that he didn't particularly enjoy his proclivity for catastrophizing, even if it did make him a highly functioning type triple-A human being with an unsettling ability to forecast market meltdowns and other disasters. He and I were a good combo that way.

That's why it was going to be such a bummer to tell him that while I'd been watching my kittens defecate all over the rainbow, I'd taken a wrong turn at happy and run smack-dab into a dead end.

As I speed walked through Dr. Sanders's office and out to the elevator, I found myself thinking about funerals, as one will do when one learns one is not long for this world. I'd gone to a single funeral in my life, but afterward, I swore I would never attend another.

Because that funeral had been my mother's.

At ten years old, Paul and I were too embarrassed to hold hands in front of other people, so we huddled together in a corner of the funeral home: he clasping the back of my dress, me grabbing at the corner of his suit. We watched our father greet this person, and reminisce with that one. Occasionally someone would approach the two of us to offer pat condolences, then quickly move on, all parties relieved that what needed doing was done. The chemical-scented air was suffocating. An eternity passed, then another. Finally someone gently pushed us to the front of the room where our mother's body lay.

The funeral home was decorated like a small chapel, and we were instructed to sit in the front pew beside our father, entirely too close to the casket. I remember thinking that I could not feel my feet, and my hands and face were tingling as well, though my ears burned from the knowledge that everyone seated behind us was trying, and failing, not to stare at the remains of our family.

Our pastor took his place at the podium and began to pray, asking God to welcome "Phillip's wife, and Paul and Elizabeth's mother" to her heavenly home. I had a different request for the head of the Holy

Trinity: I prayed that the tingling was a sign I was seriously unwell and would join my mother in very short order. I begged God to take me to her—the pre-cancer her, with a smile free of pain, reaching for my hand—because the only place I would ever want to be again was wherever she was.

My father said some words. A few other people spoke as well; I don't remember who they were or what they said. And then the room was empty, and Paul was pulling at my dress, harder now, telling me it was time.

The casket was only partially open, as though the half of my mother's body that ultimately killed her was not suitable for viewing. I told myself that if I didn't look directly at her, none of it would be real, that this terrible experience was actually happening to someone else.

But I had to, because it was the last time in the world that I would ever see her face.

Even in death, skin coated in pancake makeup, cheeks over-rouged and now sunken when they'd been swollen and stretched in hospice just days before, she was the woman who had wiped my tears when I needed comforting, and cut my sandwiches into small squares just as I liked, and told me she would love me forever and ever and still even longer than that.

She was lovely. And I knew as I reached down to touch her softly, one more time, that anything that happened next in life simply could not be as unbearable as this good-bye.

I expected my father to scold me for touching her, but for the first time that day, he had let himself go and was weeping on his knees, oblivious to his children.

Paul was crying beside me. Now he took my hand and held it so tight that it hurt. I didn't tell him to stop. We were just beginning to realize we were motherless children, and that we were all we had left.

By the time my father, Paul, and I got in the car to drive across the state for the burial, I had decided I'd had enough of funerals for one lifetime. It was a vow I almost kept: when distant relatives passed away, or a friend's parent, or a colleague, I sent large bouquets and vague apologies for my absence.

But as the elevator doors outside Dr. Sanders's office opened and I stepped into the plummeting metal box that would deposit me in the hospital lobby, it occurred to me that I could not keep the promise I had made to myself twenty-four years ago.

I would attend more than one funeral, after all. It just so happened that the second would be my own.

# TWO

Then this happened:

"Tom? Tom?" I was crying so hard that my contacts had fallen out, and I couldn't really tell if the blob hovering around the kitchen island was my husband.

The torrent of tears started the minute I left Dr. Sanders's office; it was a miracle that I managed to make it from the maze-like medical building on Lake Shore Drive to Michigan Avenue and flag down a cab without being flattened by a bus. At nearly five o'clock on a Monday evening, it took half an hour to make it to our condo in Bucktown, and as every quarter mile passed, I became more distraught. When I thought of my life—as in the big-picture, full-screen version—this was not how the story ended. I still needed to learn Spanish and quit my job and see the world and maybe adopt a child or two (I couldn't seem to get pregnant, for reasons my ob-gyn had yet to identify). The ashy particulates in the urn that would rest on our fireplace, which was soon to become just Tom's fireplace (sob!), were supposed to be at least seventy years old, not thirty-four.

"Marriage troubles?" the cabdriver asked at one point, handing me a tissue. This made me cry even harder, because my beloved Tom would soon learn he was about to become a widower. Tom! So loving, so brave. He wouldn't let me see him cry, but I could just imagine how I would wake in the middle of the night to find him weeping silently in front of his computer (he had insomnia and was often up until two or three in the morning). I felt worse for him than almost anyone, except for my dad and Paul, as they had already lived through my mother's death. Even now, her absence was as palpable as a newly missing limb; all these years later, the three of us still hadn't learned to balance or ignore the phantom ache.

"Libby? Are you okay?" Tom rushed at me, taking me by the shoulders. Thank goodness, he *was* home. Tom was employed by a small architecture and urban-planning firm that didn't adhere to strict office hours, so he often left as early as three or four in the afternoon to go wander around the city, then finished the rest of his work in our home office in the evening.

"Tom!" I wailed. "How could this happen?"

"Libby . . . ," he said cautiously, and let me go. This caught me off guard; wasn't he supposed to be stroking my hair and comforting me? "You know, don't you?"

"Of *course* I know!" My head was spinning. I knew, but how did Tom? Weren't there laws specifying that you couldn't share a person's medical history without her consent? Although I *had* put his info down on that privacy sheet I filled out before surgery. Maybe Dr. Sanders was alarmed about the way I'd fled his office and had called ahead to warn Tom.

"Oh boy," he said. "I didn't want you to find out this way. Did O'Reilly spill the beans?" he asked, referring to his best friend, who had been known by his surname as long as I could remember.

How would O'Reilly know I was dying of cancer? I was officially confused. I wiped my eyes on my jacket sleeve, then fumbled around in the drawer under the kitchen island, where I kept an extra pair of glasses. After jabbing myself with a pair of scissors, I located the glasses and put them on. One of the arms was missing, so they were slightly askew on my nose, and the prescription wasn't quite right anymore, but they were effective enough that I could see Tom's face was, well, mildly terrified. My heart lurched in my chest: perhaps he would not be quite as brave as I'd originally anticipated. *Be strong, Libby,* I commanded myself. *Tom needs you.*

"It's just that I've been seeing a new therapist . . . ," he said.

Was he? Good. I didn't think Tom was really the type to visit a shrink, but at least it would help him deal with my dying.

"Libby, did you hear me?" he asked, staring at me intently.

I blinked. "What? No. What did you say?"

"I think I might be . . . gay."

A dizzy spell came over me, and I felt my backbone smash against the edge of the cold stone counter. "Oh my," I said, reaching out for Tom's arm.

"Libby," he said, pulling me to him, "I am so terribly sorry. Are you okay?"

"I'm—I'm fine," I said, because that was what I always said when someone asked me this question.

As Tom looked down at me, his eyes were moist with unshed tears. "Thank you," he said, his voice warbly. "Thank you for saying that. You knew for a long time now, didn't you? Deep down, at least."

Up until that point, everything he'd said had been hitting me without my actually absorbing it. Now it all sank in at once. Was he nucking futs? I knew global warming was killing polar bears, the Chinese population blew past one billion several years ago, and *rhythms* was the longest word without a vowel in the English language. I did not know, however, that my childhood sweetheart, the man I had loved for nearly twenty years (twenty years!) was sexually attracted to men.

"No, no—no," I said, pulling my head back in a way that made my neck disappear, a phenomenon I was aware of only because my boss Jackie was always telling me not to do it after she made yet another outrageous request ("Libby, buy a cream-colored, brown-spotted alpaca throw for me on your nonexistent lunch hour, and please stop doing that thing with your neck because you look like a turtle, okay?").

"I'm not saying this is the end of our marriage," Tom said, hugging me tight. "I love you so much; you know that. It's just that—well, I'm trying to figure out who I am. This is something I've been struggling with for years, and I'm—Libby? Libby, what are you doing?"

I wasn't sure I could answer that question, but I had unlatched myself from him and found myself rifling through yet another drawer, this one where we kept our silverware, which still looked as shiny as it did when we selected it for our wedding registry eight years ago. I took a fork out and held it up to admire it. It sparkled in the light of the dining room chandelier—pardon me, *light sculpture*—that Tom spent a fortune on, even though we were still paying off his graduate school loans.

"It's just that—" I said, then brought the fork down on his hand, which he'd placed on the marble island.

"*Gahhh!* Why did you do that?" he yelped. The fork had fallen to the floor, so I knew it hadn't gone in that deep, but Tom was jumping around and pumping his arm up and down like he'd been burned, or, you know, stabbed. "I pour my heart out to you, and you spear me like a piece of meat? What is wrong with you, Libby?"

"What is wrong with me?" I stared at him, wild-eyed; I was feeling a wee bit feral. "What is wrong with me?!"

What was wrong with me was becoming a very long list in a remarkably short period of time. Previously, my problems amounted to incurably frizzy hair, a butt that was too big for otherwise well-fitting pants, and an awareness that although I was quite good at it, I hadn't actually enjoyed my job since Bush Jr. was in office. Now I was dying of cancer and wanted to murder my husband, who, as it turned out, was attracted to a chromosome makeup distinctly different from my own.

"You're always doing this," I told him.

Still clutching his hand, he took a step back. "What do you mean?"

I could feel the crazy coming on again. "Upstaging me!"

It was not entirely lost on me that his commandeering my big reveal was probably not the right dilemma to be dwelling on, but I couldn't seem to stop myself. It was as though the spirit of Jackie, she of the many long-winded outbursts, had slithered into my body. "Every time, Tom!" I screeched as he stared at me with horror. "Every time!"

In high school, Tom won rave reviews for his rousing performance of Curly in *Oklahoma!* while I was relegated to the understudy for Laurey, a role I did not once bring to fruition while pining for Tom from the chorus. His custom-tailored suit for our wedding was far nicer than my dress, and it was all anyone could talk about at our ceremony. If anyone could steal the thunder of my cancer diagnosis, it was Tom.

Now, I know, I know: Musicals? Designer suits? Surely, Libby, you must have been aware that your husband was perhaps not as hetero as he'd let on? But Paul had been out and proud from the minute he emerged from his amniotic sac. I knew from gay men. At least, I thought I did.

"I'm dying," I said. "I. Am. Dying!"

"Libby, please don't be dramatic," he said. "I understand that you're upset. I am, too. But we can't move forward if you're screaming at me."

"Tom," I said, eyeing the recently sharpened steak knives, which hung from a magnetic strip just above the sink, "don't take this the wrong way, but I think you should leave before I do something we'll both regret."

He recoiled. "Libby, don't you have any sympathy for me? Do you know how hard that was? I've been working on this for months now."

How lovely. Even as my tumor grew from a pea to an olive to a lime just beneath my skin—not far from the very area where the baby I pined for should have been reaching similar milestones—Tom had been perfecting his I'm-breaking-up-our-marriage elevator speech.

"Tom, Tom, Tom," I said, fingering the top of the knife bar, which was dusty; I'd take care of that later. "You lost the right to ask for sympathy about three minutes ago. Now get out of our home before I stab you again."

# THREE

Would I have gone off the deep end if the whole mess with Tom hadn't unfolded as it did? Hard to say. Tom would have come out eventually, although I suspect that if I'd had the chance to tell him my Really Bad News before he told me his, he probably would have kept his secret under wraps until after I'd died. How convenient that would have been for him. I could just imagine him telling people, "I loved my wife so much that after her untimely passing, I just couldn't feel that way about another woman again—ever. So now I date men."

But as these things go, Tom couldn't wait to open his trap, and the news that came flying out was so terrible I could barely breathe, let alone tell him about the grenade in my gut.

I can't say for sure exactly what happened after Tom left, although I do remember lying on the floor in front of the apartment door, pressing my cheek against the cool wood, and wishing that I could disappear, perhaps permanently. Tom's confession had hit me like a sonic boom delivering shock waves: *My husband is gay?* "I'm trying to figure out who I am." *Even if he sort of likes men, he loves me so much it doesn't matter . . . right?* "I'm not saying this is the end of our marriage." *Maybe I can pretend I didn't hear him.* "You knew for a long time now, didn't you?" *Perhaps we can just forget this all happened and carry on as usual, at least until I die.* "What is wrong with you, Libby?"

At any rate, I was irrational enough to decide *not* to call Paul, telling myself he was probably on his way to the Yale Club or Barney Greengrass or who knows where to wine and dine some random investor for the hedge fund he managed. (Besides, I liked to play this little game in which I waited to see if he received the distress signals I was sending out over the telepathic twin transmitter system, whose existence I had always been rather skeptical about.) When I was finally able to pull myself off the floor, I located Tom's sleeping pills in the medicine cabinet, took one, then decided to take another, and except for some sobbing and the frenzied consumption of an entire sleeve of chocolate chip cookies, the rest is a bit of a blur.

I woke the next morning in a pool of drool. A bleating ring was coming from my cell phone, which I eventually located between the couch cushions.

"Morningpaul," I mumbled. It was still dark out, but Paul was one of those psychotic types who didn't require more than six hours of sleep; since he had discovered prescription amphetamines, that number was now closer to four or five.

"What is it?" he asked, as though I'd been the one calling him. (Perhaps there was something to the twin clairvoyance phenomenon, but don't expect me to admit it out loud.)

I contemplated whether to ask him if he wanted to hear the bad or the ugly, but even with the sleeping-pill fog still hanging around my head, it occurred to me that I couldn't tell him about the cancer, not yet. I could hear his twin sons, Toby and Max, playing in the background, and in his own Paul way, he sounded sort of chipper. And that a life-sapping tumor would reduce our nuclear family to just two—well, that was news that needed to be delivered in person.

"Tom is gay," I said.

Paul hooted. "Charlie, wake up!" he said to his partner, who was not a morning person and was undoubtedly dozing nearby. "You have to hear this!"

"*That* is your first response?" I said, tears pricking behind my eyelids.

"Libs, I'm sorry, I didn't mean it like that. I'm—well, I'm gobsmacked. How on earth could he do this to you? Are you all right?"

"No," I admitted. "I'm in a very bad place right now."

"Oh, Libs," he cooed. "I hate Chicago, too. Will you consider moving out to the East Coast, preferably the United Republic of Manhattan? You would be so much happier here."

"Paul."

"Brooklyn?"

"*Paul.*"

"I'm sorry, Libs. I'm only joking because I'm upset. You know how I get. So this actually happened? What did he say? What did *you* say?!"

"It happened," I said miserably. "I might have stabbed him with a fork."

"Mad Libs, I *love* it! Though . . ."

"Though what?" I asked sharply.

Paul hesitated. "Is Tom okay? This must be awful for him."

"Tom?" I said. "Is mother-fudging *Tom* okay?" (One of the things I remember about my mother is that she despised swearing, so I figure the least I can do to honor her memory is scrub my vocabulary of curse words.)

"Libs, you know what I mean."

"Don't Libs me." I sniffed, thinking of how Tom only blurted the truth out after he thought I already knew. "And yes, he's fine."

"I'm sorry," Paul said again in a way that told me we'd be revisiting the topic sooner rather than later. "What are you going to do now?"

That was a very good question. I pushed my glasses up on my nose and eyed the clock; I had about an hour before I had to be at the office. Of course, I could call in, but that would mean I'd spend the day crying in the home I shared with the man who had torn my beating heart from my chest. Bad enough that I'd just learned my body was disease-ridden; I would be damned if my husband's accidental outing was going to be the thing that took me out of the game of life.

"I'm going to shower. Then I'm going to get dressed. Then I'm going to work."

"You will do nothing of the sort! Tell Jackie to shove it. One's husband coming out necessitates at least a full week off, if not a month."

I did a mental rundown of my day, which meant I was really taking a survey of my boss's day. Jackie, who was the head of advertising at a large media conglomerate that had a hand in radio, television, and custom print publications across the US, had a breakfast meeting with one of the company's publishers at eight forty-five; conference calls, which I would facilitate, with various heads of sales at ten, ten thirty, and eleven; then an early lunch with the CEO at the Ritz, which would buy me an hour of downtime, although I would need to pick up her gown for the Joffrey event this evening, or at least find a messenger competent enough not to get it caught in the spokes of his bike while playing bumper cars on LaSalle—

I have cancer, I realized yet again, as though for the first time. I felt around my stomach, wincing as I fingered the still-bandaged incision to the left of my belly button. If the tumor was out, but I still had cancer, did that mean there were malignant cells lingering in the area right now? Or were they already speeding through my body, like microscopic surveyors trying to figure out where to set up their next subdivision?

Where the cancer was didn't matter. The only thing of importance was that I was *dying* that very second. If I said this to Paul, he would point out that we're all dying every second we're alive. But as I mentioned, I wasn't ready to drop the C-bomb on him just yet, for reasons pertaining not only to his psychological well-being, but also my own. I needed a few days to evaluate the barren desert of my mental landscape before I started telling people.

*If only I could confide in Tom,* I thought, fresh tears springing to my eyes. Unlike Paul, he would not launch into strategy mode or offer advice I wasn't ready to take. He would hold me until I was done crying, and he would ask me what I wanted to do next, a question that—only when he asked it—always seemed to help me point myself in the right direction. But for all intents and purposes, there was no Tom anymore.

Regardless, Paul was right: I should take some time off work. But I was going to do it on my own terms.

Unaware that a good chunk of my anguish was due to something even worse than my imploded marriage, Paul was still thinking about Tom. "If it helps, I always had my doubts about him."

"You suspected he was gay?" I spat. "Why didn't you tell me?"

"Libby, love, if I suspected *that*, you would have been the very first to know. Trust me, this is as shocking to me as it is to you. I just felt that you could do better."

This, at least, was not news. A week before my wedding, Paul pleaded with me to put it off. "You're so young, Libby. Go date other guys, figure out if you really want to settle for Tom."

"I'm not settling," I told him. "I've had ten years to think about this, Paul, and I know that love like this doesn't come along more than once in a lifetime."

"Libby, that's like saying Long John Silver's has the best fish in the world when you've never even tried a Maine lobster."

"Lobster is a crustacean, and you're jealous," I said, even though we both knew the latter comment wasn't even the tiniest bit true. Paul asked me again if I was sure—really and truly sure—the night before our ceremony, though he did stand beside me as my de facto maid of honor.

I was sure then. Now, not so much. I'd always been so proud that Tom never gave himself whiplash when a woman in skintight yoga pants walked by, but clearly I'd been searching for the wrong warning signs. What else had I overlooked while I was mentally high-fiving myself for scoring such a perfect husband?

"Well, I didn't *want* to do better," I sniffed to Paul. "And I thought I was good in bed."

"Although I must vomit in my mouth a little in order to admit this, I'm sure you are very good in bed, Libs. You do know this has nothing to do with you, right? Tell me you know that."

I'd brought it up, yes, but now that we were having this conversation, I wasn't quite ready for it. "I know. I'll call you later, okay?"

"Love you."

"Love you more."

"No, I love *you* more," he said, and hung up before I could respond.


*"Liiiibbbyy!"* Jackie had this peculiar way of yodeling my name, which, despite seven years of working for her, still managed to make my hair corkscrew even tighter. She kept hollering, although I hadn't stepped into her office yet. "Do you know I've been here since six thirty this morning? I expected you to be here early to make up for that disappearing act you pulled yesterday, not to mention the day off last week. The city is full of doctors who work nights and weekends, you know. You don't see me taking off for personal appointments in the middle of the day, do you?"

In fact, two days before, she left at four to get a manicure, and yesterday I was fairly certain her noon meeting was actually a quickie with her Argentine boy toy; but I was not about to point out either instance.

Instead, I opened her door and said, "Good morning, Jackie!" Yes, it was odd to be pleasant if not vaguely chipper to this hurricane of a human being, but after facing so much upheaval in such a short window of time, it was easy—comforting, even—to fall right back into my role of well-paid sycophant.

Now, Libby, one might ask, why would you willingly work as an assistant to someone so awful? Don't you have any self-respect? I do, but as someone who watched her father nearly go bankrupt as a result of her dead mother's medical bills, I also have respect for the almighty dollar. Under Paul's careful tutelage, I had quit on four separate occasions, and each time, human resources rewarded me with more money and a fancier title. This is because while Jackie is a miserable person, she happens to be so good at luring advertisers, and so bad at keeping the staff needed to fulfill the contracts made with those advertisers, that it is worth it for the company to pay her assistant (whose résumé, for the record, reads "vice president of media management") a solid hundred and twenty grand a year. Jackie acted as if my compensation were her personal gift to me: "You know that's a man's salary, don't you, Libby? I'm breaking glass ceilings for you," she would say in her smoker's brogue, shortly before throwing her cell phone at the wall, not far from my head. Then I would spend the afternoon replacing the phone and reprogramming her data. I often reminded myself that working for Jackie was a necessary evil, not unlike a colonoscopy or a friendly fondling from airport security personnel.

"Do you know I could hire an assistant in Pakistan for eight dollars an hour?" Jackie said from behind her *Tribune*.

"But would she bring you this?" I asked, producing a vegan bran muffin from behind my back. I was still operating on autopilot, so I'd stopped at the deli as I always did, purchasing Jackie's usual and a large frosted cinnamon bun for myself. I'd heard that sugar fed cancer, but it was too late to worry about it.

"Hmph," Jackie said, and put down her paper to hold out her hand for the muffin; breakfast meeting or not, she had a weakness for freebies and carbohydrates. She shoveled cardboard crumbs into her mouth while dictating the list of daily to-dos that were to be done in addition to my already scheduled duties: call this guy, call that guy, order flowers for her mother, smooth things over with this woman, send these contracts to that company, and so on. "Jackie," I interrupted at one point. "Could you please give me a minute to jot down the last few?" I was feeling unfocused and a bit dizzy, and it was hard to keep up with her.

"No," she snapped. Ignoring my glare, she continued rattling off her demands until I had a legal pad filled with tasks that would take an e-assistant a month to complete.

When she was done, she handed me her crumb-covered wrapper to toss out like a good little underling, even though there was a wastebasket under her desk. I narrowed my eyes and looked at it for a moment, then sighed, plucked the wrapper from her fingers, and marched it out to the trash basket near my cube. When I returned, I perched on the edge of the clear Plexiglas chair in front of her desk.

She furrowed her brow in a way that made it clear she was not pleased by my presence. Normally I let her nastiness slide off me like water off an otter's back, but as the minutes ticked by, it seemed less and less likely that I was going to be able to ignore the disease and impending divorce debacle hanging over my head. In fact, I was feeling surprisingly pissy. "Jackie," I said, glowering back at her, "I'm kind of going through some stuff, and I'd like to take a week or two off. I can work today and tomorrow as planned."

"Your personal issues are not my problem, Libby. You know we're gearing up for the big sales conference in January. And I need at least a month's notice if you're going to go sun yourself in the tropics. I mean, this week alone we have a half dozen advertorial contracts to wrap up. You can't honestly think that Mark can handle them," she said, referring to the senior accounts manager, who was, as far as I could tell, alarmingly competent.

"Jackie, I'm not going to the tropics. I have to handle something personal. I would be happy to take a leave of absence if necessary." I gazed out her window, which overlooked Lake Michigan. It was late autumn, and the waves were high and white tipped; it wouldn't be long before they were crystalline confections lining the shore. It was entirely possible I would not live long enough to see them in frozen form.

"No can do, Libby," Jackie snipped. "Now get back to work."

I stood, and this was about the time that I started wondering if the cancer had moseyed on up to my brain, because I wasn't thinking quite right. Instead, my emotions were beginning to bear a striking resemblance to those of Paul's toddlers in the midst of a tantrum: Libby *angry*! Libby *pissed*! Libby *no like this*!

Was I really going to spend the last few months of my life making phone calls for other people and coordinating charity events I wasn't even invited to? It was like playing Cinderella right up until her fairy godmother showed up.

"Go on," Jackie said, waving her hand like I was a stray dog she was shooing from her yard.

"Oh, I'm going."

She'd already turned her attention to her computer screen, and she didn't stop typing as she responded. "Every word you speak is a second you could be doing your job."

"And every word *you* speak is a second of my life that you are completely wasting," I volleyed back.

The frenzied clacking of her keyboard abruptly stopped. She swiveled in her Aeron chair and stared at me with bloodshot eyes. "What has gotten into you, you overfed milkmaid?"

If she was insulting my appearance, she was actually concerned. Fine. Let her be worried. She and Tom could sit together at my funeral and pretend that they'd shared something special with me.

"Cheap shot. Perhaps menopause is making you lose your touch?" I smiled at her. "By the way, I quit."

"Nice try," she scoffed. "It's a recession. Human resources isn't going to fork over more cash this time."

"I don't want money. I want you to treat me the way you expect other people to treat you. But I can't wait around to see if that will ever happen."

She glared at me as I started for the door.

*"Liiibbby!"* she yelled. "Libby?"

Outside Jackie's office, I stopped briefly at my desk. A framed photo of Tom and me sat next to my computer monitor, and a small placard noting that I was employee of the month last June hung on the cubicle partition. In the drawer there were some tampons, spare change, and business cards I never used. There was not a single thing worth grabbing.

"It's been fun!" I called over my shoulder. I felt slightly elated as I tore toward the exit sign at the end of the hall, but only slightly. Because however gratifying it was to unleash all that anger bottled inside me, I couldn't help but wonder if maybe—just maybe—I was killing off a little bit of what was good in me in the process.

# FOUR

Paul texted me while I was on the L.

PAUL: Libby, are you okay STOP Getting distinct impression that there is more to story I must hear immediately STOP Coming to get you and drag you to NYC STOP

ME: Paul, STOP! I am fine. As fine as someone newly unemployed with no references can be.

PAUL: Sassy Sissy! You finally told that old bag to jump in the lake, didn't you?

ME: Affirmative.

PAUL: Good. I was beginning to wonder

if you'd die in that G-D office. More
soon. x's!

I turned off my phone and sighed. If only he knew.

When I got home, Tom was at the stove; the smell of freshly baked brownies hung in the air.

For the briefest moment I was thrilled to see him, and not just because he'd made my favorite dessert—I could tell him all about how I had overthrown Jackie, the evil asinine dictator! Then I spotted his bandaged hand and it all came crashing back. "I don't want you to be here, Tom. And that," I said, pointing to his hand, "is overkill, don't you think?"

"Libby, I love you," he said.

I tilted my head and examined him for a moment, considering the best way to lob some of my emotional pain at him, as though it were a quantifiable entity that could be distributed between us. Then I smiled at him rather insanely. "Tom, that's very sweet, and I'm sure you *think* it's true. But, in fact, you love the dong. The wang. The cock-a-doodle-do. Because if you truly loved me, why didn't you tell me the truth years ago? I mean, ten, seven, even *five* years ago, I would have been ripe for the picking. Now? I'm almost thirty-five, Tom. I'm set in my ways. I have gray hair and cellulite." *And cancer,* I thought, although I chose to omit this morsel of information. Maybe it was selfish, but I didn't want Tom to be allowed to grieve with me. I was too hurt to share any part of myself—even the diseased bits—with him.

"That's not fair, Libby," he said. "We were raised to believe homosexuality is a sin, and I thought it was a choice. And I was attracted to you."

I winced. "Past tense."

"I didn't mean it like that," he said quickly.

A wave of nausea hit me. No, he probably didn't mean it like that. In fact, there may have never been a time in which Tom had not been imagining a physique markedly more masculine than my own while we were having sex. "So did you——?"

"No," he said firmly. "I know what you're thinking, but it wasn't like that."

I couldn't bring myself to respond. Instead, I left him in the kitchen and wandered into our bedroom. Funny, it was the one room in our apartment that we had never finished decorating: the walls were as white as when we moved in, and our comforter was the same one I'd used in college, even though it was too small for our queen-size bed. On the wall, Tom had nailed a photo of us in front of the church on our wedding day. Beside it, I had hung a picture of him and me at junior prom; we'd started dating earlier that year. On the dresser, there was a photo of me, pink-cheeked and spilling out of my bikini on the beach in Acapulco, which Tom snapped on our honeymoon. I was relieved to be done with the wedding and to begin our lives as husband and wife. I'd married my best friend. We had a great apartment and friends we loved. Tom was on his way to having the career as an urban planner that he'd dreamed of, and it wouldn't be long before the two of us would welcome a baby into our lives, or so I thought.

I'd never felt more hopeful than I did then.

*Mexico.*

The thought was an electrical current through my body. At once, I realized I needed to get moving—and fast. I went to the hall closet, located a suitcase, then returned to the bedroom.

"Libby?" Tom called from the dining room.

"Not now, Tom!" I yelled, and began opening dresser drawers and tossing his clothes into the suitcase. After it was stuffed, I went to the master bathroom and threw in Tom's cologne and various other personal grooming products. I wheeled the suitcase to the spare bedroom, which we used as an office, and finished stuffing it with papers of Tom's that looked like they might be important.

By this point, he was standing in the doorway watching me. "Libby, please stop."

"Not an option. You need to leave. As in yesterday."

The year before, Tom and I had gone skiing in northern Michigan. We were halfway down a bumpy blue run when I almost skied into a man who was splayed out in the snow. Even beneath his thick snow pants, it was clear that the lower half of his leg, which was bent at an unnatural angle, was snapped like a twig. I expected him to be moaning in pain, but as I pulled up beside him, he looked up at me with clear eyes and a neutral expression. "I just broke my leg and need to get down the mountain right away," he said, as though he was commenting on the temperature. "Would you mind flagging down the ski patrol for me?"

At the time, I was amazed at the man's reaction. Now I knew how he was feeling. I was aware that the bit of pain I was feeling was going to start hurting like hell in very short order, but for the time being, my brain and body were in self-preservation mode, and I could focus only on what had to be done next.

"But this is *our* apartment," Tom said.

"That may technically be true, but who paid for it?" I asked, so coldly that I surprised myself. Until that moment, I'd never once held money over his head, even though I'd used the sum I received from my mother's life insurance policy when I turned eighteen to make the down payment on our home, and covered more than four years of mortgage payments on my own before Tom began drawing a paltry salary as a newbie urban planner. He now paid a mere third of our monthly bill, and I continued to cover his student loans.

"Libby, please. I told you, I really want to work this out."

"Tom," I said, putting my hands on my hips, "that is not possible. No matter what you say or do, what you told me will always be with me. Always, Tom. It can never be undone. You must have known that, deep down, when you admitted it." I'd intended to mock what he said the day before, but mostly I sounded sad. "I don't have the time or energy to work it out with you. This may not make sense now, but one day it will. If you have additional questions, I suggest you discuss them with your therapist or a divorce lawyer," I said, and handed him the suitcase.

"Oh, Libby," he said. He was starting to cry.

It had been a long time since I'd seen Tom shed tears, and he looked so sorrowful that my instinct was to fling open my arms and cradle him to my chest. The scene quickly unfolded in my mind: I would say soothing things to him, and he would look at me appreciatively, then longingly as I dried his tears. We would make sweet, tender love on the bed, or maybe on the floor, and I wouldn't even mind that it was over before I was ready. Afterward, he would joke that he should really cry more often, and we would laugh together, and then I would kiss my lovely, emotional husband and tell him I loved him like a mouth loves pizza, which never failed to make him smile.

It was enough to make tears spring to my own eyes.

But this was not the time to dwell on things that would never, ever happen again. "Please do that somewhere else," I said, and pushed a now-weeping Tom toward the front door.

I expected to cry, too, after Tom left. Instead, I sat on the hallway floor feeling hollowed out and exhausted. If cancer was a gift, I wanted to return it. I didn't need a fast-acting tumor to remind me about the fleeting nature of life: watching my mother rot in a hospital bed and die in hospice before she had a chance to teach me to choose a bra that wouldn't make my ample bosom resemble missiles—let alone see me walk down the aisle with the man who would shatter my heart with one stuttering sentence—that was reminder enough.

After a while, I returned to the kitchen, ate a few brownies, then remembered the ticking of the cosmic time clock I was now observing and the fact that although I didn't have concrete plans, let alone a job to occupy my day, there was plenty left to accomplish. I sat down at the computer and began.

# FIVE

Even with Tom out of the apartment, I still felt tethered to him. Unlacing some of our financial ties seemed to be the next best step toward securing my independence, even if said independence would be, quite literally, short-lived.

The legality of emptying most of our joint savings into a new online account registered to yours truly was questionable, but I decided I had the ethical right of way: I had been the one to stash cash all those years. After transferring the funds, I logged onto my retirement and life insurance accounts and made Toby and Max the new beneficiaries. Though it was tempting, I ultimately opted against canceling Tom's school-loan payment, which was drawn directly from our checking account. After all, he would end up paying it himself when I ran out of money, after I died, or when we divorced, whatever came first.

There was the sticky matter of the mortgage, which was in both our names. I didn't know how I would convince Tom to sell, but somehow, some way, I would. The apartment had been our haven for eight years, and like the tar-stained drywall of a smoker's home, it reeked of Tom and Libby—a couple who no longer existed. If I couldn't burn it to the ground, it would have to be sold. A quick e-mail exchange with a friend who was a Chicago real estate shark confirmed that the condo would be an easy sell.

I was on my way.

The only problem was, cutting Tom off financially had released some of my anger, and that opened up a space for the loss that had been hovering in the background. As soon as I shut my computer, I found myself hunched over, sobbing so violently that I was worried I might vomit. Eighteen years: it was more than half my life, and thanks to Dr. Sanders's medical briefing, I was hyperaware that I would never have the opportunity to spend more time without Tom than with him. Now all of it—my epic high school crush, our long-distance college relationship, the wedding, moving to Chicago together, our anniversary celebrations, the many holidays spent with Tom's insufferable family, and yes, obviously, the sex—felt like an incredible farce, particularly in light of my new expiration date. It was as though I'd just watched a priceless piece of jewelry wash away in the swell of the ocean's tide. There was nothing I could do to change what had happened, but I could not stop myself from desperately wishing I could rewind my life and do it all over in a way that was the exact opposite of my past.

Although I was exhausted—the crying, no doubt, and probably the cancer, too, making my white blood cells run laps around my body—I forced myself to go out for lunch. I wandered down Damen and stopped at my usual coffee-and-pastry place.

Jeanette, the regular barista, greeted me from behind the espresso machine. "Hey, Libby. Don't usually see you here during the day."

"I'm taking a personal day," I said.

With her long dreads and various facial piercings, Jeanette was a relic of Bucktown circa pre-yuppification. "Fun!" she said, thwacking the espresso pod against a bucket filled with old grindings. "How's Tom?" she added. (He and I went there a lot.)

"Oh, Tom?" I said, fingering one of the shrink-wrapped cookies on the counter. "He's dead."

Jeanette spun around. "Oh my God!"

"Not literally," I said, and reminded myself to lay off the hyperbole. "Just to me."

"Ohhh," she said. I saw her mental wheels turning: *Libby's clearly traumatized. So sad—they were cute, reading the Sunday paper over lattes and strudel. Although he was better-looking than her, and that never works.* "I'm sorry."

"Eh," I said with a wave of my hand, "don't be. My two-year-old nephews have bigger penises than Tom." This, too, was hyperbole, and I was aware that it was odd to say such a terrible thing to a woman who, aside from my preference for whole milk in my coffee, knew next to nothing about me. I had always held my tongue and tried to think the best about people, but something strange had happened. I would soon be nothing but a memory to others, and for reasons I couldn't quite understand myself, I didn't want anyone—not my brother, not my ex-boss, not this barista—to remember me as lie-down-and-take-it Libby.

Jeanette laughed. "Good for you, then! Life's too short."

"Isn't it?" I said, and slipped a ten in her tip jar.

On the way back to my apartment, I fell into step behind two women speaking to each other in Spanish. For all I knew, they were discussing industrial waste, but the florid words fell off their tongues in a way that made me envious. I'd studied German in school, and although it had been billed as a practical business language, I had yet to find myself in a situation in which there was an opportunity to *sprechen Deutsch*. Meanwhile, I'd traveled to three Spanish-speaking countries and had fallen more in love with the language on each trip. Obviously there wasn't time to master it, but I had an idea about how to capture a pinch of Latin magic before I died.

First, though, I wanted to verify that this wasn't all an overreaction on my part. I went home and called Dr. Sanders's office. "Hi, this is Libby, er, Elizabeth Miller. I was in yesterday and Dr. Sanders said I had cancer. I'm just calling to find out what type of cancer, exactly, I have. I know it was lymphoma, but I can't remember the rest. Can you check my chart?"

"I see," said the receptionist. "Hang on one second." I heard some rustling, and then she asked me to hold again. A few minutes later, Dr. Sanders got on the line.

"Elizabeth—"

"Not that you'll need it for future reference, but I go by Libby."

He sounded upset. "Libby, I understand this is very unfortunate—"

"Yes, it is," I said. "Now can you please tell me the name of my cancer again?"

"Subcutaneous panniculitis-like T-cell lymphoma."

"Uh . . . can you spell that?"

He did. I thanked him, then pressed the End button on my phone.

A second opinion from Dr. Google confirmed that my diagnosis was, indeed, the worst sort of news. The aggressive form—as mine was—spread rapidly and was generally resistant to chemo. On top of it all, this particular form of cancer was rare enough that agreeing to treatment was essentially volunteering to be a guinea pig whose claim to fame would be a postmortem appearance in medical literature. Thanks, but no.

I removed my shirt and stared in the mirror. How long would it take before the worst happened to me? The skin around my bandage was starting to look not unlike the center of an undercooked pork loin. I got back on the computer and poked around some more, ultimately determining that if anything, Dr. Sanders had sugarcoated my prognosis. If I was lucky, I was looking at three to six decent months of life, followed by six to twelve wretched ones, then a swift kick to the old bucket.

I had a rough idea of how to proceed, but for inspiration, I popped *Y tu mamá también* in the DVD player and splayed out on the sofa. My sophomore year of college, I shared a room with an international student named Isidora, and she introduced me to the tragic beauty of Spanish-language cinema. Most of my favorite films—*Lucia y el sexo*, *Los amantes del círculo polar*, *Piedras*—were set in Spain, but I had a particular weakness for the Mexican *Y tu mamá también*.

In it, the thirty-something Luisa meets two teen boys at a wedding, and they boast about a secret beach called Heaven's Mouth, telling her she should come with them to find it. After learning that her husband has cheated on her, Luisa does just that. The three of them dance and drink and have lots of sex. There's more to the story, but—sorry if I'm ruining it—Luisa stays on at the beach and dies of cancer soon after, which she never told the boys about.

Although it was probably the ninth time I'd seen the movie, it felt especially poignant on this particular viewing, and I sat sobbing as I watched Luisa walk into the frothy waves. "Life is like the surf, so give yourself away like the sea," she said in a voice-over, and I curled up in the fetal position and wailed like a humpback, even though I wasn't sure what, precisely, she meant.

I was going to find out. I was going to go to Mexico while I still could.

# SIX

There was just one teensy problem: my passport had expired. And I hadn't noticed, because Tom and I hadn't traveled in . . . gosh, how long had it been? A while. When we were younger, we went everywhere—Crete, Austin, Buenos Aires, Boston. In fact, Tom said he knew he wanted to marry me because we traveled so well together; it was a sign we were truly compatible, he claimed. But we hadn't been able to make our vacations match up since he started working. Now I wondered if this had less to do with our respective calendars and more to do with Tom's not wanting to have vacation sex with me. My cheeks burned as I recalled his reaction when I wanted to make love twice in a row during a trip to Paris. "I'm not a machine, Libby," he said, and even though he immediately apologized, I slouched under the covers on our lumpy hotel bed, mildly aroused, moderately irritated, and severely mortified by my inconsiderate, overactive libido. (I could just hear Paul saying, "You know this has nothing to do with you, right?" Well, I did now.)

The defunct passport was momentarily disheartening—I didn't have six weeks to wait while the State Department issued a new one—until I discovered that for an extra fee, I could speed the process to just two weeks. *Yes,* I thought excitedly, *that's exactly what I'll do.* I walked to the drugstore and had a new passport photo snapped, and although the photo made me appear eerily cadaverous, I took the L to the post office and submitted it along with a check and the necessary forms.

When I got home, I ate a microwave burrito while searching for beachfront properties along Mexico's far eastern coast, which was supposed to be gorgeous in the fall. Thanks to what was apparently a fresh surge of drug-related violence, ticket prices were down and waterfront properties were cheap. I bought a round-trip flight that would have me in Mexico for a month and a half, then put down a deposit for a small cottage on a private beach in Akumal. If I tired of Akumal, I could head to Cozumel or Tulum or any number of places, although the specific location was really beside the point: the only things I needed for spiritual redemption were sand and water, authentic Mexican food, and buckets of margaritas. (I didn't really drink, but I intended to start.)

After Mexico, I would fly directly to New York, where I would finally tell Paul about the big C. Then he and I would drive to New Hampshire, where our father lived, and together we would deliver the news. The three of us would visit my mother's grave one last time, and then I would die quietly, surrounded by the people I loved. Admittedly, the specifics of my post-Mexico plans were murky. When the pain became unbearable, I would theoretically put heavy rocks in my pockets and wander into a large body of water, or maybe find a nice warm oven and stick my head in. In reality, I knew myself well enough to know that I couldn't go through with that, and so Paul and Dad would end up watching me suffer for at least a short while. This, more than anything, was devastating, so I tried not to give it too much thought.

It was after eight when I finalized my itinerary. I decided not to prolong the misery of the day any longer and took two more of Tom's sleeping pills.

I crawled into bed, but visions of white sand and mariachi bands danced through my head, making sleep impossible. I gave up and made a giant bowl of popcorn, devoured it, then logged into my social network of choice and changed my marital status to single, even though I was aware that this would set off waves that would trigger a minor social tsunami. Fine. Let everyone be worried. My failed marriage could be a smoke screen for my failing health, which I didn't intend to inform anyone about. When my mom was dying, long-lost relatives and distant church friends crowded our home, and later the hospital, eating up the precious few hours that we had left with her. This time, it was my march into the great beyond, and I was calling the shots. The first rule of the cancer club: there was no cancer club, and therefore there would be no well-wishers rubbernecking at the scene of the tragedy, reminding themselves how fortunate they were without absorbing any real loss.

By nine, I was getting loopy—the couch was feeling not unlike an underhydrated waterbed, and when I looked in the mirror, my face seemed freakishly large—which should have been reason enough to put myself back to bed, but I kept hearing an odd noise in the background. Did the upstairs neighbors get a grandfather clock? Was that a gong?

No, it was not. It was my phone. The number was blocked, but I picked up anyway. "Nice try, Tom," I scoffed.

"Libby?" It was Jess, O'Reilly's wife. She was the closest thing I had to a best friend. I had trouble opening up to people I wasn't related to or sleeping with, a problem Paul shared and attributed to our freaky twin closeness; but because our husbands had been best friends since childhood and I had known O'Reilly since high school, Jess and I warmed to each other over many, many years. I sometimes questioned our friendship, particularly when she was trying to pry into my psyche to get me to confess all the ways that I must secretly be dissatisfied, when the truth was, up until two days ago—provided Jackie wasn't chucking something at me or I wasn't thinking about how I was on the losing side of thirty and still didn't have the children I had always wished for—I was pretty darn content.

But Jess was fun and easily the most stylish person I'd ever met, which made most of our outings feel sort of like sociological field trips. (Some women spent six hundred dollars on a single pair of shoes; who knew?) Now, however, I was annoyed with her because if O'Reilly knew about Tom's true sexual preferences before I did, that meant Jess did, too.

"This is Libby," I said, as though I didn't know it was Jess on the other line.

"Libby, are you okay?"

"Of course, I'm okay," I said. (I may or may not have been slurring.)

"But how are you doing?" she asked, too gently.

"How am I doing? How am I *doing*? My husband just told me he was imagining a manwich while he was between my legs. How do you think I'm doing, Jess?"

"Oh," she said. I honestly think she expected me to be bubbly about it, which was more my fault than hers, since effervescent was basically my M.O.

I heard her whisper something.

"Mother trucker!" I spat. "Is Tom there right now?"

Jess didn't respond.

"Listen, it's nice of you to check in on me, but I'm kind of in the middle of something." I murmured a few sweet nothings to the invisible man sitting next to me on the couch, which was now feeling like a raft on a very choppy sea. "Ooooh! You are *naughty!*" I cried, then hung up. Tom didn't want to sleep with me, so it didn't matter anyway, but in my Ambien-addled mind, I'd just made it clear to Jess, O'Reilly, and Tom that I had already moved on.

Then I got another idea, which is about the point at which things really started to go south.

# SEVEN

Ty Oshira had worked with me for three years. Rather, he worked on the other side of the floor I was on, and because he was some sort of marketing genius, he had fairly regular dealings with Jackie. "And how is our lady of perpetual discontent?" he would say under his breath as he tiptoed up to my cubicle. "Full of grace!" I would respond, giggling like a schoolgirl. Ty was clever, charismatic, and—how do I put this delicately?—the hotness.

I had a crush on him, the kind that has the primary purpose of making the workday more palatable. This crush was fueled by a healthy dose of interest on his part. I'd caught him stealing glances at my rear end more than a few times, and when I finally dragged Tom to our holiday party, Ty, who was reasonably hammered, cornered me at the bar, pointed across the room to Tom, and said, "*That guy* is Mr. Libby Miller?" as though Tom wasn't four inches taller than Ty and handsome in his own right.

The last year Ty and I spent as coworkers, our casual-if-flirty acquaintanceship morphed into a friendship of sorts. We would often grab coffee and occasionally had lunch when Jackie was out of town. Ty would tell me about how awful it was to be a thirty-five-year-old man still on the dating scene; I would try to assure him that married life wasn't all it was cracked up to be, so unconvincingly that he would howl with laughter and accuse me of being a lobbyist for a pro-marriage organization. He wasn't wrong. I loved Tom and wouldn't have dreamed of cheating on him. But I would be lying if I said I didn't love the way Ty made me feel fresh and fascinating—a woman to be won over.

Then Ty left to work for another agency, and that was the end of that, until I ran into him on the street last spring. "Libby Miller, full of grace," he said, breaking into an irresistible grin.

"Hey, Ty." I blushed, knowing that this chance encounter meant I would have to work hard to keep his face from surfacing during intimate moments with Tom over the next month or so. "How's the job going?"

"Well, the publisher doesn't accuse me of being mentally disabled, so that's a start," he said. Then he smiled deviously. "And how's that husband of yours?"

"Fine," I stammered. "He's fine."

"Well, if that ever changes, look me up, Libby Miller," he said, then strode away, like he hadn't just stamped a question mark on my heart.

I had a conundrum. Even if I had the time to try, there was simply no way to save my marriage. Yet I didn't want to die having slept with just one man in my preternaturally short life, particularly given what I now knew about that man. To be honest, I would have been happy with a frenetic make-out session (as getting naked would be tricky; I didn't want to have to explain my bandaged abdomen). I just needed someone—someone who was definitely not Tom, but who was also not a random serial killer—to affirm that I was an interesting, desirable person with a perfectly healthy sex drive. I was pretty sure that person was Ty Oshira.

The problem was, I didn't believe in cheating. And quickie divorce, as it happens, isn't actually quick; I would have my passport long before I could expect to serve Tom with papers that would dissolve our union. (Tom had insisted on including "till death do us part" in our vows, even though I found this incredibly morbid. I hated that on this final item of business between us, he would probably be right.)

I was going to have to do things the old-fashioned way.

Now, I wasn't planning to *kill* him. If I were going to meet up with God in the near future, I didn't want Tom to beat me to the punch. Besides, all my stabby urges had been replaced by a wobbly melancholy. I was devastated when I woke each morning and remembered, yet again, why Tom wasn't lying beside me. At one point I found myself simultaneously cursing him and reaching for the phone to call him and tell him all about how my terrible husband had wronged me, as if there were two versions of him: the impostor who had just hurt me, and the real Tom, who would damn impostor Tom and make it all better.

Beneath my morose feelings was a not-unwarranted sense of urgency; and even deeper still—and I know this sounds strange—a beacon of optimism shone through. I was going to die, which was extremely unfortunate, but presumably I would see my mother again soon, just as I'd been waiting to do my entire life.

Moreover, I could have been hit by a car an hour after Tom told me he was gay, and that would have been that. As much as I hated to admit this, even to myself, terminal cancer did offer one parting gift: a sliver of extra time in which to alter my narrative.

I put on my favorite outfit, a burgundy sweater dress and high-heeled leather boots that Jess talked me into buying last year. Then I removed my wedding band, which I should have done three days before. I dangled it over the toilet bowl, daring myself to let it hit the white porcelain and disappear in a whoosh of water.

Tom had picked out the ring for me. I didn't see it for the first time until he was putting it on my finger at our wedding ceremony. "Do you really like it?" he asked me eagerly, moments after the pastor declared us husband and wife.

"Yes," I whispered, running my finger over the smooth gold. It was neither thick nor thin, and unlike the lovely engagement ring that had been my mother's and was now mine, the band was not ornate in any way.

It was, I thought at the time, exactly like the love Tom and I shared: simple and easy.

Now I knew there was nothing easy about our love, nor much else in life. I stopped waving my hand precariously over the toilet and tossed the ring in my makeup bag.

An hour later, I marched through the doors of Tom's office.

"Libby! Long time no see!" said Alex from behind the reception desk. Alex was my kind of person: too smart for his job, but wise enough to know that complaining wouldn't help him fly the coop any faster.

"Hey, Alex," I said, reminding myself to smile. "Is Tom around?"

"Yep," he said, then rang Tom, who was out to the lobby like a shot. While I fully own that I maimed him and kicked him out of our home, I was still shocked to see that—why, yes, he actually seemed irritated that I showed up at his workplace.

"Bad timing?" I asked.

"No, of course not," he said, leaning in to hug me.

I bent back like the reigning limbo champion of Eastern Illinois. "No, no, no," I chided playfully, well aware that Tom would catch the edge in my voice.

"Let's go outside," he said.

"Let's not," I said, directing him into the cube city that made up his workplace.

"Libby, what's this about?" he asked under his breath as I walked to his desk.

If he was worried that I would out him to his coworkers, he needn't have been. "I told you, I don't want you at the apartment."

"Uh, okay," he said, fidgeting with the buttons on his shirtsleeve. "So . . . are you here to talk? I was hoping we could do that sometime soon."

"No, I am not." I could have spread it out, made a scene. But I'll admit—I wanted it to be over. "It turns out that the State of Illinois decided that divorce should be a long and painful process."

"I already told you. I don't want a divorce."

"You don't, Tom, but you will," I said. I felt a sob bubbling up from deep within me. I swallowed it and steadied myself. "So without further ado—"

I glanced around to see if his colleagues were within earshot, and darn if he didn't duck like I was about to pull out a gun.

"Get up, fudgewit," I said sharply.

He rose slowly.

"Tom Miller," I said, "I, Libby Miller, divorce you. I divorce you, I divorce you, I divorce you."

I was expecting shock, but as my eyes met his, all I saw was hurt.

*This is not your fault, Libby,* I reminded myself. *Don't let his pain emotionally derail you. He's the one who threw you on the tracks.*

"Good-bye, ex-husband," I said quietly. Then I turned and left his cube without looking back—not to make a point, but because I was not certain that I would be able to keep myself from rushing at him with apologies, acceptance, and absolution for us both.

. . .

Slightly shaken but still committed to my original mission, I arrived at Ty Oshira's office just as Chicago began to take lunch. The office occupied the bottom half of a brick row house tucked in a tony neighborhood just outside of downtown. I rang the doorbell, said Ty's name into the black box as prompted, and was immediately buzzed in. I found myself in a sitting room filled with antique furniture and large oil portraits, any one of which would appraise for more than my net worth.

Ty entered through a set of mahogany double doors. "Libby," he said in a tone that was kind, but hardly oozing with the eager testosterone I'd been anticipating. "What brings you here?"

"Hi, Ty," I said, flustered. We were already off script—and why was his expression one of platonic curiosity?

"Let me guess: things with Jackie aren't going so stellar," he said with a smile.

*Tom,* I thought with panic. *You mean Tom. Remember?* I laughed nervously. "You could say that."

Just then, a woman walked through the doors. I'd like to describe her as waddling, but alas, even at a good seven to eight months pregnant, she was all but gliding on air, a lithe goddess with a basketball of fertility attached to her abdomen. She was very pretty, and she beamed at me as though we were old friends. Then she put her hand on Ty's lower back in a decidedly un-coworker way. I was momentarily puzzled—had I confused his home and work addresses?

"Libby, this is Shea Broderick," Ty said.

I stared blankly. "As in—"

"Broderick Media," said Shea, just as Ty said, "My wife."

"Oh," I said. "Oh, my goodness. How wonderful."

"Isn't it?" Ty said, grinning at Shea. "We were just married a few months ago."

"It looks bad, doesn't it?" Shea smiled. "With me being forty, and Ty's boss to boot. But I couldn't have known when I hired him that we would fall in love."

If she was forty, I was fast approaching four hundred. No wonder my body up and quit on me.

"Libby, can you blame me?" Ty said.

I opened my eyes wide as though I understood completely, even as I began to pray for the rapture: *How's now for you, God? Because now is definitely a good time for me.*

"I mean, in the past year alone, Shea has funded literacy programs for—how many kids is it, baby?"

"Oh, you, stop it!" Shea said, all faux humble.

"Seriously! Libby, did you know that almost forty percent of people in Chicago proper can't read?"

No, I did not, I told him, as I glanced around for a window to jump out of, never mind that the door was right behind me; rational thinking was now a distant, almost unfathomable memory, like a land before e-mail.

"It's true!" Ty enthused. "And with Shea at the helm, Broderick Media has funneled nearly a hundred thousand dollars to the city's most effective literacy program. I mean, it's just astounding." He tilted his head back, regarding me like I was a rescue puppy wagging my tail and begging him to pick me. Which was not entirely off base. "You should come work for us, Libby."

*Us.* I wanted to throw *us* in a bonfire. I wanted to stuff *us* in a bottle and toss it into the Gulf of Mexico during hurricane season.

Instead, I plastered on a deranged smile. "You know, I'd love to, but I just quit on Jackie to start my own nonprofit. For, um, children who've lost parents to cancer. That's why I'm here, actually. I was hoping you and Shea could give me some pointers," I fibbed, as though I hadn't just learned that in addition to running one of the few profitable publishing companies in Chicago, Ty's secret wife just happened to have a heart of gold.

"Mentoring is one of my core competencies!" said Shea. "I'd love to chat more, but right now, baby Broderick-Oshira is *starving*! You know how that is."

I did not.

"Do you have a card you could leave, Lizzy?" she asked sweetly.

Again, I did not, and Ty didn't tell Shea that she had just mangled my name. He seemed relieved that I was about to exit his personal Eden. "Well, I should be able to look you up," he said, extending his hand.

It was cold as I shook it. "Yes, I'm easy to find online," I told him. Just search the obituaries.

# EIGHT

The thing about life is, you think it's going to go on forever, that there couldn't possibly be an end to your story, at least not in the foreseeable future. But then around the time you—and by you, I mean me—should be having the stirrings of a midlife crisis, a stranger in a white coat tells you that you are no longer a member of the general population and do not have another forty-five-and-a-half years to warm up to the idea of dying.

Cue my end-of-life crisis.

Really, *crisis* is a kind way to describe what I was going through; it was more like a full-blown meltdown, although at the time I thought I was being quite reasonable. And while I would like to blame the cancer and Tom's untimely outing, or even Cool Hand Ty and the Rejections (which would be my band name in my next life, I decided), it was really Shea who hurtled me to the front line of my emotional Chernobyl.

Because Shea, with her company and charitable donations and mother-fracking fertility, was the embodiment of everything I was not, had never been, and would never, ever get a chance to be.

*What have I done that has made a real impact?* I wondered as I sat shivering on my deck, which overlooked row after row of condos and a malodorous McDonald's. I sent the occasional hundred dollars to my local public radio station. There was the time in tenth grade that I successfully petitioned for my high school to stop dissecting fetal cats in the biology lab. Last year, I teamed up with the IT department to create a shared network that allowed my colleagues to access one another's files from any location, leading to fewer vacation- and illness-related workflow interruptions. Being chained to my desk most days, I didn't have the opportunity to use the network myself, but I was told it was a lovely innovation.

Nothing, I concluded. Unlike Shea, I had not done a damn thing to crow about, let alone be privately proud of, and that was far more awful than learning that my supposed life partner had relinquished his role.

I contemplated taking another sleeping pill or seven, but called Paul instead. He picked up on the first ring. There were people in the background, lots of them, and they sounded shmacked.

"Where are you?"

"A bar. I'm out with some of my coworkers. Market's closed for the week, remember?"

"Uh, yeah," I said, only then recalling that it was Friday. "Well, can you put on your money goggles for a few more minutes?"

He laughed. "They never come off, Libs. Is this about divorce lawyers? Because I already looked into it. It'll run you about twenty-three thousand, give or take a few. Mediation's a fraction of that, but if you want to take Tom to the cleaners, I suggest spending more up front."

"He's worth nothing."

"You can say that again, sister."

I blinked hard, trying to keep the tears at bay. It was pointless; Paul could smell my sob from eight hundred miles away. "Oh, Libby. I know you don't like it, but I'm sending you a psychic hug right now.

*Mmm-mmm!* Okay, now hold on, I'm going outside so I can hear you better."

When the commotion died down, I asked him how much money I would need to live on for a year. I probably wouldn't last that long, but just in case, I didn't want to be a burden, not even to Paul, who had roughly a trazillion dollars tied up in investments and property but who also had two children to care for.

"Are you taking a year off?" he said with a mix of delight and horror. Paul became comatose when he wasn't working, and had two smartphones on his person at all times. But he liked the *idea* of downtime and was constantly telling me to take a break.

"Affirmative."

"What are you going to do with yourself?"

"I'm going on vacation. Then maybe I'll come see you and spend some time with Dad," I said vaguely. If our mother's ovarian cancer was any indication, I would also lose half my body weight, pretend not to be in horrific pain, and compensate by sleeping for fifteen to twenty hours at a time. But Paul would learn this soon enough.

"Perfect! The twins will be so happy to see you, and we can do career brainstorming while you're here. I think you would make a brilliant hedge fund manager."

"If that was true, I wouldn't be calling you to figure out how much cash I need."

"I do see your point. So . . ." He muttered a few numbers to himself, then rattled off a figure that was higher than I was expecting. "I want to double-check this when I have my computer in front of me, but I'm assuming you'll need to front your own health coverage and will end up paying the entire mortgage on your own. You've been following my plan, haven't you?" he asked, referring to the budget he created for Tom and me several years ago.

"Of course. Paul?"

"Hit me."

"Wh—"

"Ow!" he exclaimed, and in spite of myself, I laughed; I'd been falling for that stupid joke since we were kids.

"Seriously, though. What if I sell the condo?"

"And come live with me for a while? I could turn the whole bottom floor of the brownstone into a private apartment for you."

"Maybe," I said vaguely, as I had no intention of actually moving in with him. "How much would I need then?" I wanted to liquidate as many assets as possible. Also, the idea of Tom being homeless was appealing.

Paul gave me another number, one that was much lower.

"Awesome. One last question. I want to give, um, some money away. You know, try to boost my karma and lower my taxes for the year," I said, asking God to forgive me for this and the many fibs I'd had to tell over the past several days. "How would I find a good charity?"

"Check out Charity Navigator. They have a full rundown of who's legit. Look for an organization that has at least a B-plus rating."

"You know everything," I said. I was starting to see the light again.

"It's a burden, I tell you."

"I love you the most, Paul."

An hour later, I emptied half my savings. I would've unloaded the entire account, but since there was a chance I'd have to split it with Tom if I lived long enough to legally divorce him, I stuck the other half in a cash deposit.

I couldn't find a well-established charity specifically for children who had lost parents to cancer; and while I briefly contemplated turning the lie I told Ty and Shea into truth by forming some sort of foundation for that purpose, I ultimately decided my money would be better off with people who knew what they were doing. So I chose two nonprofits dedicated to cancer research—Memorial Sloan Kettering Cancer Center and St. Jude's Children's Research Hospital—and sent each one a check far larger than any I had ever written before, specifying that the donations were in memory of Charlotte Ross, my mother.

Which got me thinking. Though I was prone to prayer and put my faith in God, I could not say with absolute certainty that I believed in the afterlife—although I sure as hell hoped it existed. I wasn't so much interested in meeting my maker as I was in seeing my mother again. As this possibility drew nearer, however, I was getting a tad panicky. Had she been watching my life from afar? What would she say about my choices? The two donations seemed inconsequential. Surely I could pay tribute to my mother in an even bigger and more meaningful way.

Yes. Yes I could. And I would do so by ridding myself of all the treasures I would not be storing up in heaven.

I went on Craigslist and placed an ad:

DIVORCE SALE! MID-CENTURY FURNITURE!
LIGHT SCULPTURES! MODERN ART! DIRT
CHEAP PRICES—EVERYTHING MUST GO!

Then I called my Realtor friend. "Libby?" he said curiously. I'd already reached out to him about the condo, but he probably was not expecting me to contact him at nine on a Friday night, especially as we hadn't seen each other since a mutual friend's engagement party a few years ago.

"Raj, I want to move forward. Can you still sell the apartment for me?"

He perked right up. "So you're going to go through with it! How soon?"

"Yesterday."

"How much do you want?"

"Enough to make the mortgage disappear," I said, and told him what I still owed.

He whistled. "Nice. You guys bought before the height of the market, so you'll probably pocket close to a hundred."

"Dollars?"

"Thousand, Libby. A hundred thousand."

I exhaled. "Tell me more."

"I can get it listed this week, but you're going to have to make sure the place is as clean and clutter-free as possible."

"Not a problem. It'll be all but empty, and I'll be out of town for the next month."

Raj and I were friends online, and he'd seen my recent status update about being single. "Libby, I hate to ask, but—"

"Tom's not happy about it, although I've paid for ninety-eight percent of this place. Even so, he's on board." I'd have to get the locks changed and forge Tom's signature. That was regrettable.

On the other hand, I was going to make it rain for kids with cancer. Heck, by the time the condo was unloaded, Shea's measly literacy donation would look like a lemonade stand.

More important, I would no longer be a worthless chunk of carbon, but rather a daughter who had done at least a little something to show that her mother's death had not been entirely in vain.

# NINE

"Mary and Joseph, Libby. Have you lost your mind?" said Jess. She glanced around my apartment, which was barren. I had planned to hold the Death and Divorce Sale all day, but an interior designer armed with a moving van and a couple of beefy guys showed up first thing that morning and nearly cleared me out. "This is really yours?" the designer kept asking; apparently putting Salvation Army prices on Scandinavian furniture makes it appear as though you're not doing business on the up-and-up. Though my initial goal had been to unload everything as quickly as possible, I realized the designer had the ability to pad my charity fund, and I tacked an extra thousand bucks onto her bill. She didn't open her trap again.

I wouldn't have buzzed Jess up if I had known it was her, but I thought she was another buyer swinging by.

"Seriously," she said, aghast. "I think you should see a professional. Like, today."

I followed Jess's eyes to the dust bunnies clustered where the cream sectional had been not an hour before. "Maybe," I allowed. I examined her outfit du jour. "Then again, I'm not the one wearing a feather in my hair without a hint of irony and carrying a bag made from llama foreskins."

"It's ostrich." She sniffed. "And I've been calling you. I'm sorry about the other night, but avoiding me isn't going to make this better."

"I'm not trying to make anything better."

Now it was her turn to regard me skeptically. "While I find that hard to believe in theory, the state of your apartment says you're telling the truth. Where's your furniture?"

"I'm redecorating," I said, unable to suppress my smile.

"Libby, that is not nice. That furniture meant a lot to Tom."

"A shame the same could not be said of our wedding vows." I laughed, but it came out hollow. "Besides, you and I both know that I paid for nearly every single thing here. Er, that was here. I believe I'm entitled to do as I please with it."

"I suppose you are."

"Is Tom staying with you guys?" I asked.

"Yeah. For a little while." She looked around for a place to sit, but the only options were the coffee table—a long glass number that was both ugly and unstable—and the floor. "You want to go outside for a smoke?"

"Sure."

I hadn't sold the patio set yet, so we sat on wicker love seats facing each other, Jess puffing away. She'd been trying to quit for years, mostly because O'Reilly hated the smell, but she still had a few a day and reasoned that she would kick the habit for good when she got pregnant. Jess had been putting off pregnancy for as long as I could remember, and she was two years older than me.

"So you knew for a long time," I said.

She exhaled a thin plume of smoke. "No. I only found out last week. But I did wonder."

I winced. Jess had suspected it. Why hadn't I?

"Oh, Libby, don't make that face," she said, pressing her half-finished cigarette into the small glass dish I kept out for her. She didn't like to smoke them all the way down; too gauche or something. "It's not like I caught him sneaking into a gay club."

"Then what? What was it?" I said. I was starting to cry again, which was annoying.

"To be honest, I don't know. I just felt like . . ." She stared at the golden arches peeking over the condo garage. "I always felt like he was a little in love with Michael," she said, meaning O'Reilly.

"You did?" I said, wiping my eyes with the back of my hand.

"Um, yeah." She laughed. "I mentioned it to Michael once, and he was really upset with me, so I never said anything ever again, but I think he secretly agrees with me. He was so shook up when Tom came out to him. I mean, if you were in the dark, then Michael was at the bottom of a cave with a fully functioning flashlight that he refused to turn on. I'm not saying he's homophobic," she added quickly, probably thinking about Paul.

"I know," I assured her. "And trust me. I get it. You think you know someone . . ."

"And then you find out you really don't. Not at all," she said, and reached into her bag for another cigarette.

I almost blurted it out. Part of me wanted to unload the horrible thing that was pressing down on my chest like an anvil. But I wouldn't want Jess to tell anyone, and that would be asking her to lie quietly under the anvil with me.

"Jess, I would say we should stay friends, but I'm planning on leaving Chicago, and I don't think I'll be coming back for a very long time."

Jess was about to lift a match to her cigarette, but she put it on the table and came over to sit next to me. "Libby, I love you, but I worry about you sometimes."

"Why is everyone always saying that?"

"Well, why on earth would you think geography will end our friendship? We've been friends for, how long is it now?"

I counted in my head. "At least twelve years."

"Exactly." She put her arm around me and I tried not to stiffen; like I mentioned, I wasn't crazy about people other than Tom touching me. "The weirdness will pass, you know. One day you'll wake up and you won't feel like showing up at Tom's work and making a fool of yourself."

I scowled. "I didn't make a fool of myself. I just wanted him to know our marriage was officially over."

"Whatever you need to tell yourself to get through this," she said jokingly, then gave me another sideways hug. "But really. Things will start looking up. I just know it."

"That's very sweet, Jess." I was losing steam again. "I only wish it was true."

After Jess left, I started boxing up what was left of the apartment, which was mostly in piles on the floor (although the contents of our bedroom remained untouched; I couldn't bring myself to let anyone in there, and besides, I needed a place to sleep until I flew to Mexico). I would mail a few things to Paul's. The rest would go in the trash or would be donated.

I shouldn't have, but I found myself sprawled across the bed, flipping through our wedding album. Tom, in his spiffy suit that he had no business buying on a credit card that would take two years to pay off; me in my mother's wedding dress, which had to be let out significantly but was gorgeous all the same. We were both grinning wildly, faces plump in the way that gave us away as closer to twenty than forty.

Paul was right: we were too young to be making such a major life decision. And while I may have been too foolish to know better, somewhere in his soul, Tom must have—he just *must* have—known he would one day betray me with his truth, and yet he went and married me anyway. I'll be honest: when I thought about this, I literally wanted to kill him, in the most grammatically accurate rendition of the phrase.

I flipped through a few pages of the album before pausing at a photo of Tom and me standing in the middle of a busy downtown street. We were on a strip of raised concrete that divided one direction of traffic from the other, but with my wedding dress spread out over the cement, it looked like we were parting the cars. Tom had tipped me backward to kiss me; just behind my head, a bus, blurred by distance and speed, charged toward us. When I saw the shot after the wedding, I thought it was cute. Cute! Like, *Look, my marriage is so strong that this two-ton city bus can't shatter it!*

That girl, who couldn't identify a metaphor if it ran her over? Who believed her future held a house full of laughing children and a husband who would love her for the rest of her life?

I didn't know her anymore. I wondered if I ever really had.

# TEN

After my mother died, I wanted to die, too. I don't often think about that time; mostly I pretend it never happened. Our family has almost no photos from the year that followed the funeral, but the few that exist reveal an uncomfortably overweight girl with short, self-shorn hair; her brother, who, while thin and hauntingly beautiful, was every bit as uneasy in his skin; her father, a bereft middle-aged man with a lightning strike of gray running through his curls; and a shadow where a wife and mother should have been standing beside them. You can see why I don't like to reminisce.

In the end, I recovered, as did Paul, and we did it by hiding away from the world—ditching our friends, dropping activities we'd once excelled at, doing the bare minimum in school, burying our noses in novels, and cultivating a disturbing appreciation for horror flicks (which appalled our father, who nonetheless handed over his Blockbuster card because he worried that saying no would cause even more trauma to our fragile psyches). What little we spoke was to each other or Dad; slasher films aside, we wanted to protect him as much as we motherless pubescent humans were able, and ignoring him would have had the opposite effect.

This is all to say that isolation worked, so it's not terribly surprising that after my adult life fell apart in the span of a few short hours and continued to crumble in the days that followed, my instinct was to re-create the people-less bubble that once brought me peace. I needed to get to a better place so I could live like I was dying. Which is surprisingly difficult to do if you *are in fact dying*, as opposed to, say, singing along to some canned song written by a guy who has never had anything more serious than the stomach flu, or reading a fridge magnet to remind yourself that if this were your last day on the planet, you would have a tub of Cool Whip for dinner—dessert first and all that—then go line-dancing with your friends.

I didn't want to sing. I didn't want to gorge myself on imitation dairy or put on cowboy boots. But if I could just ignore the world for a month or two, I was confident that I would eventually be able to fully immerse myself in life's little pleasures while I still had a life left to live.

If the voice mails I received in the thirty-six hours following the Death and Divorce Sale were any indication, solitude was a tall order.

PAUL: "You know I don't like it when I don't hear from you every day. Call me or I'm going to send a diving crew into the Chicago River to look for you."

DAD: "Paul told me about Tom. I'm so sorry, honey. I love you. Call me when you get a chance."

JACKIE: "Libby, you cow! Come back before I send a messenger to drag you here by the hair. The holiday ads will kill me if I don't have an assistant, so stop sulking and get your bovine butt in the office. *Now!*"

PAUL: "Libs? Knock it off and call me."

PAUL: "Libs. *Today.*"

RANDOM MEDICAL RECEPTIONIST: "This call is for Elizabeth Miller. Elizabeth, Dr. S—" (*Delete.*)

JACKIE: "Libby, this is not amusing. Get your dimpled a—" (*Delete.*)

PAUL: "Regret to inform you that if you do not pick up your phone soon, I will be forced to get on a plane and come find you. Although that would require getting in a large hunk of metal and catapulting myself into the air at the mercy of a plebeian who makes a mere hundred and fifty-six thousand dollars a year to operate said metal, and as you are well aware, I'd rather wax my sac than do that. So call me, okay?"

JACKIE: "I spoke with HR. There's an extra fifteen thousand in it for you—" (*Delete.*)

RAJ: "The listing's live and I've already had a few inquiries. I can start showing as soon as you're ready. Talk soon."

TOM: "Um." (It sounded like he dropped the phone.)

TOM: "Me again. Are you okay? Can you please call me?"

DAD: "It's me again, Libby Lou. Please call me when you can."

I texted Paul a photo of the empty apartment as proof of life, then hopped up on the kitchen counter and called my father back.

He sounded like he was trying not to sound tired. "Hey, kiddo. Paul told me about you and Tom. I'm . . . I'm just really sorry. You deserve better."

"Thanks, Dad," I said, and even though I promised myself that I wouldn't, I sat on the other end and cried. "There, there," he said at one point, which made me cry even harder.

"Sorry," I sniffed when I could finally speak again. "Let's talk about something else. How's Dolores?" As far as Paul and I could tell, my father had been dating Dolores for about two years, but he insisted on referring to her as his "friend."

"Oh, she's good. We went to see a movie last week," he said. I pictured him sitting in his small cedar-shingled bungalow, watching the Tigers in his Red Sox town, then going to bed alone. Even more than I regretted marrying Tom, I regretted not going to visit my father more over the past few years. I'd been wrapped up with work, and trying to get pregnant, and—well, every excuse was lame, and now none of it mattered. Maybe I would shorten my trip to a month so I'd have more good time with him.

"I'm thinking of going to Mexico, Dad," I told him. I didn't supply that I'd quit my job and already booked a ticket.

"Mexico? Honey, isn't that a bad choice, seeing as how the two of you went there on your honeymoon?"

I hadn't really thought of it that way, I confessed as I ran my hand along the countertop, which was cool to the touch. Tom claimed white soapstone was overdone to the point of being tacky, but it was one of the few features of the apartment I really liked.

"Every time you see a taco or sombrero you're going to think of Tom," my father said. "Is it okay if I say his name, or is that too much?"

"It's okay." I pictured Tom snorkeling beside me in the Gulf of Mexico. A giant stingray had just passed beneath us, and Tom, knowing I was panicking, calmly took my hand and gently tugged on it, signaling for me to follow him back to the shore. When we surfaced, he wrapped me in a dry towel and hugged me tight until my teeth stopped chattering. That was the thing about Tom: he always made me feel safe and warm. Now, when I most needed that sense of security, it was no longer available to me.

"Okay, good, because if I tried not to, I would probably end up saying it all the time. Anyway, honey, why don't you go somewhere else? Like Hawaii. No, that's too romantic, and that wouldn't be good . . . hmm."

"I'm still here, Dad," I reminded him. He was in the habit of talking to himself, which was getting worse as he got older.

"Sorry, kiddo. Oh! I know. Puerto Rico. Go to Puerto Rico," he said. "One of the best beaches your mother and I ever went to was on the southern side of this little run-down island called Vieques."

"Really?" I asked. He did that on occasion—surprised me with some story about my mom that he'd never mentioned before, as though he was saving it up for just the right moment.

"Yep. The navy was there then, and the locals weren't too thrilled about that, but I read in the paper that the government moved out a few years ago. Anyway, unless things have changed, it wasn't a couples' destination, and it was terrific. There was this bay where the water lit up at night, and there were horses running wild all over the place . . . your mother always said she wanted to go back one day."

"Huh," I said. The lit-up bay bit made him sound a little touched, but I was nonetheless intrigued.

He continued. "I think you'd like it. Everyone speaks English and Spanish, so that's easy, and it's a US territory and you don't have to worry about changing your money into pesos or what have you. Although I do worry about you traveling alone. Maybe Paul could go with you, or your friend Jen," he said, meaning Jess.

"I'll look into it, Dad. Thanks for the suggestion."

"You're welcome. You know I love you, right, Libby Lou?"

I felt the sobs coming on. "Dad, I've gotta let you go, but I'll see you soon, okay?"

"I hope so, kiddo. I really do."

Even as I cried, I noticed it again—that speck of hope shining through. After all, my father had just provided me with the most inspired idea I'd had since stabbing Tom. My days were numbered, and I was wasting time in a city that was home to my sort-of-ex-husband, my should-have-been lover, and the doctor who'd given me the worst news of my life—but I didn't have to stay. And why should I, when there was a Spanish-speaking, non-passport-requiring, solace-providing beach destination just a short plane ride away? Of course, I would be wasting money by abandoning the Mexico trip, but for once I didn't care. The cash couldn't go with me when I crossed over.

Yes, I would go to this Vieques Island and find out why my mother had loved it. I would go right away.

Tom ambushed me as I was leaving for the airport.

"Where are you heading, Libby?" he said, stepping out of the stairwell in front of our apartment.

I smiled out of habit, but then the more evolved neurons in my brain reconnected, and I remembered that this man was no longer my ally but rather the enemy.

"Fire!" I yelled, because I once read this was the fastest way to get help if you were being attacked.

"You can't keep running," he said, although he took a step back. He was probably afraid, and rightly so, that I would pull a kitchen utensil out of my coat after I finished accusing him of arson.

"Watch me," I retorted, attempting to skedaddle. With two large suitcases attached to my person, this was a bit of a challenge.

Faced with my imminent departure, Tom lunged forward to grab my arm. I jerked away, which sent the larger of the two suitcases tumbling. I'm sorry to report that my hand was still firmly clamped around the handle, so away I went—bump, bump, bump, belly-down on the stairs, the synthetic carpet grabbing at my incision like Velcro. I gritted my teeth, willing myself not to cry out in pain. The suitcase and I landed in a pile in front of the ground-floor apartments.

One of my neighbors, whose name was Bill, maybe, or Will, stuck his head out the door, probably curious to know who was making such a racket at eight in the morning. "Hello?" he said. Then he looked down at me. "Yeesh! Are you okay?"

Out of the corner of my eye, I saw Tom approaching. "Help!" I cried. "My ex-husband is trying to kill me!"

"Knock it off, Libby!" Tom said, although he had gone to the trouble of carrying my second suitcase down for me.

With some effort, I stood up. There was a searing sensation radiating from my stomach, and I was fairly certain that half of my stitches had just been ripped out, but I was going to have to learn to get used to pain. Perhaps the Brookstone store at the airport sold self-hypnosis CDs.

"Should I call someone?" Bill-or-Will asked, glancing at Tom, who was now standing next to me.

"Only if you hear me scream again," I said. Then I turned to Tom and opened my mouth wide, the corners of my lips curling upward in a creepy clown smile.

The neighbor closed his door, although I was willing to bet he was lingering on the other side, waiting to see if our marital strife would play out as comedy or tragedy.

"Libby," Tom warned. "Please stop it. I just want to talk to you. I need you to know that this isn't your fault. Your behavior tells me that you don't actually know that. I think you should see a psychologist."

"My fault?" I said. "My fault?! At what point did I give you the impression that I think *I* am the reason you are attracted to men?"

"Can we please go somewhere else to talk about this? Like our apartment?" He sounded exasperated.

"See, that's the thing," I said. My stomach really hurt, and it was hard to separate that from the anger I felt toward Tom. "You insist on talking to me when I clearly do not want to talk. You tell me I should see a shrink. You're a control freak, Tom, and you think that this—you ending our marriage—is something you can control. Well, I've got news for you: the show's over. How I react is entirely up to me. *Me!*" I yelled, channeling my nephews yet again. "*Not* you."

He looked almost as surprised as when I'd forked him. "I'm sorry, Libby. I was only trying to be helpful when I said you should see someone. You should, you know. You're not acting like yourself."

"The Libby you knew is dead, Tom," I said. "And by the way, I changed the locks. Until I get back and hire an attorney, you'll need to find somewhere else to live."

I took my luggage and rather ungracefully maneuvered it through the front door, down the sidewalk, and onto the curb. Then I stuck my fingers in my mouth and whistled for the livery cab I had called to take me to O'Hare. The rest of my life was waiting, and I did not intend to be late.

# ELEVEN

Great mother of pearl! Liquor was powerful stuff. While I wasn't sure I liked it, I had a feeling it might come in handy as I prepared to meet my maker. Historically, I had no strong feelings toward alcohol one way or the other, but aside from the occasional beer or celebratory glass of champagne, I'd largely avoided it because Tom's father was an alcoholic, and not the jolly, highly functioning type. Even mild inebriation made Tom uncomfortable.

But his concerns were no longer my own, so after learning I had two whole hours to kill before my flight, I pulled a move that was decidedly un-Libby-like: I walked into an airport bar, sat down, and told the bartender to serve me what he would have if he were making a drink for himself. (In hindsight, perhaps this was not the best idea, as the bartender's capillary-spidered cheeks said he'd spent the better part of his life downing highly flammable spirits.) "Dirty martini," he said, pouring the contents of a silver shaker into a deceptively small cocktail glass with a flourish. I didn't know what to do with myself, so as bitter and medicinal as the martini was, I set about drinking it as though each sip would make it more appetizing. Which proved to be true.

Five minutes later, it was gone, so I ordered another one, which I drank slower as the room began to tilt ever so slightly. Gin seemed to supply a gentler buzz than Tom's sleeping pills (though I brought those with me, too, just in case). On the other hand, I knew that if I finished the second martini, my carry-on would never make it with me to the gate, so I left half the murky liquid in the glass, paid my bill, and went wandering through the terminal.

Many believe O'Hare International Airport to be the very inferno Dante spoke of, but I don't mind it. The bookstores are good, the food isn't half-bad, and while you encounter the occasional screaming traveler, most people who pass through are distantly friendly in that Midwestern way. Also, there's a Brookstone, which I located roughly four and a half miles from my gate. The store was fresh out of self-hypnosis CDs, and much to the saleswoman's frustration, I didn't see the point of buying soothing ocean sounds when I would be on the beach the following morning. So I plopped down in a massage chair and treated the contents of my stomach to a reenactment of the bartender's martini mixing.

I'd just closed my eyes when I heard someone squeal my name. "Libby?! Libby Ross Miller, is that *you?*"

*No, no it most certainly is not,* I thought, sinking lower into the leather seat and pushing my feet against the floor in a desperate attempt to make the chair swivel. Alas, it was nailed firmly to the floor, so I opened my eyes and confirmed what I already knew to be true. It's funny, isn't it, how a person can gain or lose a ton of weight, get her nose done, or do any number of things that would make it difficult to recognize her across a crowded room—but she says one word and you can immediately identify her? So although I had not seen Maxine Gaines in a good fifteen years, all I needed to hear was the first syllable of my name to know exactly who was calling it from behind a stack of self-massage tools.

As she rushed at me, I reluctantly stood to greet her. "Libby, OMG! How *crazy* to run into you after all these years!" she screeched.

While I trusted plenty of humans who didn't deserve it, those who eschewed full words in favor of spoken acronyms did not make the cut. "Yeah, crazy," I said.

Maxine and I were friends in high school, probably because I was one of the few people who would tolerate her insufferability; her hyper-achieving goody-goody act made my church girl seem like a delinquent who was just a few bad decisions away from becoming an after-school special. I wasn't sad when I stopped hearing from Maxine once she went to college *out east*, as she coyly and constantly referred to Princeton, although I accepted her friend request a few years ago, largely because I hadn't understood the nebulous, passive-aggressive way that online friendships often work.

"I've actually been thinking about you! Are you still in Chicago?"

"Not really," I said. "I'm kind of between continents right now."

"Wow! And here I thought living in New York was exciting. I'm still waiting to run into Paul, by the way. I'm practically right around the block from him and *Charlie* on the UWS." Her tone told me that while she was plenty proud of her ivy matriculation and New Yorker status, she was even more impressed that my brother's partner happened to be an actor on one of the top crime procedurals on network television.

Maxine zeroed in on my naked ring finger even as I ogled the engagement boulder teetering off the back of her hand, which I had already seen close-ups of online. "I saw that you and Tom are no more," she said, making a pouty face. "Are you *okay?*"

I smiled stiffly. "I'm peachy. People change." I didn't believe this, but given my circumstances, I longed to, and it was a sufficiently vague explanation for why my marriage went the way of the stegosaurus.

"Do they, though?" she said, opening her anime eyes even wider.

"Yes, they do," I said.

Her half smile dripped with pity. "If you say so."

"I *do* say so. That's exactly what I say."

I kept waiting for her to announce that she had a flight to catch, but she just stood there. Judging me.

"If it makes you feel any better, I always wondered about Tom. Did he cheat on you?" she asked, raising a penciled-in eyebrow.

A petite growl escaped from my throat, which Maxine seemed to misinterpret as me struggling not to cry.

"Oh, Libby," she said, leaning in to hug me, "I won't pretend to understand why God has allowed such monumental challenges into your life, but know that I'll be praying for you."

As she attempted to squeeze the stuffing out of me, I decided to invoke my Fourth Amendment–mandated right to protect against unreasonable search and seizure and casually let my teeth rest on her bony shoulder blade.

She pulled back rather violently. "Jesus Christ, did you just bite me?"

"*Bite* you?" I said, flashing my canines pleasantly. "Sheesh, Maxine. Maybe people don't change." I shook my head, then sat back down in the massage chair. "Now, if you don't mind, I'm going to try to unwind for a few minutes before I get on a plane to paradise. I'll tell Paul to be on the lookout for you on the Upper. West. Side," I said, slowly enunciating each word. "Adios!"

She opened her mouth, closed it, and walked away. I really couldn't have asked for a better outcome.

Even so, I was a potent combo of sad and irate after Maxine left. People did indeed change, and I was exhibit A. While I wouldn't necessarily describe myself as a fount of charisma, it used to be that you could seat me next to your mumbling grandmother or lecherous uncle at your wedding and know they would later report that I was a model dining companion. But in the past week, almost every human interaction I'd been involved with had taken a wrong turn— and worse, my behavior seemed compulsive. While being blunt and occasionally aggressive was extremely satisfying in the moment, I was ashamed afterward. I had to return to a more pleasant version of myself so that I wouldn't sully everyone's good memories. Lord willing, I would find a way on the beaches of Vieques, surrounded by a bunch of strangers who—if they had any sense—would bite back, then forget all about me.

When I was sure Maxine was nowhere in sight, I wandered over to my gate, and after what seemed an eternity, boarded the plane. I'd requested a window seat, so I pressed my face to the Plexiglas and watched the skyline disappear as we rose above Chicago and headed over Lake Michigan.

It was amazing, that lake—one of the biggest in the world, so expansive that an air traveler could easily mistake it for the sea if she didn't know better. When Tom and I moved to the city in our early twenties, I made him drive me up and down Lake Shore Drive night after night, and even though gas sapped our already anemic budget, and Tom's clunker was constantly threatening to quit, he took me because he was just as enamored as I was. Traffic at all hours of the day; twinkling skyscrapers stacked thick against the sky; the beautiful western coast, which we saw as the right side of the lake because it was everything that our childhoods in the suburbs of Grand Rapids were not. The city was our beginning.

I had purchased a one-way ticket to San Juan, and from there a one-way ticket to Vieques. When the month was up, I would probably fly directly to New York. If I was able to sell the apartment remotely, as I hoped, it was entirely possible that I would never see Chicago again. As the plane continued to ascend and the lake vanished beneath the clouds, I found myself praying that one day—one day soon—this would no longer feel like a loss.

. . .

Several hours later, the plane descended over vivid blue-green waves and delivered me to the San Juan International Airport.

A man with a handwritten sign greeted me at the gate. With dark curls and deeply tanned skin, he looked Latino, but didn't have so much as a hint of a Spanish accent. "You're Libby Miller? Great," he said in a way that made it impossible to discern whether he was being sincere or sarcastic. The wraparound shades he wore, even though we were indoors, did not help. He took my carry-on from me. "We'll get your checked bag, then head to the tarmac."

"Tarmac?" I asked. Thanks to my new friend gin and the exhaustion plaguing me, I had fallen asleep shortly after takeoff and slept most of the flight. Now I had cottonmouth, a pounding headache, and the linguistic capacity of a second grader.

"Private planes use different runways from the commercial carriers, and they usually don't have gates," he said. "You did book a charter flight to Vieques, right?"

"Right," I said, massaging my temples.

"Great. Do you have to use the bathroom or anything? There isn't one on the plane."

"I'm good," I said, though this had not been true for more than a week. I tagged after him to the baggage claim. Once we located my suitcase, we wound through a series of halls, eventually coming to a security checkpoint where a uniformed woman barely glanced at my license. A set of stairs deposited the two of us onto a blazing hot field of cement. The roar of jet engines shot through the air, and I covered my ears. The man pointed at a battered pickup truck at the edge of the lot, indicating that was where we were heading.

When we reached the truck, he threw my suitcases onto the bed, then opened the passenger door for me. The truck didn't have the name of the airline on it, and I hesitated as I imagined Paul chiding me for not being more cautious. *Eh,* I thought as I thanked the man and climbed in. Not that I wanted to miss out on my vacation, but the Grim Reaper was lurking just offstage anyway. If this guy wanted to drive me to a secluded beach and strangle me—which seemed highly unlikely, as he barely seemed to register my presence—then it would probably be no worse than, and possibly preferable to, death by overzealous cell colonization.

I was hoping for air-conditioning, but the man rolled down the windows and I spent the next few minutes pretending to be entranced by palm trees while wondering if I was sweating hard enough to make it look like I wet my pants. We pulled up near an airstrip where a row of planes was parked. The man grabbed my suitcases and began walking to a small plane. Scratch that—a plane so minuscule you could park it in the average suburban driveway. He pulled down a panel that made up the better part of the right side of the plane and suddenly I understood Paul's fear of flying all too well: this thing was a tin can with wings, and I was about to allow it to hurl me into the sky.

The man started up a rickety set of stairs attached to the panel, both suitcases in hand. When he reached the top, he turned. "Coming?"

I looked at him, confused. There wasn't a single other person in sight. "Where's the pilot?" I asked.

"You're looking at him," he said. I was indeed, and he was wearing deck shoes, a pair of khaki shorts, and a linen shirt that was two washes away from becoming a rag. I must have done the disappearing-neck trick because he said, "Hey, look, I'm doing you a favor. It's my day off and I could have said no when they asked me to fly you, which would mean you would've ended up on the ferry. And trust me, unless you want to lose your lunch, you don't want to take the ferry on a windy day like today."

I wasn't sure whether to be embarrassed or irritated. "I didn't have lunch," I said. "And thanks, I suppose." I climbed in after him. "I'm the only passenger?"

"Yep," he said. He turned around to face me and finally lifted his sunglasses. His dark brown eyes met my own, and he stared at me for what seemed to be longer than a socially acceptable length of time (though to his credit, I didn't look away, either). Something odd in me had just begun to flutter when he pivoted and pulled the glasses back over his eyes. "Sit where you want," he said.

"Okay," I said flatly. There were just a handful of seats to choose from; I took one behind him to the right, which had a decent view out the tiny cockpit window as well as the side window. Shades firmly in place, he swiveled back around and ran me through the emergency procedures, which involved little more than a seat belt and a prayer, then handed me a large pair of noise-blocking headphones. "It's a quick flight, about twenty-five minutes, but it's loud. And Puerto Rico gets busy in the fall, so it can take a while to get out of San Juan."

He wasn't kidding. We sat on the runway for the better part of an hour as large sweat stains formed in the pits of my T-shirt, and my jeans papier-mâchéd themselves to my thighs. I cursed myself for not taking two minutes in the terminal to change into a dress, then chided myself for caring. After all, I had bigger fish to fry than body odor, and besides, I would never see this alleged pilot again.

Even so, I had nothing else to do, so I kept stealing glances at him. I couldn't tell how old he was; his hairline was just starting to recede and his sideburns were threaded with gray, but acne scars pocked his cheeks slightly, which gave him the air of a teenage boy. He sat facing forward, saying nothing, which was aggravating, although the aggravation itself was grating because my goal was to be left alone and there I was, not even enjoying this rare triumph.

Finally, he said something into a headset, then yelled back at me, "Green light. We're going up."

Up we went. Once again I found myself over the turquoise sea, staring at the lush green landscape and long yellow beaches that make up Puerto Rico's northeastern coast. I was curious to learn more—in my haste, I hadn't even bothered to buy a travel book—but the pilot proved to be a piss-poor tour guide. "You can't really see the rain forest from here, but it's out there . . . ," he droned. "To your right is Fajardo, which is where the ferry runs from . . . that lump of land in the distance is another island called Culebra."

Even so, there was something magical about the altitude; we were up in the air, but so close to the water that I could see passengers on the boats we flew over. In spite of Maxine, my headache, and the unpleasant events of the past week, my spirits rose significantly. I had made many wrong decisions recently, but this trip? It couldn't have been one of them.

As the plane began to descend, bringing us closer to the water, the pilot looked over his shoulder at me. "Isn't it great up here?" he shouted.

"Yes!" I shouted back. "I love being away from the rest of the world!"

He smiled. "Exactly!"

Buoyed by my newfound sense of well-being, I was feeling generous. Gregarious, even. "By the way, I didn't catch your name."

"Shiloh," he shouted again.

*That's an unusual*—I didn't have time to finish my thought, because there was a loud *thud-thud-thud*, followed immediately by a shredding noise, which coincided with the plane lurching from side to side.

Adrenaline coursed through my veins as stomach acid surfaced in my gullet. "What was that?" I whimpered as I stared out the window at an inauspicious plume of black smoke billowing out of an unidentified location.

"Nothing," he said, but then he started yelling into his headset. "Carib Carrier seven three two. Emergency. Bird strike to air intake. Requesting landing at VQS. May attempt water landing. Alert Coast Guard."

We began to drop. Rapidly. At which point I began to freak out ever so subtly. I grabbed my phone from my pocket and texted Paul: I LOVE YOU. XOXO. Then, as further evidence of my mental infirmity, I texted an identical message to Tom, adding, IT'S OKAY, exonerating him just in time for my demise. I considered calling my father, who didn't text, but realized that this would amount to him listening to me scream as I flew into the sea.

The man I now knew as Shiloh yelled at me again. "Tighten your seat belt, tuck your head between your arms, and lean into your lap. Now!"

As the plane careened toward the water, I had a singular thought, and this thought branded me a liar.

Because all that stuff I told myself about not caring if I was strangled and being ready to see my mother again? Lies. Damn lies.

No, as I begged God for a miracle, the truth rang clear through me: *I don't want to die.*

# TWELVE

The plane skidded clumsily and hit something—the ground? the sea?—with a tremendous crack. My head smashed against the back of the seat in front of me, then jerked back as we tipped precariously to the left. I held my breath, waiting for the worst, the engine to explode, the water to seep in and deliver me to a watery grave. But all was silent, save a faint rumbling coming from the front of the plane.

Shiloh let out a whoop, then turned to me. "We made it! You're okay?"

"Am I okay? Are you fudging kidding me?" I spat. To say his celebratory mood ticked me off was pretty much the understatement of the century. "You almost just killed us. We almost just *died*."

He undid his seat belt, then reached back to unlatch mine, like I was a child. "We need to get out of here in case the engine decides to blow. And for the record," he added, quickly opening the panel door and all but pushing me down the stairs, "the flock of pelicans attempting to get a bird's-eye view of the propeller almost killed us. *I* just saved your life. Do you have any idea how hard it is to land a plane like this on the side of a beach with absolutely no warning? If we'd stayed in the air another two minutes while I attempted to make it to the airport, you would be fish food right now."

Continuing to yap, he took my hand and pulled me through the shallow water we'd landed in. I glanced over my shoulder and saw that the plane was smoking, at which point I yanked my hand away and started to run for the beach—just in case God was still making up his mind about whether I should be granted a few more months on the planet.

"Hey!" Shiloh yelled, running after me. "Wait up!"

When the sand turned to patchy grass, I figured I was safe and collapsed onto the ground. Shiloh jogged up, and only then did I realize there was a trickle of blood coming from his face.

"I think your nose is bleeding," I said, shielding my face in case he got too close.

He reached up to touch it. "So it is." He wiped it with the corner of his shirt, then sat next to me and tilted his head back as he pinched the bridge of his nose. "Thanks."

I hugged my knees to my chest to try to stop shaking. "Don't mention it. So . . . now what?"

"Now we wait. We just landed on the part of the old naval grounds that are still off-limits to the public, and the control tower knew we were about to crash, so you'd better believe we won't be here by ourselves for long." He put his head back down and took his sunglasses off to examine me. "Lizzy, are you all right?"

Our eyes met again, but instead of triggering strange flutterings, it somehow reiterated that my current circumstances were not a bad dream, but instead reality. And reality, as it turned out, did not agree with me. "Libby!" I snapped. "My name is *Libby*!" Then I sort of stopped breathing.

I'd never suffered a panic attack before. Had I known mine would have me clawing at my chest in a futile attempt to get air into my lungs, I would have scurried into the brush so I could humiliate myself privately. Alas, I didn't know what was happening to me. As I gasped and scratched at myself, Shiloh watched me with interest. Not worry. Not amusement. Just interest, like I was a nature documentary he just happened to land on while channel surfing.

When it became clear I was about to choke on my own terror, he began to pat my back, and only because this was something Tom did when I was upset did I allow him to continue. "Whoa. Whoa there. It's okay, Libby," he said, saying my name as clearly as possible so I would catch that he got it right this time. "Pretty sure I know what's happening to you. You're having a panic attack. I've been there. That was a bad situation, and I'm really sorry."

*A panic attack?* I thought incredulously, but I couldn't get the words to come out of my mouth.

"Look," he said, continuing to pat me with one hand while pointing at a distant dirt path with the other. I squinted, attempting to focus, which was difficult with so little oxygen making its way to my frontal lobe.

Then I saw them—the wild horses my father told me about. There were four, galloping majestically through an opening in the trees. They trotted across the narrow path and disappeared into a clearing on the other side, gone as fast as they had come. And at once, so was my panic attack.

"Wow," I whispered.

"You feel better," Shiloh said. He smiled, and now that his sunglasses were off, the lines around his brown eyes showed that his smile was genuine.

"I do," I admitted.

"Distraction. Works every time. I learned that from an old friend back when I was having trouble coping."

I flushed. "Thanks. And sorry for yelling at you. It's just that I don't want to die. I lied to myself about it, and I thought it was fine, but now

I'm sure I was wrong, and I really just want to live, you know?" I wasn't really making any sense, but I couldn't shut up.

Shiloh looked at me curiously. "But you're alive. You didn't die."

"I'm *going to*," I explained. "I have cancer." A rush of relief washed over me as I shared the worst news of my life with a stranger.

"Damn," he said, and let out a low whistle. "That sucks."

"Yeah. And it's not even ovarian, which is what killed my mom, but some rare super cancer that's especially lethal for women my age. Twenty-nine," I added slyly, and then I knew the panic attack had fully passed.

He grinned. "See, and I would have put you at twenty-two."

"Guilty as charged." I was tempted to ask him how old he was—my current guess placed him well into his forties—but even though he knew my terrible truth and had been permitted to touch me, I wasn't going to get too cozy.

A government truck pulled up at about the same time a Coast Guard cruiser began to circle the shore. A police officer got out of the truck and approached us. "You're the pilot?" he asked Shiloh, who nodded. The officer pulled out a pad and started asking questions while I zoned out. Paul and Tom had both called me back, and I hadn't picked up because I wasn't sure how to respond to either of them. Paul was probably freaking out, but he would freak out even more once he found out that I was in Puerto Rico and hadn't told him about it. As for Tom—well, I didn't even want to go there.

"Miss? Where are you heading?" the officer asked me.

I could barely remember my middle name, let alone recall my itinerary. I grabbed my phone and opened my e-mail. "Island Motors," I told him, once I'd located my reservation confirmation. "I'm supposed to pick up a rental car."

"I'll give you a ride if you like," he said.

I looked at Shiloh. "Go ahead," he told me. "I still have to deal with dispatch and the Coast Guard."

My eyebrows shot up. "Given that your current means of transportation is your two legs, and I would prefer to never get into a moving vehicle with you ever again, I wasn't asking you for a ride. But I smell like dirty socks, and I was hoping I could get my luggage."

He glanced back at the plane, which no longer appeared to be smoldering. "Let me check." He jogged back to the shore, where a couple of Coast Guarders were milling around. He returned a few minutes later with a sheepish expression. "They've got a bunch of clearance stuff they need to do. So probably not until this evening. But I'll tell you what. You tell me where you're staying, and I'll make sure our company gets it delivered to you."

I peered down at my filthy T-shirt and frowned. "Is that my only option?"

"Afraid so."

"Okay." I was reaching for my phone to find the address to the beach house when it began to ring. Blech. "Cripes, Tom," I muttered.

"Tom's your boyfriend?" Shiloh asked.

I flushed, embarrassed that I'd been overheard. "Um, no. He's not." I caught his eye, but this time, I looked away quickly. Because this guy—the one who almost just killed me? He was very attractive—if you liked the sinewy, weathered type. And the expression on my face just informed him that I did.

It was a good thing I'd never see him again.

# THIRTEEN

"This your first time in Vieques?" the police officer asked.

"How can you tell?" I shouted, my head half out the window, like a dog coming home after a week at the kennel. Vieques was verdant, beautiful, and largely untouched by humans. There were cinderblock houses scattered among the rolling hills and dotting the roads, and we passed the occasional grocer and restaurant. On the whole, though, it was miles of solitude hedged by sea. Heaven.

"Good luck," the officer said when he dropped me off at the car rental place.

*"Gracias!"* I responded.

I rented a Jeep because I'd read that a vehicle with four-wheel drive and the ability to withstand a pothole or thirty was the only way to get around here. I almost never drove; Tom liked to, so I let him and took public transportation or a cab when I was on my own. Now I realized I'd done myself a terrible disservice. As I puttered along, the other drivers whizzed by at what seemed to be eighty miles an hour. Nerves got the better of me, and my hands began to shake again. With no navigator and only a paper map for reference, I made one wrong turn after another. I was about to drive myself into a ditch and call it a day when I spotted the street sign.

It was hand-painted on a panel of wood, sort of like the type people like to post in front of their vacation homes—*Retirement Road*; *Had Her Way*. This sign read *Calle Rosa*. It was a long dirt path canopied by trees and vines. Half a mile down, I located the driveway and turned in. Then I saw it in the distance: the stretch of beach I'd been waiting for.

I parked the Jeep at the foot of the driveway and climbed out. My feet crunched on the gravel as I strode toward the pale pink stucco house where I'd be staying.

"Took you long enough."

I jumped as an older woman emerged from behind one of the large fronded palms in front of the house.

Her laugh was broken glass on concrete. "I'm kee-ding! You're Libby, no?"

"Yes," I said, extending my hand. "You're Milagros?"

Her skin was soft and crepey beneath my fingers. "Ay, *gringa*," she trilled. "Mee-lah-grohs."

"Milagros," I corrected myself, trying not to frown at the woman who would be my landlady for the next month.

She gave me a toothy smile. "*Muy bien!* You'll be just fine, *mija*. Come on," she said, waving for me to follow her farther down the drive.

"So that's not where I'm staying?" I said, pointing at the house.

"No. That's *mi casa*." She led me to the back of her house and down a winding path, until we hit a similar but markedly smaller pink house (which, judging from the crumbling stucco and the wavy metal roof, could more accurately be described as a fancy shack). "This," she said, unlocking the wrought iron door, "is yours." She handed the key to me and motioned for me to step in.

There was a small living room, a tiny bedroom, and an eat-in kitchen. But off the back of the kitchen, a large glass-walled porch opened directly onto the beach. It was the entire reason I'd chosen this property, and unlike the rest of the house, it looked exactly as the online photos depicted it.

Milagros crossed her arms and regarded me. "You don't like it?"

"It's perfect."

She beamed. "Good. Because you already paid for it, and I don't do refunds."

I inquired about the bathroom, which I hadn't seen yet, and she directed me to a small door next to the bedroom. I looked in and tried not to gasp. It was a glorified broom closet with a sink and a toilet better suited for a preschool.

"Um . . ."

"No bath," Milagros said.

I sighed, catching an unfortunate whiff of eau de B.O. on the inhale. I could always bathe in the sea.

Milagros hooted. "You are too easy, Libby!" she said, slapping her thigh. "The shower's the best part. Follow me."

She unlocked a door off the end of the kitchen, which led to a garden surrounded by a stucco wall as high as the house itself. Though tiny, the garden was filled with birds of paradise, orchids, and dozens of other tropical plants I'd never seen before. At the end nearest to the beach, there was a cement stall. I stepped inside to find an expansive outdoor shower lined with vivid blue tiles and—just in case I needed to be reminded that I was newly single—two enormous shower heads.

"Is it safe?" I asked Milagros.

She pursed her lips. "Nothing in this world is safe, *mija*. But it would take a lot of effort for someone to get over the wall and into this garden. I've lived alone for forty-one years now. When you're a single woman, you've got to use your head. Hell," she said with that jangled laugh of hers, "when you're any kind of woman, you've got to use your head. Don't leave your purse on the back of your chair, don't wear your jewelry to the beach, and don't flash your money around." She examined me. "You okay?"

Come to think of it, I wasn't feeling so hot. "I just need to sit down," I told her. On top of my most recent brush with death, I hadn't had a proper meal since . . . yesterday? I couldn't actually remember the last time I ate, which may have been the first time in thirty-four years that I was able to make that claim.

"Here," Milagros said, guiding me to the sofa on the back porch. "Sit. I'll be right back."

I sank into the sofa and surveyed my surroundings. The place was sheer Caribbean kitsch: old wicker furniture topped with weathered floral cushions, candy-colored walls decorated with cheesy prints of seashells and boats and sunsets. Tom would have an aneurysm if he had to sleep there for a single night. I loved it.

Milagros returned with a frosty glass, which she pressed into my hand and instructed me to drink. Coconut water! Was anything ever so delicious?

"Now eat these," she said when I finished, handing me a plate full of crackers spread with a thin reddish-orange paste.

"Is this guava?" I said, my mouth jammed full of food.

She nodded. "I put fresh fruit and milk in the fridge, and coffee and granola in the cupboard. When you need groceries, there's a place about a mile from here, but there's a better one closer to Esperanza. I can tell you about any restaurant on the island, too, so if you're not sure, just ask me. You feeling better, *mija*?"

"Much better," I assured her. "Thank you. Now, I hate to ask, but do you have a T-shirt I can borrow?"


I got in the shower as soon as Milagros left. Although the water made my incision sting and my lone toiletry was the bar of soap I snatched from the bathroom sink, I soaked myself until the shaft of sunlight shining through the roofless shower had almost disappeared. What a day. What a *week*. While I was profoundly grateful to still be alive, I didn't know what to make of contradicting emotions racing through me. I was proud of myself for getting out of Chicago and excited at the prospect of my month in paradise, even if I had barely made it there.

But the more I thought about it, the more Maxine's comment—*I always wondered about Tom*—gutted me. She may as well have said, "Stupid Libby, I've known he was gay since high school! How could you not?" It was a valid question. I'd slept next to the man almost every night for the past decade and had called him my own for nearly twice as long. I truly believed he loved me in every way that a husband should love his wife.

And I had been wrong.

No amount of improved communication or couples' counseling was going to fix us. Tom and I were over. Absolutely, irrevocably done. The more I thought about it, the more it seemed that what I'd said to Jeanette in the coffee shop was true. Tom wasn't dead, but this felt an awful lot like death.

I got out of the shower, wrapped myself in one of the stiff towels I'd found in the closet, and walked back into the house. I was halfway across the kitchen when something skittered across the far edge of my peripheral vision.

On instinct, I ducked behind the cupboard island that divided the kitchen from the small dining space.

"You can get up," a wary voice called. "It's just me."

*Me?* This suggested I knew my attacker. Which, if memory served, was statistically most often the case.

"Shiloh," he said.

I groaned.

"Yeah, I sense that you're happy to see me," he said. "The good news is, I have your suitcases. So you can put some clothes on."

I stood up slowly, intending to peek over the edge of the counter to see if I could run to the bedroom without being seen—then shrieked when I realized Shiloh had walked over and was peering down at me. "Whatcha doin'?" he asked.

I pulled my towel tighter around my chest. "First you try to crash our plane, now you're trying to give me a coronary. You just let yourself in? What if I was naked?" I said indignantly, even as I mentally chided myself for failing to lock the screen porch just minutes after Milagros told me to be careful.

"I'm confused," he said, grinning. "Is that supposed to sound like an adverse outcome?"

"Creep," I retorted, although I wasn't really feeling threatened by him. (Paul would say this was on account of my faulty people reader. "You'd find something to like about Charles Manson," he groused after I mentioned I didn't think his ex-boyfriend—who, admittedly, exhibited bunny-boiling tendencies—was as awful as Paul made him out to be.)

"Guilty as charged," Shiloh said, borrowing the phrase I'd used on him earlier that day. "But I happen to be the creep who brought you your stuff. Otherwise you'd be sitting in your own stink for another forty-eight hours. No one else was available to bring your bag by."

"As you so rudely discovered, I've showered, and now I smell perfectly fine, thank you very much." I eyed him suspiciously. "I hope you're not doing this because you feel sorry for me. Because you know about . . . well, you know."

He leaned in to sniff me—the nerve of this guy! "You do smell better, and no, I didn't bring your luggage just because of the 'you know.' I happen to be a fairly decent person." He glanced around. "So what are your plans for your time on the island? Are you meeting people here? Is this Tom character making an appearance in the near future?"

I stuck my chin out. I may have even pouted. "He most certainly is not."

"Good, because you didn't sound too excited about him calling you. What are you doing for dinner tonight?"

"Finding something in the fridge," I said. "Given that I survived a near-death experience today, I'm not really up for exploring."

He gave me a half smile. "Life is a near-death experience. But suit yourself," he added lightly, as though I'd just rejected the offer he didn't actually make. "Your suitcases are on the porch. See you around, Libby."

I opened my mouth, but he was gone before I could get the words out.

# FOURTEEN

It wasn't enough that he almost scared the pants off me twice in one day. No, Shiloh had to go and inform me that nearly crashing into the Caribbean—to say nothing of the cluster muck of cells sapping away my life force—was no different from the unpleasantness of everyday existence.

Well, that pithy pilot was lucky I hadn't assaulted him, I thought to myself the following morning. Which was progress on my part, I reasoned as I pulled off the T-shirt I'd slept in and stood before the bedroom mirror. It was a cheap full-length, and the wavy glass narrowed my waist while lengthening my incision, making it look even worse than it already did. I'd removed the bandage a few days before, thinking that some air would do the wound good, but the two-inch gash remained red and angry.

Stepping into my bathing suit, I commanded myself to stop thinking about Shiloh and cancer and anything that remotely rankled. I was going to the beach, and darn it, I was going to enjoy it.

This time I heeded Milagros's warning and left everything of importance in the house, triple-checking the door to make sure it was locked. It was still early, and aside from an absurdly fit woman jogging barefoot down the shore, I was alone. I laid my towel out on the sand and headed for the water. The waves were cool as they rushed against my legs, then warm as they retreated back into the sea, so I waded in deeper. My incision stung, but I dove into the surf, determined to make friends with pain—or at the very least, to learn how to ignore it. Sure enough, the discomfort let up, so I went back under, holding my breath while the sea enveloped me, filling my head with its blunted gurgling sounds. Saltwater seeped into my mouth as I surfaced. I felt invigorated and alive, or whatever it is to be aware of your body as it is pacified by a fresh burst of oxygen and momentarily oblivious to the disease eating away at it. For the next few weeks, at least, I was going to be fine.

Except it didn't appear that way, because Milagros, clad in a short orange housedress, came running down the beach hollering my name.

Reluctantly, I trudged back to the beach. "What is it, Milagros?" I asked as she approached the water's edge.

"Ay, Libby, I thought you were drowning! *Por favor*, be careful. The tide is very strong right now. You see those waves?" she said, pointing into the distance.

"Those are, like, a mile out."

"They'll suck you right under," she insisted. "Don't go in past your belly unless you're at a roped-off beach."

"Okay," I said, trying not to sigh and failing miserably. Luisa instructed me to give myself away like the sea, but come to find out, I was only able to do that in designated swimming areas.

"*Bien*. Oh, and, *mija*? I take drinks on my back porch every day at six. Join me if you can."

Take drinks. This woman was too much. "Okay, Milagros," I agreed. "See you then."

.   .   .

While Paul inherited our mother's sharp cheekbones, dark hair, and warm complexion, my resemblance to her was evident only in my medical files. As such, even with SPF four hundred slathered on, my pale skin was no match for Vieques's proximity to the equator; after an hour on the beach, I was forced to head back to the house. I changed into a sundress and attempted to make myself presentable, then drove to Esperanza. Though it was not yet noon, the tiny town was bustling: families roamed about, smiling and squabbling in equal measure; bronzed surfer types in bodysuits toted boogie boards and kiteboarding equipment toward the water; and couples held cameras at arm's length to snap nauseatingly gleeful selfies.

With no small effort, I parked the Jeep on the side of the road. Then I secured my wide-brimmed hat and sunglasses and set off on foot. As far as I could tell, most of the town proper was situated along a strip on the island's southern coast. As I walked from one end of the strip to the other, I passed dive shops and trinket stands, white-tablecloth restaurants, and food trucks parked along the grassy stretch dividing the road from the beach. After weighing my options, I stopped at a restaurant with generic fare and private dining verandas overlooking the water.

"Just you?" asked the hostess.

"Just me," I said. You would think I'd know how to dine alone, but you would be wrong. Although I'd devoured many a sandwich on a park bench during lunch, I'd never intentionally sat down at a real restaurant and eaten by myself. Given that I was traveling solo for an entire month, it seemed a good time to learn.

I pretended to study the menu, but the words blurred together, so when the waitress came to take my order, I blurted out the first thing that registered—a pulled pork sandwich with yucca fries, whatever those were. She left, and I looked around awkwardly. It was not unlike the airport bar. I didn't know what to do with myself, and I hadn't even thought to grab a book from the selection I'd packed. After some time, I settled on the water as an appropriate place to stare.

Maybe a leisure vacation was a bad idea. There would be countless opportunities just like this, during which I had nothing but thoughts of impending doom to occupy me. As I watched a ship depart from a marina not far from the restaurant, I found myself thinking of my mother—at the end, but before things became really bad. She quit her job as an elementary school teacher to concentrate on her health and spend time with us. During those months, she napped a lot and went for chemo; but every day, Paul and I each got at least an hour alone with her. She and Paul often went for walks or headed to the library or comic book store. She and I spent most afternoons baking, even though I rarely saw her take more than a bite of the things we made.

One summer afternoon—or perhaps it was several, conflated by memory—we stood side by side at the counter making chocolate chip cookies. The sun streamed into our small yellow kitchen. Her hair was long gone, and she had wrapped her head in an ivory scarf; with the light on her face, she looked angelic. "The secret is to put a pinch of salt on top of each cookie before you put them in the oven," she whispered in my ear. "Remember that, okay, Libby Lou?" I didn't understand that she was preparing me for life without her. I didn't *want* to understand. I thought it would always be like that: her taking us to Chuck E. Cheese's, and falling asleep with us in our beds, and pulling us out of school to drive us across the state to see a park or lakefront beach where she'd played as a child. I couldn't comprehend that she was stuffing us full of happiness to prepare us for the famine that was to come.

The waitress must have put my food down in front of me while I wasn't paying attention, because she startled me by returning to see if it was okay. I glanced down at the untouched plate and stuck a suspiciously pale fry in my mouth.

"Nothing's ever tasted so good," I told her, but of course, I was referring to the cookies.

. . .

Paul called as I was finishing lunch. "Where are you?" he said.

"What do you mean, where am I? I'm in Chicago," I said blithely, just as a large bird landed on the veranda banister and let out a ridiculously tropical-sounding caw.

"Oh, are you?" he said dryly. "Am I also to believe you just purchased a toucan?"

"Ha, ha. No." I hadn't planned on telling him where I was just yet, as I was still feeling vulnerable and was pretty sure that spilling the beans on one thing would prompt me to unwittingly share other secrets, including a particular revelation that started with a *c* and ended with *ancer*. In retrospect, I probably should have let Paul's call go to voice mail, but I didn't want him to worry, especially after my panicked text message the day before.

"Come on, Libs. As if your freaky-but-sweet message yesterday wasn't alarming enough, now you're going to try to convince me Chicago has been invaded by exotic fowl? You know I can have the tech guys at my firm run a GPS data search on your cell and pinpoint your exact location in four seconds flat."

"I hope you're joking, because that is fricking creepy."

"Not as creepy as me being forced to read your mind. Give it up, Libs. *Estás en* Meh-hee-ko?"

Unlike me, Paul had been smart enough to study Spanish in school, which he mastered in about two months before moving on to Mandarin.

I exhaled loudly so he would sense my wrath over the transom. "I'm in Vieques."

"Is that near Bogota?"

"Ask your security guys."

"Libbers," he said playfully. "Stop being cranky and throw your beloved brother a bone."

"Fetch this, Toto. I'm south of Cuba and east of the Dominican Republic."

"*Puerto Rico?* How the heck did you end up in Puerto Rico? I hope there's a cabana boy next to you right now."

"That was him you heard crowing earlier."

"Libs on the loose!" he said with delight. "Vacationing by yourself. I'm proud of you."

"Thanks. I'm proud of me, too, if only because I managed to royally tick Tom off when I ran into him on the way to the airport."

"Oooh, the element of surprise. Brills. How long are you going to be there?"

"I don't know," I responded truthfully.

"When you do leave, will you please come to New York to see us?" Paul persisted.

"I will."

"Hurrah! You just made my entire week better, which is no small feat, considering the Dow plunged two hundred points last night."

It pained me not to tell him that the stock market wasn't the only thing plunging, but I knew that if I told him about the plane, it would undo years of therapy he'd undergone to deal with his fear of flying. Instead, I said, "I'm here to help."

Paul got serious. "Are you hanging in there? Because you know it's okay if you're not, right? You don't have to be perky all the time. This Tom crap is pretty awful."

"I'm not perky all the time," I grumbled.

"I can hear that, sweetie, and I'm going to take it as a sign of improvement. It's just that—one sec." I heard him say something in an official-sounding voice, and only then did I remember that he was in the middle of his workday.

"Hey, I know you're busy," I told Paul when he returned. "We can talk again soon. And next time, I won't wait so long to call."

"You'd better not," he scolded. "Anyway, what I was trying to say is that I want you to know that I love you, and so do Charlie and Toby and Max. It's all going to work out okay. I promise."

I almost fell right off my rattan chair. If Paul had traded our I-love-you-the-most game for the kitten-and-rainbow routine, I was officially in trouble.

# FIFTEEN

I didn't make it to Milagros's for drinks the first night, but I wandered over to her place the following evening. I found her on the tiled patio behind her house, chatting with an elderly man.

"I'm sorry," I said when I spotted them lounging in a pair of chairs. "I didn't realize you had company."

She waved me in. Her patio was lined with potted fruit trees, many of which had colorful orchids hanging from their branches. "It's my party and everyone's invited. Libby, this is my cousin Sonny. Sonny, *esta es* Libby." She pointed in the direction of the beach house to indicate my provenance, then turned back to me and mock whispered, "Sonny is deaf in both ears."

"Milly!" Sonny squawked.

Milagros whacked him on the back. "Just kidding, Sonny! Libby, can I get you something to drink?"

"I'm good," I said, but she was already well across the patio. I sat on a carved wooden bench across from Sonny. "Hi," I said.

His face lit up.

"Do you live near here?" I asked.

He laughed like I'd just made a sidesplitting joke. I bit my lip: Was he screwing with me?

"I wasn't joking," Milagros said, coming up from behind me. She slipped a drink into my hands and leaned in conspiratorially. "The man can't hear a thing. If he shows you his dentures, that means he's just playing along."

"Oh." I glanced at Sonny, who was grinning at me with large ceramic teeth.

"Eh, Milly," he said, and began telling a story—or so I imagined, as he was speaking in Spanish. Milagros cackled along with him, occasionally interjecting a sentence or two. I smiled the way humans will when bearing witness to others' happiness, even though at that moment I was ill with envy. I wanted to live into my seventies or eighties or however old these two were, so I could tell long-winded tales to my cousins (who I technically couldn't stand, but that was but a minor detail to be hammered out over the next four decades of this alternate life I was wishing for myself). I wanted a chance to be wrinkled and deaf and without a care in the world, confident I had lived fully and completely in the way that only the old can.

"Libby, you really need to learn *español*. This is so ridiculous that I couldn't translate it if I tried," Milagros told me, wiping tears from her eyes with the back of her hand.

She was right about Spanish. I'd spent the morning exploring the shore, and as I tossed a pound of seashells into my bag and dug my toes in the sand and snuck glances at what I was certain was a couple doing the dirty in the ocean, I contemplated what, exactly, I would do during the rest of my vacation. (As I have mentioned, I didn't put much thought into this before hopping on a plane out of Chicago.) By the time I dragged my sunburned butt back to the house, it had become painfully apparent that beachcombing could take up only so much of my time.

"I was hoping to do just that," I told Milagros. "Do you know of any Spanish tutors on the island?"

"Tutors? Tutors?!" she said, and I flushed, wondering if I'd made some unintentional gaffe. She pointed her finger at me. "*I* can teach you Spanish."

"Really?"

"Really. I taught English for forty years."

I was already in command of the English language, but judging from Milagros's enthusiasm, I thought it best not to clarify. "Okay. That would be great."

She clapped her hands together with delight. "*Bien.* We can start whenever you're ready."

I thanked her, then lifted my glass to my lips and took a small sip. I had to will myself not to gag as I swallowed. "What's in this?" I coughed.

"Rum, *claro.*" She chuckled. "If you don't like it now, you will in an hour."

My eyes watered as I took another drink. "Uh-huh."

At one point, Sonny drained his cup and walked off without saying good-bye. When it became clear he wasn't going to return, Milagros looked at me and said, "So, Libby. What are you running from?"

I frowned. "What makes you think I'm running from something?"

"Single woman rents a beach house for a full month, with no plans to meet friends or family? I'm no detective, *tú sabes,* but I'm not stupid either." She laughed, then leaned back in her chair, waiting for my answer.

So I told her—mostly. "Well, let's see. I recently learned that my husband of eight years is attracted to men."

"*Dios mío,*" she cried.

"Yeah, not great news. I found out less than two weeks ago," I said, and took another drink of the cocktail, which tasted not unlike lighter fluid.

Milagros mistook my sipping as a sign of enthusiasm. "Here," she said, producing a pitcher from beneath her seat. "Have a little more."

"I really shouldn't," I said as she filled my glass.

"If ever there was a time, this is it. Now tell me, what happened after you found out?"

I took another sip. "I quit my job, emptied our home so I can sell it, and booked a ticket here."

"*Ay, mija*, I know about bad husbands," Milagros said. "Let me tell you about my third, José. I got really sick at work one day. My boss told me to go home because he was worried I was going to infect all my students. I had a fever and could barely walk, but when I called José to see if he could pick me up and drive me home, he didn't answer. So I took the bus back and dragged myself into the house. When I got to my bedroom, who did I find but that *hijo'e puta* with my best friend—"

I gasped.

"—and her husband, too!" Milagros whooped. "I mean, *qué* pervert! Sorry if that's your kind of thing," she added.

"It isn't," I assured her. "What did you do?"

"With Miguel? *Claro*, I divorced him," she said, crossing her arms.

"Miguel? You mean José?"

"Miguel, José—what's the difference? All that's left of that man is my version of his story. What I'm trying to say, *mija*, is that eventually the pain goes away. Then one day you think about it and it's funny. *Te prometo.*"

"That's what everyone says." I did not volunteer that I no longer had the luxury of waiting around for such a transformation to happen.

Milagros again topped off my glass and motioned for me to walk with her to the beach. "Don't worry, it's safe," she said as she locked the patio gate behind us.

We stood in the sand, drinking silently as the sun lowered in the sky, cutting wide swaths of sherbet pink and cornflower blue in its wake.

Three months ago, Tom, Jess, O'Reilly, and I had celebrated the end of summer by commissioning a charter boat to take us out on Lake Michigan. The evening seemed to stretch forever, until we glanced up and saw that the sun had dropped, almost at once, and was hovering just above the skyline. Within seconds, it was between the jagged teeth of the city's buildings—then gone before we'd really had a chance to take it in. I was beginning to feel that, like the sun, my life had slipped past when I was turned in the wrong direction.

"Why Vieques?" Milagros asked after a while.

"My father told me that my mother loved it here."

She nodded, understanding what I had not said. "I lost my *mami* too early, too. Yours was a smart woman to love this place."

I watched as the western waves swallowed the last of the day's light. I'd barely made it to the island, but I *had* made it before it was too late. Certainly that meant something. Didn't it?

# SIXTEEN

I woke the following morning with an excruciating headache, rum scum coating my tongue, and the urge to do something constructive. I suppose when you've already cashed in ten of the estimated hundred and eighty days left of your life, there's a smidgen of pressure to push through your hangover and make it count.

I downed a bowl of coconut granola, threw on some sneakers, and applied bug repellent to my skin. Then I hopped in the Jeep and headed for a hiking path I'd read about in one of the tourist booklets lying around the beach house.

The path was part of a recently formed national park on a section of the old naval grounds, but other than a metal sign designating that it was open to the public until ten p.m., it was almost impossible to differentiate the park from any other overgrown area I'd encountered thus far. I left the Jeep in a lot adjacent to the sign, then ventured over to what appeared to be a dirt trail. As per usual, Paul's voice whispered in my ear, warning of predators, but I hummed loudly to drown him out. What could be nearer to God than nature? Surely here of all places I would be safe and protected.

As I stepped over a downed tree, I found myself imagining what life was like for the island's early inhabitants, before there were roads or vehicles or Quick-Marts for purchasing drinking water that wouldn't cause a bout of gastroenteritis to be reckoned with over a hole in the ground. As I forged ahead, the path became increasingly unkempt, and branches whipped against my face as spiky vines lashed my limbs. Smelling a meal, swarms of thumb-size mosquitoes deftly maneuvered around my swatting and jammed their stingers into my skin, as though the DEET I had applied were barbecue sauce.

I wasn't trying to be a pioneer woman. I didn't go camping and fishing for fun, nor did I even *pretend* to enjoy rugged outdoor activities, as my former colleague Corey did because her husband was disturbingly aroused by camouflage-covered mammaries. But I *was* trying to learn more about why my mother found this lot of sand in the middle of the sea to be so magical, and the verdant parks were part and parcel with the island's identity. So I pressed on.

It wasn't long before the narrow path deposited me at two wider trails, both of which looked well maintained, as though they might even be the handiwork of a landscape architect. I was elated: finally, a hike I could manage! I chose the path on the right.

I'd gone about a quarter mile when I heard a loud rumbling. For a moment I expected to see more wild horses—perhaps a whole herd, I thought as the noise drew nearer.

Instead, I found myself staring down a very different sort of horsepower as a yellow pickup truck barreled straight at me. A group of kids were yelling out the windows, and as the vehicle approached, I saw that the truck bed, too, was filled with rowdy teens. I stepped to the right, out of the center of the path, but then the truck veered left, directly into my path. Did the driver not see me? Was this some sadistic game of chicken? The only thing I was sure of was that I needed to move. Immediately.

With seconds to spare, I jumped into the bushes behind me, scratching every square inch of uncovered skin in the process. My pulse whooshed in my ears, and I struggled to breathe. If I hadn't moved, they would have hit me.

*They would have hit me.*

There was laughter as the truck spun its wheels in the dirt and turned onto another path, disappearing into the trees.

I remained huddled in the bushes in case the teens wanted to return and finish me off. It seemed appropriate to burst into tears, but I was dry-eyed, which was unusual for a chronic crier like myself. I sat still and stone-faced, not even bothering to fight off the bugs feasting on my flesh.

Then a bloodcurdling scream shot through the park. It took me a moment to realize that it was my own, and it was about to happen again. As a deep and furious anger I hadn't even known was in me unleashed itself, I screamed again and again, until my chest burned and I was too hoarse to scream anymore.

If this had happened even three weeks earlier, I would have been mortified to make such a spectacle—even in the middle of miles of uninhabited vegetation. But now it didn't matter. I wasn't sure *anything* mattered. I had been a good person who had lived an honest if uninspired life; but in case I'd missed the previous two warnings, the universe sent a bright yellow truck to inform me in no uncertain terms that one way or another, I was going to die—and soon.

# SEVENTEEN

A few moronic teens would not be allowed to ruin my vacation; at least that's what I told myself the next morning as I drove to Isabel Segunda, Vieques's primary town. Even after a solid night's sleep and a long shower, the previous day's shock had not worn off, but I was confident that a good cup of coffee, a baked good or three, and a change of scenery would help soothe my nerves.

Isabel Segunda was larger than Esperanza, and filled with pastel-colored shops, government offices, and more churches than I had ever seen in a single location. After strolling up and down a few blocks, I came upon a blindingly pink café, from which the scent of heaven itself—baked dough and sugar—wafted out. I walked in and sat at one of the bar stools that lined the U-shaped counter.

"What smells so good?" I asked the woman behind the counter.

*"Mallorcas,"* said a voice.

I did not turn around as I responded. "Really?"

"Yeah, that's really what they're called," Shiloh said, perching on the stool next to me. His hair was damp, as though he, too, had recently showered, although his T-shirt was at least two decades old, and his cargo shorts looked like they might walk off without him.

"No, *really* as in, you *really* couldn't have picked a different place to get coffee?" I muttered, barely looking at him. "Don't you have a plane to fly into the ocean or something?"

He smirked. "Actually, I'm on leave while the FAA investigates our little incident. So no, I will not be expertly landing a plane next to the beach in order to save your life again anytime soon." He turned to the server. *"Hola, Cecelia. Dos mallorcas, por fa, y tres cafecitos."*

Just when I'd girded my loins, he had to go and speak Spanish. "Mind telling me what you just said?" I asked.

"I ordered you a coffee. You *do* drink coffee, don't you?"

"I am to coffee as you are to pelicans," I said. "I hope you asked for one of those mahor—"

"May-jor-ca," he said. "And of course I did."

"Excellent. So, given your spicy accent and knowledge of the local baked goods, I'm guessing you live here?"

He grinned. "I live a lot of places. My company has an apartment that I stay at between flights. The rest of the time, I stay at my place in San Juan."

"The vagabond life. Interesting choice for a man your age."

"I'm forty-two, and that's a pretty judgmental thing to say for a, uh, twenty-nine-year-old woman traveling by herself."

It was my turn to grin. "My male chaperone wasn't available this month."

"I bet he wasn't. Something tells me that Tom guy would have been happy to escort you here."

My smile evaporated. I didn't want to think about Tom, which was proving far more difficult than I'd anticipated. I'd spent six thousand, five hundred, and some odd days with him (not that I was counting). Wasn't the newfound knowledge of my Lilliputian lifespan enough to banish him from my mind?

"Sorry," Shiloh said quickly. "I see that that one's off-limits. No more talk about the guy whose name rhymes with bomb."

In spite of myself, I laughed. "Thanks." When I looked up again, those warm brown eyes of his were staring at me again, with no intent of looking away. I felt a jolt of wanton, unsettling excitement, then glanced away with relief as the server slid white ceramic plates toward us, each topped with a huge buttered bun dusted with powdered sugar. She placed three small paper cups of coffee between the plates.

"Those are the smallest coffees I've ever seen," I said to Shiloh. "Please tell me you ordered two for me."

"You're welcome to them, but I'm warning you, this place has the strongest espresso on the island."

"If you say so."

He sipped one, then turned to me again. "Hey, I never did ask you. What brings you to Vieques?"

"Lots of things," I said vaguely. I bit into the bun, which all but dissolved on my tongue.

"Not bad, right?" he said.

I nodded and washed my mouthful down with a swig of coffee, which was every bit as strong as Shiloh had warned. "So you've been here"—he counted on his fingers—"four days now? Have you had Isla's conch fritters yet?"

"What's a conch fritter?" I asked.

"Oh, my. You've never had a conch fritter? We'll have to fix that. Do you have plans tonight?"

I eyed him suspiciously. "Maybe. Why would you want to go to dinner with *me*?"

He cocked his head. "As you keep pointing out, I almost killed you. It's the least I can do, don't you think?"

*Sure, since you know I have cancer.* "Okay," I agreed, but only because I had nothing else to do. (That was my story and I was sticking to it.) "You know where I live."

He winked. "That I do." He pulled his sunglasses out of his front pocket, grabbed the bun from the plate, and took one of the coffees. "See you tonight, Libby."

I watched him saunter away. He had broad shoulders and a high, firm ass. I had an uncanny capacity for catastrophe and a history of choosing the worst possible partners, both real and imagined.

It wasn't until he was gone that I realized we hadn't agreed on a time and I had no way to contact him. In fact, I didn't even know his last name, and frankly, I was in no position to attempt to act like a normal human for a sustained period of time.

This was a very bad idea.

Just after seven, I heard tires rumble in the gravel outside the beach house. After one last glance in the mirror, I swung the door open and found Shiloh standing there.

"Hello," he said lightly. He had on the same shorts from earlier, but had swapped his T-shirt for a crisp butter-colored button-down. I was wearing a sundress, which I felt stupid about, as it seemed very date-like and this was not a date.

"Hello," I said as I locked the door behind me. "Do you want to drive or should I?"

"Why don't I, since I know where it is?"

"That's fine," I said, standing stiffly in front of his Jeep. The easy-if-barbed banter of our café conversation was long gone, and I lamely tried to think of appropriate ways to interact with him, which made me even more uncomfortable.

He opened the passenger door and offered me his arm, which I accepted, but not before adding, "You don't have to do that."

"I know," Shiloh said, giving me a curious look as he closed the door behind me.

"So, Chicago," he said as we backed out of the drive. "I haven't been there since I was in my twenties. Is it still cold?"

"Like the Arctic."

He laughed as though this was actually funny, and I decided I was right about the cancer pity. I'd have to put an end to that. "How'd you end up there?" he asked.

I tugged a curl, then sat on my hands so I would stop fidgeting. "Um . . . honestly? My ex. His best friend was already in Chicago, and he thought it would be a good place to launch his career."

"And you?" he asked. "What did you think?"

I wanted to be with Tom wherever he was. But there was no way I was going to admit this. "I thought I would like it. And I did, until a few weeks ago." I was grateful when he didn't ask me to elaborate.

We pulled up at a restaurant tucked into the hillside, right off the side of the road. The banisters and awnings were strung with holiday twinkle lights, and as we entered, I saw that most of the tables were in an open-air courtyard.

"*Hermano*, how's it going?" the bartender called to Shiloh.

"*Bien*, Ricky, *bien*," he said, and started rambling in Spanish. At which point he stopped being the guy who almost killed me and started being the one I wanted as my main course. Yes, I'd heard his romance-language routine at the café, but this was different. He was having a full-blown conversation, and it shifted his whole demeanor. His hands flew around. His laughter deepened. He oozed confidence and, you know. Sex.

"Sorry about that, Libby," he said as the hostess seated us at one of the booths in the open-air courtyard. "He's chatty."

"And you're very fluent in Spanish," I said, a bit accusatorially. It wasn't that his being bilingual was such a surprise. It's just that his English lacked the lilt I'd grown accustomed to since landing in Puerto Rico, so I had assumed he was from somewhere else. "You're Puerto Rican?"

"Yeah," he said. "My mom's a Nuyorican—her parents were from here—but my dad was born and raised in Fajardo."

"And were you raised here?"

"My parents split, so I was shuffled around way more than most kids like to be."

"Oh. Sorry."

"Hey, what can you do? Anyway, that was ages ago for this old man." He smiled, and as I instinctively smiled back, a sharp zing shot through my hinterlands. I glanced away, acutely aware of the inappropriateness of the tingles I was feeling. My already pathetic judgment (see Ty, et al.) had undoubtedly been further weakened by the week's events. What's more, Shiloh knew I was going to die soon, so any relations between us would be laden with sympathy—or worse, the understanding that I would be an easy and extremely short-term lay.

I was relieved when the waiter appeared, although slightly disappointed when he started speaking to us in English.

"Am I allowed to order for myself?" I asked Shiloh, eyebrows raised.

"As long as you order the you-know-whats."

I glanced up at the waiter. "An order of conch fritters and the tuna steak."

"And to drink?" the waiter asked.

"Something strong."

"I'll have the same entrée and a Corona," Shiloh said.

The waiter brought me a tumbler filled with guava juice and rum, which was tastier than Milagros's rocket fuel, and which relaxed me to the point that I was able to chat about trivial things with Shiloh until the fritters arrived. (For the record, they were as edible as anything battered and deep-fried, but not particularly earth-shattering.) I had just started on my tuna when Shiloh asked, "So, is this trip a pre-chemo celebration?"

My head jerked up in surprise, and then I put my fork down—just to be on the safe side. "Pre-chemo? Um, no. I'm not going to get treatment."

He looked stunned. "You're not? Why not?"

"Because I don't want to do that to myself."

"It's not that bad. Definitely preferable to dying."

"I told you already, the doctor said it wouldn't matter. I'm toast."

His eyes flashed with an anger I hadn't seen in him before. "Ef your doctor. Get a second opinion."

"I already consulted Dr. Google, who confirmed that no second opinion is going to stop my guts from turning to rock-size tumors while my skin falls off," I said matter-of-factly.

"You don't know that for sure." His face was getting slightly red, and a thin layer of sweat had formed on his brow. I wondered if someone close to him had died after receiving bad medical advice.

I shrugged. "Listen, I appreciate your concern. But I've had more than my fair share of experience with cancer, and I want to live out my final days in the most pleasant way possible. Chemo and radiation don't exactly fall under that umbrella."

He took a long swig of beer, then held my gaze. "If God, or whatever you believe in, wanted you to be dead, why aren't you at the bottom of the sea right now? I'm a decent pilot, Libby, but now that I've had a few days to sit on it, I'm going to call that landing a minor miracle."

"So all that talk about life being a near-death experience was crap, huh?"

The heat of his anger was instantly replaced with a cool distance as he sighed and leaned back in the booth. I, too, was having a quicksilver shift, as desire gave way to a rush of irritation.

"You are exasperating," he muttered.

"Lucky you, you won't have to deal with my exasperating tendencies after this evening," I shot back.

The waiter came over to take our plates. "How about dessert?" he asked. "Or another drink?"

"No," Shiloh and I said at the same time.

# EIGHTEEN

I would spend the rest of my vacation in solitude. After all, I had tried human connection and failed spectacularly. Sequestering myself away from all potentially irritating and/or murderous people, I reasoned, was the only way to protect what was left of my dignity and enjoy the little time I had left on my trip.

Said plan was rudely interrupted by Tom's repeated calls. (I *did* turn the ringer off, but it was not enough to silence the repetitive buzzing or dim the screen glowing in the middle of the night as Tom phone-stalked me with a vigor he had never applied to many aspects of our marriage, including but not limited to adhering to our budget; attempting to fix things that broke in the apartment; and marital relations, particularly of the nonmissionary variety.) Seven calls later, I realized that he would not leave me in peace until I spoke with him, so the evening after my dinner with Shiloh, I finally picked up.

"Libby, why have you been avoiding me?" Tom.

"Gosh, I just don't know, Tom."

"Tell her you're sorry, you idiot." O'Reilly, hissing in the background.

"What the hell is O'Reilly doing listening in on our conversation?" Me, obviously.

"Li—" Tom.

"Listen to me, you piece of spit. If you're going to have the balls to break up our marriage, then have the balls to deal with the fallout."

"But I told you, I don't want to break up our marriage."

"He loves you, Libby!" O'Reilly.

"You're my best friend." Tom.

"I thought I was your best friend!" O'Reilly, who I was certain was blasted. Apparently Tom had been forced to lower his liquor standards because O'Reilly was sheltering him.

"No, Tom, I assure you that I am not. Best friends share secrets with each other." Me, attempting to ignore my eyeballs, which had started to drip in an unfortunate way.

"I am so sorry, Libby. I never meant to hurt you."

"He really didn't, Libby!" O'Reilly, hollering in the distance.

"Shut up, Michael." Jess.

"I don't care if you're sorry, Tom. Sorry doesn't help at all. Please, do not call me again unless you're able to borrow a vehicle from Marty McFly and go back in time and undo our entire relationship. Now go away." Me. Click.

I went for a stroll on the beach to try to shake it off. *You are bigger than this, you are better than this,* I told myself, but that only made me think about Tom's mantra phase, during which he read stack after stack of self-help books in an attempt to catapult himself out of his internship rut and into a real job. In hindsight, it occurred to me that Tom's positive self-talk probably had very little to do with employment.

How long had he been deluding himself? The very morning of my D-day, he woke me up by kissing me and telling me he loved me. (Just thinking about it made me start to cry again. Did he suspect that he would soon tell me the truth? Was his love really guilt sandwiched in the affection that comes from spending so many years with another human being?) The whole thing was incredibly confusing. During childhood, Paul liked trucks and guns and football, all the stereotypical boy things, but we were barely into our first month of kindergarten when he proudly told my parents that he wanted to marry Michael Jackson. Our family was religious—church on Sundays, prayer before meals, memorizing large chunks of the Bible together—but though those around us were quick to condemn homosexuality, my parents never tried to convince Paul that the way he felt was wrong, so he never tried to hide who he was. Thus, the concept of coming out later in life seemed like something that happened on television.

Moreover, though Tom's father was a mouthy drunk who didn't hold back on his views of any and all perceived forms of sexual fornication, Tom happily flouted him in so many obvious ways—his calm demeanor, his big-city life and love of beautiful things, his alcohol aversion—that it never occurred to me Tom would feel the need to conceal such an integral aspect of himself.

While I might have given him a mouthful on the phone, I sort of felt bad for him. I *definitely* felt bad for us. If only it had happened at a time when we could have worked through it together in some sort of healthy manner—not that I would attempt to turn him straight, as I knew I was more likely to run into my mother riding a unicorn down Michigan Avenue than to expect Tom's sexuality to be deprogrammed, like it was a DVR. But I didn't want to hate him. I wanted to comfort him, as I had when his father showed up to his graduation party trashed, or when he was fired from his first postgrad school job after three disastrous weeks.

Correction: I wanted to *want* to comfort him.

Or perhaps this desire was the ghost of Libby past, trying to deceive me as she had so powerfully managed to do in so many aspects of my life.

. . .

Raj called on the way back from my walk. "You won't believe this!"

"Try me."

"You have three offers on the apartment."

I smiled; the universe did owe me a favor. "Who offered?"

"Two couples and a single mom."

"Excellent. Let's go with the single mom."

"Don't you care what they're offering? The mom's offer is the lowest."

"Get the papers drawn up."

"You're in charge," he said, but I knew he was not pleased.

"I'll up your commission to seven percent."

Raj grunted.

"Eight."

"Deal."

When I returned to the beach house, I saw that Milagros had tacked a note to my door. "Spanish, six p.m.?" it read. Cocktail hour was as good a time as any, and despite my vow of solitude, I did want to learn Spanish. At least Milagros wouldn't lecture me about the disease she didn't know about.

I went to Milagros's patio as instructed. Again she had a visitor; this evening it was a young woman jiggling a small girl on her knee.

"*Gracias*, Milagros," the woman said and reached into her pocket.

Milagros waved off the woman's attempt to slip her what looked like a bill. "*De nada, de nada,*" she insisted, and the woman hugged her and left with the little girl trailing behind.

"I was just reading Vicky's palm," Milagros explained. She patted the chair where the woman and her daughter had just been. "Here, sit down."

Tentatively, I obliged.

"Now give me your hand."

"What about our Spanish lesson?"

"We'll get there. Now let's see," she said, taking my arm and unfurling the fist I didn't realize I was making. She stared at my open palm for a minute, then ran a finger down the long line closest to my thumb. "*Esta es*—that means 'this is.'"

"*Esta es,*" I repeated.

"Good!" she said enthusiastically. "*Esta es tu linea de la vida.* Your lifeline, *mija.*"

"Okay," I said hesitantly.

"*Vida,*" she insisted. "Try saying it."

"Vee-da."

"*Ay,*" she said.

"*Ay,*" I said.

"No," she laughed. "That's me talking to myself. I was going to say that you have a nice, strong lifeline. Like mine," she said, holding up her hand so I could see the deep crevice running through the maze of wrinkles that composed the map of her palm.

"Well, that can't be accurate," I said, taking my hand back.

"Why's that? You don't want to get old like Milly?"

"It's just that I have a health condition," I mumbled.

"Whatever it is, that hand of yours says you're going to beat it."

"You're just saying that because you don't want to make me feel bad."

"No," Milagros said, shaking her head. She took my hand again and stuck her pointer finger into the center of the line. "This is where you're at in your life right now, more or less. See how there's a break? Usually a circle or spot there means sickness, but a split like that means heartache. Your break is wide, so it's bad, and it means a lot more than anything I would see on your love line," she said, pointing at the swooped horizontal line across the top of my hand. "Although that does tell me that you, like me, have bad taste in men."

I managed a small laugh, even though I was thinking about Shiloh and how icy he was as he drove me back last night.

"Now, don't get all sad on me, *mija*. See these?" she said, poking at almost imperceptible lines just under my pinky. "I see *niños*. Children. A happy future."

I didn't like the direction this was taking. "I can't have kids."

She gave me what Paul liked to call *the look*. "There are ways. But enough of that. I'll tell you more when you're ready." She walked inside her house and returned with two glasses of sangria, which we drank as she attempted to teach me basic greetings and how to ask for directions *en español*. I left an hour later with a promise to return in a few days for my next lesson.

Palm reading was nothing but a bunch of mumbo jumbo, the type of fortune-telling voodoo my Sunday school teachers had warned would send me straight into the arms of the devil. But what if Milagros was half-right? The heartbreak aspect was certainly accurate. What if I should have had a chance to live a long life, but that chance had been intercepted by some cruel karmic force—or a bad choice on my part? What if those long hours at the office had sent stress hormones pinballing around my body until they wreaked so much havoc that my cells began to spontaneously multiply? What if years of eschewing sweat-producing activities and ordering fries over salad had finally caught up to me? Because let's be honest: guilt was playing on repeat in my head, and the lyrics sounded a lot like *It's all your fault, it's all your fault, nah nah nah nah nah, this is all your fault.*

I ate dinner at home and decided to call it an early night. My stomach hurt, badly, and I was increasingly dubious about my ability to withstand pain for long periods of time. If I could ride out the rest of my vacation with the help of Advil and Ambien, perhaps Paul would find me a pain specialist in New York to help me through the worst of it. Doctors were handing out OxyContin like candy these days, weren't they?

As I crawled into bed and waited for sleep to set in, I wondered if I really had it in me to make it through the next three weeks without assistance. I was my mother's daughter, but as with her high cheekbones and dark hair, I had not inherited her grit or gumption. I felt that I could not handle one more bad thing, which only deepened the guilt and shame, especially when I thought about all the people in the world suffering far worse things at that very second.

I pulled the covers tight around me and tried to breathe into the pain, like I'd heard women were often advised to do during labor. I wanted insight into my mother's experience, and now I had it. There was no one but myself to blame.

# NINETEEN

After eight days in Vieques, my carnation-pink sunburn finally peeled
away to reveal skin best described as "palest tan," so I decided it was safe
to sunbathe once again. I pulled on my tankini, grabbed the makings
of a light lunch, and walked out my back door and onto the beach.

It was a busy Saturday, and beachgoers stretched out for a mile in
either direction, while a man with a cooler on wheels strolled back and
forth calling, *"Agua! Cerveza!"* I located an open spot close to the water,
spread my towel across the sand, and lay back, instantly sated. The day
was dazzlingly bright but not too hot, and the heat felt delicious on
my skin.

I must have been there a good thirty minutes before a cloud rolled
in and blocked the light. I frowned, hoping a storm wouldn't surface
before I had a chance to flip over and toast my back.

"Hey," said the cloud.

My eyes flew open.

Shiloh laughed. "Sorry! I didn't mean to startle you."

"Sure you didn't," I said. "What brings you to my beach?"

He sat down next to me in the sand. Even behind his omnipresent shades, I could tell that he was in a good mood. "*Your* beach? Well, let's see . . . boredom?"

I smirked. "More like you broke into my house and couldn't find me to terrify, so you decided to wander until you spotted your target."

"Maybe," he said. "Seriously, though. I'm sorry about the other night. I shouldn't have pried."

Ah-ha. This was a pity visit. "You don't have to feel sorry for me."

"That's not what I said." The flirty combativeness he'd just been using on me had been replaced with what I felt was a too-gentle tone of voice.

"True," I said. "Even so, I hope you know that you don't have to check up on me. I'm fine."

"Who's checking up? I'm in Vieques for the next few days, and I was going to the beach anyway."

I regarded him. He looked sincere, but as I mentioned, I no longer regarded myself as an accurate judge of character. "So why did you? Pry, I mean?"

He shrugged. "I like you, Libby. You're not like most women I fly into the sea."

"Har, har," I said, though the fourteen-year-old in me was thinking, *Oh. My. Gosh. He said he likes me!*

"Will you let me make it up to you? I want to show you something pretty amazing."

"Let me guess: in your pants."

He laughed. "Whoa, there, lady. I don't know what kind of little boys you've been spending time with, but I'm not trying to trick you into doing anything smutty."

Really? This was disappointing. At the same time, our last outing had not gone well. As I tried to come up with a reason to say no, I found myself staring at his forearms. Which were strong, and led to an equally strong pair of hands, which looked alluringly nimble. Even if he did have some kind of savior complex, I decided it was worth it to give him another chance.

"Okay," I agreed. "What should I wear?"

"What you have on now is perfect."

"You *are* a pervert!" I said, pulling my towel around me. I was kidding, but also aware that the only thing between him and my jiggly bits was a thin layer of fabric.

"We're going boating. Although you should bring a T-shirt and shorts, too." Intriguing.

"What time?"

"Um . . . let's say six thirty. Looking forward to it." He stood and brushed off his shorts, then began walking back toward the road.

"Hey," I called after him.

He spun around. "What's up?"

"I don't even know your last name."

He wore a mischievous grin. "So you don't. It's Velasquez."

"All right, Shiloh Velasquez," I said. "See you tonight."

Several hours later, we were driving through a series of back roads. Neither of us spoke, but the silence wasn't as awkward as before.

"Here we are," he said as we pulled into a sandy lot where a few other cars were parked.

As I got out of the Jeep, I spotted some plastic kayaks propped outside a shed. Just past the shed was a row of bushes and trees, which parted in the center, revealing water not two hundred feet ahead.

"Are we going kayaking?" I asked. "Because I'm not very sporty."

"Good, because I'm not either. The only thing I'm actually good at is flying."

"Debatable," I grinned.

"Your point," he said, smiling back.

It was getting dark, and Shiloh held up a can of bug repellent and nodded toward the water. "It's no accident that they call this place Mosquito Bay. Let me spray you." He looked me up and down. "You're probably going to want to take off your shirt and shorts."

I blushed, grateful that it was nearly dark out. "Okay," I said, and stripped down to my tankini. Goosebumps surfaced as he coated my arms and legs with the chemically cooled mist.

"Will you?" he asked, handing me the can. Then he took off his shirt, at which point my entire body began to blush. There is something extremely intimate about a man removing half his clothes, standing with his lean, tan body outstretched, and waiting for you to do something to him. Even if that something is spraying him down with an industrial-strength pesticide.

"Thanks," he said, oblivious to the drool pooling in my mouth.

I swallowed and attempted to sound blasé. "Not a problem."

We walked to the shed, where he handed me a red kayak and took a yellow one for himself. Then he grabbed an oar and a life jacket for each of us.

"We can just take these?"

"Yeah, the guy who runs this outfit is a buddy of mine. He's already got a group out there, and he knows we're coming."

We dragged the small boats down a path to a murky-looking pond resembling the small lake my family used to vacation at. "What is this place?" I asked him.

"It's a bay connected to the sea, but it has an entirely different ecosystem from any other body of water on the island. Than in the world, really. You'll see," he said as he pushed my kayak away from the shore.

This sounded vaguely ominous, but I decided to invoke old-school Libby. "Great!" I said cheerfully, and began to paddle.

The water was still and clear, and it was easy to navigate the small plastic boat. It was getting late, though; by the time we reached the center of the bay, the sun had disappeared, and the moon was barely a sliver in the sky. "Are we going to be able to find our way back?" I asked over my shoulder. That was when I realized the water around Shiloh's kayak was sort of glowing. And—whoa—mine was, too. "What the . . . ?"

Shiloh laughed heartily. "I was wondering when you'd notice. It's bioluminescence. The bay is filled with tiny organisms called dinoflagellates, and they glow when they're disturbed. It works best with your body, though." At once, I remembered what my father had told me about the bay, and how I thought he'd sounded mildly demented at the time.

"Want to get in?" he asked.

"Really?"

He nodded toward a group of kayakers on the other side of the bay, who were climbing out of their boats. "Although I can't promise not to drown you, I promise I'll try not to."

I carefully lowered myself into the water. It was tepid but dense—thick, even—and my body bobbed in place with little help from the life jacket. Shiloh paddled over and tethered our kayaks together with a rope. Then he dropped out of his kayak and swam around to me, leaving a blue-green stream of bioluminescence behind him.

"When Spanish explorers first came to Vieques, they thought the glowing meant the bay was possessed by the devil, so they tried to block it off," he said, pointing toward a narrow passage at the far end of the bay. "That trapped the leaves of the mangrove trees lining the bay, which the dinoflagellates feed off. So the organism grew stronger and brighter, and the Spanish left the whole area untouched. That's why it's still like this today."

"That's amazing," I murmured, watching my hands glow as I lazily dog-paddled in place.

"I didn't want you to miss it, and if you go when the moon is too full, you don't get the full effect. Now," he said, swimming even closer, "lie back and look up."

As I leaned back, my legs floated to the surface, as though my entire body had been rendered weightless by this magical water. I gasped as the sky came into view. It was a deep black carpet blinking with some of the brightest, whitest stars I'd ever seen.

"Not a lot of light pollution out here," Shiloh said. I could tell from his tone that he was pleased that I was wowed.

"And to think that they're not even there," I said, mostly to myself. It was my dad who first told me it was likely many, if not most, stars burn up long before we see them; all that's really left is their light, making its way through the ether.

"That depends on how you look at it," Shiloh said.

"How's that?"

"Well, technically, we're seeing balls of nuclear fusion from billions of years before we were born. But as far as I'm concerned, I'm experiencing them at this very moment, so they exist in the present. They happened in the past, but they're still real now."

"Huh." I stared at the sky, thinking about space and time and my mother, who was both my past and my present, and who, for all I knew, was up there twinkling somewhere.

He asked if I knew why stars shine. I confessed that I did not.

"They're big clusters of plasma held together by their own gravity, and they can't help but continually crush themselves inward. Their self-destruction creates friction. Which comes to us as light."

"I didn't know you were into science."

"I do make my living testing Newton's laws of motion."

"Touché."

"Anyway, I like astronomy. It has a lot to tell us about the human condition."

I wasn't sure what he was trying to get at, though I suspected it had something to do with my cancer. But I didn't want to ruin the moment with an explanation I didn't want to hear, so I swam around on my back, and soon forgot all about it.

Which was incredibly easy to do. Around me, my skin glowed; above me, the sky was lit with remnants of the past. And to think that my mother had been here—she had swum in this water and seen this very sky! I could not help but feel incredibly grateful that I'd stayed alive long enough to experience it.

"Thank you for this," I said to Shiloh quietly.

"You're most welcome," he said, and when he reached through the water for my hand, I gave it willingly.

I was slightly disappointed when he released my hand a few minutes later and suggested we head back. Disguising my reluctance, I agreed, and we paddled to the shore, toweled off, and got in the Jeep as though we hadn't just had a moment. (*Which might be exactly how he was viewing the situation,* I told myself.)

"Thanks again," I said as he pulled up in front of the beach house.

"No problem. Thanks for coming with me." He looked at me, then back at his steering wheel.

"Okay. I'll see you around," I said, and let myself out before he could reach across to open my door.

"Sounds good," he said behind me.

I could hear his Jeep idling in the driveway as I unlocked the front door, but I didn't turn around to wave good-bye. I was tough! I was a diamond encased in an impermeable layer of shellac! I did *not* need a forty-two-year-old half-baked crush to make sweet, sweet love to me, gosh darn it.

These affirmations did not stop the tears from coming as I let myself into the empty beach house. It wasn't even Shiloh, per se, who was the problem. It was the whole of it: the once-in-a-lifetime experience at the bay. The aching loneliness of being discarded by a husband who couldn't even admit he'd discarded me. The end of my life, drawing nearer and nearer still.

I walked to the porch, my sandals slapping against the tile as if to remind me I was alone. I did not bother turning the lights on.

I threw myself down on the wicker sofa and watched the waves through the glass.

I put my arm across my forehead like the heroine of a Victorian novel and cried.

I cried and cried; and when that was through, I cried some more. I could feel my face swell with salt and sorrow, but I could sooner lasso a star than stop.

Then I heard a rapping on the glass window, and I peed myself—just a little.

I wiped my eyes and opened the door. "Damn it, Shiloh," I said, trying not to sound choked up.

"Libby," he said, and he took my puffy face between his callused hands and kissed me in a way that I had never been kissed before. It was rough. It was tender. It was absolutely, undeniably *not* the kiss of a man who didn't truly like women.

Now, I know, I know: it's not fair to compare the men you sleep with. Really, it's not, even if one of those men turned out to not prefer your particular gender.

But as Shiloh picked me up and carried me back to the sofa; as he kissed me until I almost tore my clothes off for him, then took me to the bedroom and undressed us both; as he entered me and made me cry out with primal pleasure, there was no way not to acknowledge what I'd been missing.

And I thought, *Thank you, Tom.*

Thank you for your awful, terrible, heartbreaking timing. Because without it, I would have never ended up in Vieques, where I would finally—dear God, *finally*—get properly laid before it was too late.

# TWENTY

Shiloh was stretched out beside me, eyelids half-mast as he ran a finger up and down my arm. "Libby?"

"Mmm-hmm?" Having died the little death three times in a single night—my all-time personal record—I'd already passed blissed-out oblivion and was on a fast track to unconsciousness.

"I need to tell you something."

Suddenly I was wide awake. "Please don't say you have herpes," I said, although STDs fell somewhere between splinters and parking tickets on my end-of-life list of concerns. I was certain he was straight, but what if he had weird fetishes, or a criminal record, or—

"I had cancer," he said. "It almost killed me."

Suffice to say, this was not the bombshell I'd been expecting, though it did explain why he'd been so worked up at dinner the other night. "Wow—I'm so sorry. What kind? When?"

"Leukemia. Sixteen years ago."

"Cripes. You were young. Leukemia is curable, isn't it?"

"Well, I'm lying here next to you, right?" he said with a small smile. "And usually, yeah. Mine was pretty bad, though. Lymph nodes, bones, groin," he said, waving in the direction of his lower extremities.

"No one said it, but basically the doctors, my family, my wife—they were all expecting the worst."

Wife? His ring finger was bare. I let it slide. "So what happened?"

He kissed my shoulder. "I lived. To this day, I'm not sure why, but I did. I mean, I was in my twenties and I really, really didn't want to die, but that's true for most people with cancer, right?"

I nodded, grateful he'd phrased it like so. One of the few things that seriously pissed me off was when someone talked about how so-and-so would *definitely* survive cancer because he or she was a "fighter" or "too good to die." While I understood the temptation to think a winning personality can tip the scales toward survival, it still made my blood boil. Because my mom? She was the best person I'd ever met. She would have had her hands and feet amputated if it meant staying alive to see Paul and me grow up. She didn't die for lack of trying; she died because cancer is a serial killer. "You're okay now?" I asked Shiloh.

"Um, yeah. I guess. My marriage fell apart before I was even done with chemo, but I'm alive. Although"—he made an exaggerated frown—"I lost a ball."

I peeked under the sheet. "Pretty sure I saw two."

"The right one's fake."

I started laughing. "You mean you have neuticles?"

"Neuti*cle*," he said, tickling me. "And you weren't complaining a few minutes ago."

"Are you infertile?"

"As far as I know, the left one works just fine. But I don't have any secret children, in case you're wondering."

"That's a relief." I laid my head back on the pillow. "So this is why you were so upset with me the other night."

"I guess, yeah. I'm not trying to tell you what to do, Libby. Even if we'd known each other all our lives, that's not the way I operate. But I'm guessing I'm not the only one who wants to see you try your best to live. And I still mean what I said about the plane thing. Usually I'm not big on fate and all that jazz. But I don't know. I just . . ." He trailed off. Then he lifted the sheet again, and pointed to my stomach. "By the way, I'm pretty sure that's infected."

I quickly yanked the sheet over my abdomen. I'd been trying to keep the wound out of sight, but clearly wasn't doing a bang-up job. "No, that's what it looks like when it starts getting really bad."

"Are you sure?"

"Yes," I said, trying to sound firm even as I began to wonder if he could possibly be right. "So now that we're trading info, I need to tell *you* something."

He frowned. "About Tom?"

"Yeah."

I gave him the rundown, from the cutlery incident to the cash liquidation to the fact that Tom didn't know I was sick. Afterward, Shiloh looked thoughtful, but not upset. "Well, I've never slept with a married woman before, but this seems like a good time to start."

"Sorry," I said for the seventh time.

"Libby, it's okay. Are you all right, though? I mean, aren't you concerned that Tom has a lot to do with why you said no to treatment?"

I shook my head, thinking of Tom's blurry face coming into focus in the kitchen, of how less than a minute's delay on my part had resulted in an entirely new narrative for both him and me. "I decided that before he told me."

"Yeah, but I'm sure you weren't the first person to initially say you were going to skip treatment. The difference is, you're sticking with it. Any way you shake it, your husband coming out plus cancer is an insane amount of stress for one person. It's no surprise you freaked out on the beach."

"I did not freak out," I said crossly.

He kissed me lightly. "Okay, cutie. Just don't be so set on your decision this early in the game. Think about it, okay?"

*Cutie.* Unless "Libs" counted, Tom had no pet names for me. I kind of liked it. Even so, Shiloh's gentle nudging made me wonder if deep down, he wanted to take me on not just as a lover, but also a charitable endeavor.

I sighed and nestled into the crook of his arm. "We'll see."

I woke the next morning to a dent where Shiloh had been sleeping. I heard clanging in the kitchen and smiled. A note would have been sufficient, but a warm body was that much better.

He was standing in front of the espresso machine, which I still hadn't figured out how to use. "*Hola.* I made you a coffee."

"Thank you." I stood there for a few seconds, wishing I'd slipped my bra on before coming out in nothing but a T-shirt and underwear, then sat at the bar. He handed me a small cup and stood across from me drinking the coffee he'd prepared for himself.

"Gotta take off soon," he said. "I have to go to San Juan to take care of some things."

"Sure."

"That's it? Sure?"

"Were you expecting a different reply?"

"I guess not," he said, looking at me quizzically. Then he leaned across the bar and kissed me, which led to some spirited groping. "I really enjoy spending time with you, Libby," he said when we came up for air.

I smiled. "I enjoy it, too. Let's do this again soon."

He ran his hands through his hair and grinned back at me. "Absolutely."

My smile faded as I listened to his Jeep pull out of the driveway. I went to the bedroom, lifted my shirt, and stood before the mirror. My stomach was markedly less enthusiastic than I was about the evening's adventures with Shiloh: it felt as though a very angry squid had worked its way beneath my skin and was attempting to breach the walls of my intestines. I located Advil in the cupboard and took three. I would have to begin prophylactic self-medication, for I had every intention of sleeping with Shiloh again in the immediate future, and I was not going to let this festering fatality stop me.

I didn't see Shiloh again that night, which I told myself was for the best, even as I did frantic, libidinous calculations in my head. I had just nineteen more days on the island, and with the way my wound was weeping, there was no guarantee all those days would be sexually salvageable. "Nothing gold can stay," Paul was fond of saying. As per usual, he was right, even if his wisdom had been pilfered from Robert Frost. I figured this, if anything, earned him a phone call.

"Aw, you finally remembered little ol' me," Paul said by way of a greeting.

"Cease ye sulking, for I bear glad tidings."

"Go on."

"I'm getting laid!"

"Excuse me for a second." He made a gagging noise into the receiver. "You've now successfully dislodged nine hundred calories worth of burrito. Thank you for speeding my weight-loss efforts."

"Whatever, Paul. First of all, you don't have an ounce to lose. Second, didn't you tell me to find myself a cabana boy? Be happy for me."

"I *am* happy for you, even if I'm less than interested in the particulars. Who's the guy, and where'd you meet him?"

I recalled nose-diving into the shallow end of the Caribbean and decided it was best if I again self-censored. "It's a long story. But he's a pilot here, and he's Puerto Rican."

"Ca-ramba!" Paul said. "Seriously, though, Libs, be careful. You don't know this guy from Alejandro."

"His name is Shiloh, and I do know him. And I'm always careful."

"So says the girl who put her apartment on the market without telling its legal co-owner, then packed a bag and headed to an island in the middle of nowhere without even informing her beloved brother."

"Hmph. I said I was sorry."

"And all is forgiven, dear sis, provided you watch your back with any and all men who so much as glance your way."

I flushed as I recalled Shiloh pressing me up against the tiles in the shower, proving that we were both sportier than we'd given ourselves credit for. "My back's never been better," I assured Paul. "Promise."


"*Hola, mija,*" Milagros said when I let myself into her courtyard. "You're looking *muy linda* this evening. Love agrees with you."

"Love?" I said. "Who said anything about love?"

"You share a driveway with old Milly. I can see when certain male visitors leave early in the morning."

I frowned.

"*Ay,* don't be angry. Think of me as a built-in security system. Besides, I'm not looking through your windows or coming over. Just making sure you're okay."

"All right," I conceded, if only because this fact would make Paul happy. "Thank you." I handed Milagros the bottle of rum I'd purchased at the convenience store down the road.

"*Y gracias a ti.* Let's have some now," she said and went to the kitchen. She returned with two small glasses, which she filled with two very generous pours of the amber liquid.

"Cheers," I said, and took a sip. It made me cough, but the liquor spread its heat through my chest and into my stomach, the latter of which instantly stopped hurting. Forget painkillers—I was going to have to drink around the clock.

"Anyway," I told Milagros, "you can't be in love with someone you don't even know." I knew Shiloh's last name, that he'd survived cancer, and that he was the proud owner of one saline-filled testicle. However, I had no idea about the everyday minutiae of his life. What was his place in San Juan like, for example? Did he have siblings? What was the deal with his wife?

*"Mija,"* said Milagros. "That's not how it works. Do you respect him?"

"Yes," I admitted.

"Do you miss him when he's gone?"

"I suppose."

"Well, then, there you go. Though you might need more than a week to make a decent decision."

A week didn't sound so awful to me. Since walking into Dr. Sanders's office, most of my decisions had been made in less than an hour—and more often than not, in a few short seconds.

Milagros continued. "My point is, don't count it out just because it's new. I only knew my last husband, Luis, for two months before we got married, and I'm pretty sure that if he hadn't hit his head and fallen into the sea during a fishing trip, it would have been forever for the two of us."

"I'm sorry, Milagros."

She waved off my sympathy. "That was long ago. This man who's been visiting you, he looks nice, and you deserve to be treated well. He does treat you well, doesn't he?"

"Yes," I said. At the very least, I was no longer concerned that I was a pity lay. "But . . ."

"But what?" she said. "Time will tell you the rest."

I held out my glass. "If you say so, Milagros."

# TWENTY-ONE

Shiloh came by the next morning as I was rolling out of bed.

The sun hit me square in the face when I opened the door, and I squinted at him like a mole rat. "You're up early."

He leaned in to kiss me. "Hi to you, too. Do you have plans for the day?"

"Let me think." I scratched my head. "Um, that would be no."

"Great. How do you feel about going to San Juan and maybe spending the night?"

"Depends on how we're getting there. Because if you say 'plane' . . ."

He laughed. "I can't fly right now, remember?"

"That doesn't mean you don't have a pilot friend who wants to see if we're death-proof."

"We'll take the ferry. Puh-lease?" he said, mock begging.

I looked him up and down. He was in another ratty T-shirt, but the thin cotton accentuated his chest muscles in a most appealing way. And although I could detect only the faintest hint of soap, his pheromones must have been powerful because I had to stop myself from sniffing him. I wrapped my arms around his waist. "All right. But don't kill me."

.  .  .

The ferry was every bit as choppy as Shiloh had said it would be; by the time we docked in Fajardo, I was amazed that the toast and coffee I'd eaten for breakfast hadn't resurfaced. Fajardo was a good forty-five minutes from San Juan, and the cab ride from one city to the next did little to soothe my stomach. While the driver himself was adept, the other cars wove around us in a way that made me wax nostalgic for Chicago traffic.

As we traveled away from Fajardo, the landscape shifted from lush mountains to freshly paved roads and cul-de-sacs to crowded housing projects where laundry dried on cords and children clustered on stoops. An hour later, the driver dropped us off at a bustling neighborhood a stone's throw from the sea.

"This reminds me of some of the beach towns outside of LA," I told Shiloh as we walked past a café.

He nodded. "This neighborhood is called Condado. And this," he said, unlocking a wrought-iron gate, "is where I live when I'm not in Vieques."

Behind the gate was a well-tended garden shaded by large palm trees, and beyond that, a stuccoed building with canopied terraces on each floor.

"Charming."

"Don't say that before you've seen my apartment," he said, and led me up a set of stairs.

We stopped in front of a thick wood door, which Shiloh opened. "It's not much," he said as we stepped inside, "but it's mine."

I loved it on sight. Large windows bathed the terra-cotta-tiled floor in sunlight, and the sky-blue walls were hung with framed music festival posters and Puerto Rican folk art.

I admired an intricately designed guitar-like instrument that was placed on a stand in the corner. "Do you play?"

"The cuatro? I wish. That was my grandfather's."

"It's beautiful."

A teak platform bed tented with mosquito netting took up the majority of his bedroom. "I don't have air-conditioning," he explained of the netting, "although being this close to the water, I don't really need it."

I nodded and attempted not to look at a photo on the narrow dresser, which showed Shiloh with his arm around an attractive woman.

He gave me a look that said he knew exactly what I had been thinking. "That's Raquel—my *sister*. Carla was my ex-wife, and you won't find photos of her here. Or anywhere, for that matter."

"Does your sister live in Puerto Rico?"

"No, she's in Arizona. I don't see her or my niece and nephew very often, although they come here for Christmas most years."

"And your parents?"

"My dad's still here. And my mom's in New York City. I fly out there as much as I can."

"No kidding. My twin lives in New York."

"You have a twin? I can't believe you didn't mention her before. What's she like?"

"She's a he. Paul. He lives in New York with his partner, Charlie, and their twin boys."

"You're full of surprises."

"Yes, I am," I said slyly.

He gently pulled me onto his bed. "Tell me more."

I would have liked for us to stay tangled together beneath that cloud of mosquito netting for the remainder of my life, but Shiloh seemed excited about whatever he had planned, so I slipped on a dress and sandals while he showered. When he came out, he was dressed in a white linen shirt, linen pants, and a pair of loafers.

"You clean up nice," I said.

"I do make an effort on occasion." He brushed my curls off of my shoulders, then ran his hand along my back, sending shivers up my spine. "Are you sure you're feeling up to this?"

He had caught me wincing earlier; I'd have to be more careful about that. "I'm fine," I told him. "I swear."

"If that changes, you'll tell me. Right?"

"Of course," I chirped, ignoring the mild but persistent throbbing in my lower abdomen.

Old San Juan was a postcard of a city, with tropically colored colonial buildings stacked side by side on narrow streets paved with deep blue cobblestones. After walking along a path overlooking the water, we ducked onto a side street, where Shiloh led me to a tiny bar. The walls were plastered with photos of famous people and what was presumably the family who owned the bar.

"Legend has it this is the birthplace of the piña colada," Shiloh said.

"Is that true?"

"I don't know, but José here makes a mean drink," he said, reaching across the bar to clasp hands with the bartender.

"You know everyone in Puerto Rico," I said.

He squeezed my thigh lightly. "No, I'm just taking you to my favorite places."

This was comforting. If he had other girlfriends on the side, he wouldn't be parading me around town. Plus, he'd shown me where he lived. Not that it mattered, I reminded myself; we had a few more weeks to play couple, and then it was on to the end.

José slid two tall frosty glasses toward us, each filled with an icy mixture so pale yellow it was nearly white. Sweet without being heavy, the drink set off every pleasure receptor in my body. "I think I'm in love," I told him, face still in my glass.

Shiloh smirked. "I'm fond of you, too."

I kicked him under the table. "Not so fast, tough guy. I'm still trying to reconcile your fine body with your homicidal tendencies."

He leaned in to whisper in my ear. "How many more times do I need to replicate this afternoon to make you forget about the plane mishap?"

I smiled broadly, then kissed him, surprising myself. I wasn't usually the type for affection of the spontaneous or public variety. Then again, I was not the type to sleep with random men while I was still legally married. And yet.

After we finished the piña coladas, Shiloh and I walked a few more blocks to a brightly colored restaurant where a band was playing. We were seated and ordered wine and paella. After the waitress left, Shiloh motioned toward the dance floor. "Come on."

*"No puedo,"* I said, mimicking Milagros during our last lesson.

*"Sí, tú puedes,"* he said, pulling me out of my chair. He stopped and glanced at my stomach. "Wait, are you feeling okay? Because if you're not—"

"Very clever use of reverse psychology there, Dr. Velasquez."

"I'm serious, Libby. We've already done a lot today. If you're not up to it, it's not a problem."

For once, my cancerous abdomen wasn't the issue. The issue was that I was about as graceful as a buffalo mid–accidental cliff dive. "I can't dance," I confessed. "I have, like, four left feet."

"You're in luck, because Puerto Ricans happen to be born with a right foot, a left foot, and dancing hips. I could salsa before I could walk. I'll teach you."

He gyrated exaggeratedly in front of me and I laughed. "Okay, but you'll have to lead."

"Not a problem." He put one hand on the small of my back and took my right hand with the other. "Watch my feet for a minute. Then look up and let me guide you with my body."

I blushed as he moved me back and forth, again and again, until I managed to operate my limbs in a manner that might charitably be described as dancing.

"You're not half-bad," Shiloh shouted over the music.

"For a *gringa*!" I said, mostly delighted that I had not yet broken one of his toes.

"Exactly." He laughed and spun me around.

The tempo slowed, and he pulled me close. "What's next, Libby?" he asked quietly, his cheek almost touching mine.

*Best to play dumb,* I thought. "After dinner? Maybe we can call it an early night."

He chuckled. "Sure. But I mean after Puerto Rico."

He'd seen me stark naked, with all my divots and dimples highlighted in the bright light of day. He'd witnessed my postsurvival meltdown on the beach and my sobbing like a sad sack on the porch. But sharing how I planned to spend my final months felt insanely revealing, and I fought the urge to duck under the nearest table.

"I'm going to see my brother in New York," I said noncommittally. "Hey, would you mind if we went back to the table? I'm kind of thirsty."

"Of course," he said, guiding me across the room. We sat down, and I downed an entire glass of water before looking up. When I did, he smiled and said, "So, New York, huh? I hear they have some pretty good hospitals there."

"That's what I hear," I said, dabbing at my mouth with a corner of a cloth napkin.

"That's what I hear, too," he said, and reached for his wineglass.

The waiter delivered our paella, and Shiloh and I feigned an unusual amount of interest in consuming it, pausing between bites to discuss meaningful topics such as whether I liked mussels, and if the rice had been cooked long enough.

But.

After we returned to his apartment, stripped down, and took to each other like coyotes on carrion, we were lying there panting. And he looked over at me and said, "Has it occurred to you that maybe it isn't your time?"

I squinted at him, still kind of light-headed from the sex we'd just had. "Given what you've told me about your feelings on fate and fatality, I'm going to assume you don't really believe that."

"No," he confessed. "I believe we have absolutely no way of knowing. But I think it doesn't hurt to assume we're going to live until we're absolutely ready to die. You're not ready. You can't convince me you are, Libby."

I pulled the sheet up around my bare flesh and said nothing.

In the low light of the bedroom, his eyes looked nearly black. "Damn it, Libby, fight for your life," he said in a low tone. "At the very least, get a second opinion."

Fists wedged into my armpits, I gripped the thin cotton sheet tightly. "That's not what this is about. This is about *dignity*. I'm fighting for my right to let nature run its course instead of letting chemo destroy what little time I have left."

"You're talking to the wrong guy about that one. Trust me, I know how much treatment sucks. Chemo and radiation almost cost me both balls—and that was after my marriage ended. Any time I have a cramp, I think, *It's back*. I have to work every single day not to let this thing that happened sixteen years ago define the rest of my life. But you know what? It was worth it. I'm alive, and I'd do it again tomorrow if I had to."

"I'm sorry that happened to you," I said, sniffing as I attempted to maintain my composure. "But this is different. You're not going to change my mind, and if that's what you're trying to do, maybe we shouldn't see each other anymore."

His sighed deeply, then put his arms around me and pulled me down so his stomach was pressed against my back. "Don't say that, Libby," he whispered as I let myself ease into him. "Aren't we having fun?"

Fun? I couldn't argue with him there. After we made love again, and Shiloh had fallen asleep beside me, I stared up at the mosquito netting, listening to him snoring lightly. In spite of our argument, I felt weirdly content. While I wasn't fond of the inciting incident that had put me there, I liked this parallel universe I found myself in. It was a place in which I was able to ignore trivial matters such as work, bills, and my gay husband, and instead sun myself with abandon, eat and sleep at will, and catch up on the carnal pleasures I'd missed during the first thirty-four years of my life.

If only my resolve about the end of my life was not eroding like the shoreline at high tide. What *would* I do? Was my decision to forgo treatment not brave at all—but rather impulsive and perhaps even selfish, as Shiloh had implied?

As I began to drift off, I heard my mother's voice, or at least her voice as I imagined it. My father had neither the foresight nor the spare cash to invest in a video camera before her death, and so Paul and I had only a two-minute clip taken by a distant relative at another relative's party to help us re-create the light, steady timbre of our mother's speech.

"I'm not worried about you, Libby," she said, placing her hand in mine. She was at the hospice, tethered to the bed by thin plastic tubes that ran between her legs and into her limbs. It was a week, maybe, before the end, and she had asked to be alone with me. "You'll be just fine; I know it in my soul. But take care of Paul, please, love? I need you to do that for me."

"Of course, Mama," I told her as I sat paralyzed, unable to shed a tear or squeeze her fingers for fear I would make her pain even more severe.

"You're the joy of my life, Libby Lou." Her words were slow and strained, as though it took everything in her to push them through her throat and off her tongue. "I love you."

"I love you more, Mama," I assured her, holding her gaze until she finally let her eyes close.

This was not the memory I would have preferred to recall, but nonetheless it surfaced regularly. Because it was the moment when I finally acknowledged—if only for a few brief minutes—that she was going to die. My pastor, my father, Paul: they all tried to warn me. I was always a pleasant child, or so I've been told. But the day my mother and father sat us down and explained that she had cancer, a switch in me flipped. Forget looking on the bright side. My subconscious decided that if I didn't acknowledge that there *was* a dark side, life's negatives would cease to exist. So when people tried to explain that my mother didn't have long to live, I nodded and mentally filed this probability somewhere between alien probings and a prehistoric mammal breaststroking through Loch Ness.

In all my recollecting, what I had not much considered was my mother's actual request. Unflappable and *über*capable, Paul had been the one to take care of everything and everyone, including me, so I had failed my mother in this regard. But it would not be a final failure, I assured myself as I curled up against Shiloh. I would spare Paul the sight of skin spread like rice paper over bones and blood, a body battered beyond recognition by the same chemicals intended to salvage what a lab test had already confirmed was unsalvageable.

By avoiding a grueling repeat of our mother's death, I would take care of Paul in the most meaningful and lasting way I was able.

Or so I told myself as I drifted into a deep and dreamless sleep.

# TWENTY-TWO

"I need to go into the office this afternoon," Shiloh said the next morning. We'd had coffee and croissants at his apartment, and had just returned from a quick walk on the beach, during which neither of us brought up our life-and-death chat. "You okay to take the ferry?"

"Of course," I said, though in truth, I wished he'd mentioned it earlier. Still, if I could dine alone, certainly I could take the S.S. *Regurgitator* back to Vieques by myself. Besides, I was acutely anxious about becoming too attached to a man I would be leaving behind in a few weeks. Milagros could squawk about love until she was blue. The main thing was that I didn't *want* to fall in love. Except I was getting confused, with thinking about the future and enjoying sex as more than a stand-alone act. It was the cancer; I was sure of it. Not only had it warped my brain, it had created an instabond between me and Shiloh that would not, and could not, last.

So when Shiloh dropped me off at the boat that would take me from Puerto Rico proper back to Vieques, I kissed him with abandon, then ran for the dock before I could ask when I would see him again. One day soon I would no longer be a part of his life, nor he mine. It was best if we both began adjusting immediately.

.   .   .

As the ferry approached the shore, I felt the sense of relief one feels when coming home. At the beach house I took a nap, and when I woke it was dark out. It was a waste of a day, but I was wiped out and a bit feverish, and needed to rest. I made myself a bowl of cereal, read for a while, and returned to bed.

Shiloh didn't call the following morning, and in spite of my feelings about healthy separation, it was impossible not to wonder if this had something to do with my refusal to give into his attempts to save me from myself.

No matter—it was impossible to dwell on anything other than the rusty knife slowly sawing through my gut. I'd soaked through my shirt, and when I put my hand to my forehead, I realized I was burning up. I took three Advil and cursed myself for not having rum on hand to chase them down.

Until that point, I hadn't really felt like I was dying, per se, but now death was all too real. As I bent at the waist and resisted the urge to dry heave, I imagined my life force seeping out of me, like heat from the windows of an old home. And to think that I was still months out from the worst of it! My mother had refused morphine until the month before her death. She kept smiling as tumors bombed their way through her ovaries, into her intestines and bladder. And how? How did she have the energy to parent two children and be a wife and see her friends, while I was struggling to get off the sofa?

If she could keep going, then I would have to as well. Gritting my teeth, I tugged on my bathing suit, slipped on a cover-up and a sun hat, and took off down the beach. I wasn't really in the mood to sunbathe, but Milagros told me that half a mile from our stretch of sand, there was a new hotel that made killer cocktails, which sounded apropos, even at eleven in the morning.

The hotel was a mirage of sparkling limestone at the edge of the sand. "Will you be dining with us?" a waiter asked as I approached the bar.

"Just drinks," I said. I pointed to the canvas lounge chairs lined up on the beach. "Can I sit in one of those and still be served?"

"Are you a guest of the hotel?"

"No, but I'm dying of cancer."

The waiter regarded me as though he didn't believe a word I was saying, but I was gripping my side in a manner that suggested I was in the middle of birthing a live cactus, and he decided it was better for me to be far from the dozen or so patrons brunching on the patio. "I'll be right over with a menu," he said, indicating that I was to choose a chair.

The piña colada I ordered seemed to dull the pain, so I ordered another before finishing the first. It was fast approaching noon, and some of the people around me had begun sipping fruity cocktails, so I didn't feel too bad when the waiter asked if he could bring a bill and I said yes—as soon as he was done fetching me a third drink. "Medical marijuana doesn't work for me," I explained when he lifted an eyebrow at my request. "This is the next-best thing."

In fact, I had not yet tried nor considered weed, and it struck me, through my hooch haze, that it might not be the worst idea. Perhaps Paul would be able to help on that front, too.

Seagulls were circling overhead, and it was hard to tell if they were after the cocktail peanuts the waiter had served, or my flesh tartare. The persistent boom of the surf mostly drowned out the gulls' high-pitched clamoring, but between the two, I nearly missed my phone ringing.

It was Tom. I answered, which I will attribute to the piña coladas.

"Libby?" As per usual, he sounded upset. "Why are you in Puerto Rico?"

I almost asked how he knew I was there, but then I remembered that I had booked tickets on one of the credit cards I shared with him and that in my haste, I had removed him from the account but failed to change the password. That would need to be fixed soon. In the meantime, I told him to leave me alone.

"Your doctor's office called me," he insisted.

My stomach lurched. "You know sharing a person's medical information without their permission is illegal, right?"

"They didn't *share* anything. They just asked if I knew how to get ahold of you."

"Good," I said, watching a spindly brown bug approach my chair. As it crept closer, I lifted my foot, then changed my mind as I was about to crush it. I nudged it away with the edge of my sandal and watched it scamper in the opposite direction.

"Are you going to call them back, Libby?" he asked, sounding too kind and concerned for someone who was no longer supposed to be a part of my life. "Is everything all right?"

"Of course, it is," I said, and it was almost believable. After all, what did *sick* mean? And what was *well*, anyway? I squeezed my eyes shut for a moment, then opened them, fixing my eyes on a vein in my forearm that was pulsing like a river. To the left of the vein was a blackened freckle, and to the right, a small white pigment-free blotch—both remnants of the summers I spent slathered in baby oil beneath a baking sun. My eyes trailed down, past the festering flesh hidden beneath my cover-up, to the subtle curve of my calf muscles and my slender ankles. My imperfect body, deemed terminally unwell, was the best it would ever be. Soon it simply would not be at all. It was almost impossible to wrap my mind around.

"If the doctor calls you again, tell them we're no longer married and give them my number," I told Tom.

He hesitated. "Okay," he said after a moment. "I know you're upset with me, but I want you to know that I'm here for you if you need anything."

Upset. Upset! Like the only reason I'd chosen to put two thousand miles between us was because he'd eaten the toaster waffle that I'd been saving for breakfast.

"I am fine, Tom," I said sharply. "Now please, stop calling me."

"Li—"

I ended the call before he could continue, not only because I didn't want to speak with him. I was having the same feeling I'd had after the plane crash.

"Ma'am? Ma'am, are you okay?" the waiter asked, regarding me as I gasped and clutched at my throat.

I turned my head in his direction and croaked, "I am not." And then, I am sorry to say, I passed out.

When I came to, an older man wearing a very small banana hammock was crouched over me. I yelped as I realized my face was mere centimeters from his rug of chest hair.

He leaned back, his skin slick with sweat. "I am a doctor. I am vacationing at this hotel," he said in a clipped accent of undecipherable origin. "The staff called me when you fainted. Are you all right?"

I was not all right, but alarmed, and very embarrassed. I sat up and brushed myself off, being careful not to meet the eyes of the waiter, who was hovering behind the doctor, undoubtedly concerned that I would die before I had a chance to pay for my ridiculously overpriced libations.

"I'm fine," I told the doctor. "It was a panic attack. Apparently I'm prone to them."

"If you're losing consciousness, I'll have to recommend you go to a hospital for evaluation as soon as possible. Is there someone I can call for you?"

"I can manage," I informed him, though this was somewhere south of the truth.

"I'll call you a taxi," the waiter said.

"No," I said.

"Really, it's no trouble," he insisted.

I gritted my teeth. "Please don't. Just bring me the check."

Ignoring the doctor's questioning gaze, I paid my bill and hobbled down the beach back to the house.

Pain is funny, isn't it, the way it's impossible to accurately recall once it's gone? When my incision wasn't hurting too much, it was easy to believe I would be able to withstand the agony all the way to the bitter end. But now it was as though I'd been ripped open anew, and I wasn't sure I could take another second of it, let alone an hour or a day. I served myself a bowl of cereal, but the thought of eating made me queasy, so I left it on the counter and went to the bedroom mirror. An ashen, exhausted woman regarded me warily from the glass. As I turned away, a sharp pain radiated through my groin and down my leg, making me wonder whether the cancer was spreading. I needed to see a doctor.

I limped over to Milagros's. "Hello?" I called through her screen door. "Anyone home?"

She swung the door open. "Ay!" she cried when she saw me.

"Tell me about it," I said. "I'm not feeling very good."

"You look like you swallowed a swordfish, *mija*."

"Funny, that's what my stomach feels like right now. Do you know of a decent doctor?"

"Do I know a doctor! Do I know a doctor!" she said, hopping around. "I know all three doctors on the island, and I'll even take you to my favorite. You let me drive you."

"I can drive myself."

She wagged her finger at me. "That wasn't a request. There are people I love living around here, and I'm not giving you the chance to run one of them over on your way."

What was the use in arguing? I got in her old Chevy pickup and let her take me to the clinic. She helped me up the stairs and checked me in, and it was all I could do not to take her with me into the examination room so she could hold my hand through it all.

Instead, I went in alone. A woman with dark curls and an unlined face introduced herself as Dr. Hernandez.

"I had a, uh, mass removed, and it hurts a lot," I told her, lifting up my shirt. "I'm going to go back to my doctor at home"—a tiny fib, I reasoned—"but I was hoping you could give me something to ease the pain until I get there."

She inspected the incision, then pressed down on it with her fingers while I gritted my teeth and willed myself not to boot her in the head. "It hurts because it's infected," she said. "You should have had these stitches out at least a week ago."

"I thought they would dissolve."

"Wrong type of stitches. I'm going to use a local anesthetic to numb you up. It's going to hurt while I do it, but you'll feel better after." She plunged an enormous syringe into my stomach, pushing it this way and that as she loaded my skin with a cold-feeling fluid.

"It—still—hurts," I gasped as she eased the needle out.

She tossed it into a medical waste bin and smiled at me. "But now it doesn't anymore, right?"

I grimaced, though the pain was giving way to a tingling sensation. Maybe local anesthesia would be how I would get through the next few months. But I'd have to find a physician—someone other than Dr. Sanders—who would agree to take a palliative, rather than prescriptive, approach. Which could be complicated.

Dr. Hernandez used tweezers to pull bloody-looking stitches from my skin, cleaned the wound out, and told me to apply ointment and new bandages for a week. Then she handed me a prescription for an antibiotic. "This should knock out the infection. You'll feel better in a day or two, but don't stop until you've taken every last pill. Your incision could get worse if you're not careful. I've seen cases of septic shock when patients haven't been compliant with their medicine."

I thanked her for this uplifting morsel of information and returned to the waiting room. "All set," I told Milagros.

She nodded, then looped her arm under mine. We left the clinic that way, with me leaning on an elderly woman for strength, and her holding me up as though I was a wisp of a girl. As she helped me into the Chevy, I began to cry. The soothing, the kindness, the subtle mothering: these acts comforted even as they reminded me of what I did not have. Because at that moment, what I longed for most was not my life before my husband came out, or even before I set foot in Dr. Sanders's office. It wasn't even Paul and my father, the two people in this world who loved me most. It was my mother.

Milagros seemed to understand that I was not crying out of pain. "It's okay, *mija*. Whatever it is, it's going to be okay. You're here. You're alive."

"That's the problem," I said from behind my hands. "I'm not supposed to be." I thought of the plane crash, and the truck on the hiking path. Cancer aside, weren't these evidence I was fated for a short and unspectacular life?

"And who told you that?" Milagros said, not unkindly. "You're exactly where you're supposed to be until it's over and you aren't anymore. Prince or pauper, that's how it works for us all."

If this was true, then why was I meant to be driving down a dirt road in the middle of a tiny island in the Caribbean? Why was I meant to die in a rapid and devastating manner, just like my mother?

I looked out the window for wild horses, but there were no hidden signs or answers. Only trees and bushes and vines, blurring into a seemingly endless line of green.

# TWENTY-THREE

My mother was buried in a suburb just outside of Detroit, three hours from our home, in a cemetery where her own parents and many of her relatives lay.

It might as well have been Uzbekistan.

It wasn't as though physical proximity to the cemetery would have allowed me to interact with her, but I was still furious. It was just one more way in which she had been kept from me.

Perhaps because of this, in the months following my mother's death—*our* death, really, as our family as we knew it had died there next to her—our father drove me and Paul to the cemetery as often as we requested. Then, after several exhausting months of weekend travel, he said no. "I'm tired, and we're beginning to outstay our welcome with my cousins," he told us, referring to the relatives we stayed with during visits. "We'll go again soon. Just not right now, okay?"

It wasn't okay with me, but instead of saying this, I decided to relay my anger by taking a pair of craft scissors to my curls. Paul, sensing a catastrophe in progress, let himself into the bathroom while I was halfway through the hack job. He didn't say anything, just held out his hand for the scissors, which I gave him.

"You can't tell Dad that this is about him not taking us to Mom," he said as he did his best to make it look like I had not stuck my head in a fan.

"Fine."

"Libby, please," he said, still snipping away, "you *can't*. He's already upset. Pretend you had gum in your hair. Tell him you were tired of kids pulling on your curls. Just, this is not about the cemetery, okay?"

I didn't respond, but when I saw my father later that evening, I smiled as wide as my face would allow, as though I were tickled to be the spitting image of a young Billy Crystal. And as he smiled back in response, I realized Paul had saved all three of us from yet another unnecessary maiming.

That was Paul: fixer of situations, savior of me. I needed him, and maybe more important, I needed to make sure that the increasingly suspicious Tom was not the one to tip Paul off about the terrible thing I was concealing.

So after Milagros brought me back to the beach house, and I had tossed back a handful of antibiotics and ibuprofen, I reluctantly called him. But when he picked up, I couldn't make myself say it. Instead, I sat on the end of my bed and cried into the phone.

"Let it out," Paul cooed. "Honestly, it's a relief to hear you cry. I know how horrible this has been for you. Keeping it all bottled up won't help."

"*Wahhhhh!*" I howled, because even though Paul was referring to Tom, it was so good to hear him confirm that what I was going through was horrible. It was. As much as the gash in my stomach hurt, my heart felt worse. Like my tumor, the bit of hope left in me had been torn out, leaving a gaping hole and an unspeakable ache in its stead.

Yet I couldn't admit this out loud. Every time I went to tell Paul what had happened, my shame for not telling him immediately only deepened. So I curled up beneath the bedspread and cried while he listened to me carry on, interjecting an occasional soothing comment.

"Are you still in Vieques?" Paul asked when the worst of the wailing subsided.

"Yes." I sniffed.

"Good," he said. "Are you leaving soon?"

"I don't know," I said. "I don't know what I'm doing. I'm such a wreck right now."

"Shhh, you're not a wreck. It's okay. Stay put and we'll figure something out. We always do, don't we?"

"Thank you," I whispered. Snot was collecting on my phone, and shame or no shame, it was evident that this would not be when I told him. "Can I call you later?"

"Of course. Just please, promise you won't pick up and fly to yet another country without telling me."

"Puerto Rico is part of the United States," I said, feeling defensive of a place that was not my own.

"So you say. By the way, I love you the absolute most."

"Yet I love you more," I said, and it was the truth.

The antibiotics began to work their magic. When I woke the next morning, I could actually manage breakfast; I even took a shower and got dressed without wincing. I walked along the beach for a while, then drove into town to have an early lunch at the café where I'd had my first solo meal. It was a sleepy weekday, and there were few people to people watch, so I pulled a novel out of my bag. I was able to lose myself in the misadventures of a pair of ill-fated lovers for a short while, but then said lovers began humping with a literary vigor typically reserved for straight-up erotica, and I became distracted by the thought of Shiloh. If only I'd met him under happier circumstances—in an alternate universe, perhaps, where I was neither married nor a ticking time bomb. But I knew that we would not have come together any other way.

I reached into my bag, grabbed my phone, and called him. He sounded sleepy when he picked up. "Hey, how are you?"

"Um. Okay," I said.

"Okay?"

"Well . . . I kind of passed out yesterday and ended up going to the doctor. But I'm doing better now, so no need to worry."

Shiloh let out a low curse. "I knew it."

"You knew what?

"It's getting worse."

*Yes, it's getting worse*, I thought. *I'm dying.* "Not true at all," I said in what I hoped was a buoyant tone. "The doctor said my incision was infected."

"See? You need to go back to the mainland, Libby. It's time to get this thing treated."

"I'll do nothing of the sort. I have almost two weeks left in Vieques, and I plan to enjoy them. Heck, I might not even leave at all." Though it hadn't previously occurred to me, the idea made sense. Vieques was my Heaven's Mouth; the longer I was here, the less I wanted to be anywhere else. It was the ideal place to end it all.

"No," Shiloh said firmly. "You're leaving. Don't make a bad decision just because you're afraid of being afraid."

I pushed my toes deep into the sand. "What a ridiculous thing to say," I said crossly. What did he even mean, anyway?

"Is it? Ridiculous, I mean? You're already dealing with pain, so it's not that you're trying to avoid."

I thought of the large bottle of horse pills in my fridge. "I *was* in pain, but I'm feeling much better. The antibiotics are practically a cure-all."

"I'm happy to hear that. But less pain doesn't mean that the cancer is gone. I think you're putting off treatment because you don't want to feel vulnerable. It's not chemo and radiation you're afraid of—it's letting yourself feel how scary it is to not know what's next. Please don't choose the worst-case scenario just to avoid that feeling. You have people to see you through this. I'm one of them."

Tears pricked my eyes. "Thank you so very much for that stunningly inaccurate analysis, Señor Freud."

"That's not nice, Libby."

"Well, I'm not a very nice person."

"I don't believe that for a second."

"Believe it, *hombre*."

"Libby," Shiloh said slowly, "I'm going to go now before this conversation takes a wrong turn. Please just consider what I've said."

"Fine."

"Thank you. I'll talk to you soon, okay? Take care." He did not say he planned to return to Vieques to see me—which was what I wanted to hear—so I didn't respond. But instead of filling the silence, he said good-bye softly and hung up.

I stared at my phone. Seconds passed, then minutes, but instead of bursting into tears or throwing the phone into the sand, I just sat there. Numb.

Love guts you, then saunters away as the vultures swoop down to steal what's left. I *knew* that. It had been mere weeks since Tom had reminded me.

But what had I done? I had run right back for another flaying— only to find myself surprised that once again, I was emptied and alone.

# TWENTY-FOUR

"Milagros? Hello?" I called through the screen door, but my voice was met with silence. It had been two long days since I'd spoken with Shiloh, and I was hoping a Spanish lesson would help take my mind off our chafing conversation. Plus, though I wouldn't admit this to anyone else, I was a bit bored. I'd eaten at most of the restaurants on the island, sorted an inordinate amount of shells, and walked the beach until my legs would take me no farther—which was not particularly far, given the way I was feeling. Could I really keep doing some version of the same for an unspecified amount of time? Especially if it meant doing it *alone*? I'd gone to Vieques on a solitary mission, but then Shiloh had come along, and being there without him felt all wrong.

Strangely, I missed work. Not the work itself, and not Jackie, obviously—but the structure to my day. The purpose. As I wandered from Milagros's house back to my own, I wondered what my purpose was, now that I was unemployed and had a markedly shortened shelf life. Maybe I could finally learn to cook, or—

A sharp pain shot through my stomach, as if to remind me of my only purpose: to survive.

*No, no, no*, I argued with myself as the word *survive* resurfaced in my mind. *That's not right. It's a biological urge at play, just like your urge to procreate with your nonfunctioning baby-making equipment. There is no surviving. There is only coming to terms with not surviving.*

Just thinking about it felt exhausting, and when I let myself into the house I immediately lay on my bed and closed my eyes. I quickly fell into a deep slumber and emerged groggy and ravenous two hours later. I fixed myself a bowl of SpaghettiOs (in a moment of acute desperation, I'd purchased four cans at the mini-mart), then went to the sofa on the back porch, propped the bowl on my stomach, and sloppily spooned Os into my mouth. Through the glass doors, I watched a kiteboarder zigzag across the water. Something darted through my peripheral vision, and although it was probably nothing but a lizard or another kiteboarder, I glanced around for a large object with which to defend myself. But when I turned again to see what sinister criminal lurked beyond the glass, Paul was staring back at me.

Lord help me, I fell right off the sofa. Paul yanked at the patio door, but it was locked. The bemused expression on his face as he waited for me to scrape myself off the floor told me at once that he had no idea about the big *C*.

He still thought this was about Tom! Excellent: I could tell him on my own time. I pushed myself up, trying to pretend that doing so did not make me feel as though my lower abdomen had been impaled. Forcing my grimace into a smile, I unlocked the patio door.

"Is it really you?" I said, touching his arm lightly, because I was still in too much pain to give him a proper hug. "You actually flew to Puerto Rico?" Paul did not fly—not when his big-shot clients invited him to Aspen, not when investors asked him to go to Europe or Hong Kong, not when Charlie had to be in Los Angeles for work. Half the reason our father had moved to New England was so he'd be within driving distance of Paul. Yet Paul had gotten on a plane for *me*. I wasn't sure whether to be flattered or concerned. (Had I really sounded that awful? Probably, I conceded.) Mostly I was relieved. My brother was here to help me make sense of this catastrophe. It was unfortunate that he was not yet aware of said catastrophe.

"Of course it's me," he said, throwing his arms around me, oblivious to how much his hug hurt me. "And yes, I set foot on a giant death trap just for you." Paul's smile faded as he examined my face. "Libs, are you bleeding?" he asked.

I touched the skin beneath my lip, looked at my finger for a second, then stuck the orange-red digit in my mouth. "Nah, that's tomato sauce."

Paul did his own version of the disappearing neck trick. "Enough of the niceties. You, sister love, are in even worse shape than I was expecting."

"I'm fine," I protested, but no sooner had I said this than Shiloh appeared on the patio walkway.

I did a little jump: he was back! And just in time to meet my brother! I waved him in. "Paul, this is Shiloh," I said as he walked into the sunroom. "Shiloh, Paul."

"We've met, actually," said Shiloh.

"You've—what?" I turned to Paul, who looked nonplussed.

"What?" he said. "I had to figure out where you were staying without tipping you off because I knew you'd try to talk me out of coming. Turns out that there aren't many pilots named Shiloh in Puerto Rico. It took me all of three minutes to track him down. He met me at the ferry to help me get over here."

Shiloh smiled thinly as I gave him a bug-eyed stare.

"Great," I said flatly. "Mind if I borrow him for a second?" I said, grabbing Shiloh's arm and pulling him into the bedroom.

"Cutie, chill out," Shiloh whispered when we were alone.

"So you didn't tell him?"

"Give me some credit. It's not my place."

I exhaled.

Shiloh looked at the door, then back at me. "You do have to tell him, you know."

"I know."

"I'm serious, Libby."

"So he can talk me into treatment?"

His eyes held mine. "That wouldn't be the worst outcome."

"We already know the worst outcome, and my body's hurtling toward it at warp speed."

"You don't know that."

"But the doctor said—"

"I know what he said. But you didn't get any of your follow-up scans, did you? Did they look at your lymph nodes yet? Run DNA tests?"

"You're surprisingly knowledgeable for someone whose last brush with disease occurred around the same time as the Iran-Contra affair."

"Enough with the jabs, Libby," he said, too calmly. "Your brother is in the other room waiting for you, and the longer we're in here, the more curious he's going to be about what's going on."

I almost hit him. Almost. But then my lower lip started trembling and a fog of sadness rose through my chest and head, emerging as tears.

"Now what am I supposed to do?" I whispered.

"You go out there and spend time with Paul," Shiloh said, putting his hand on my upper back gently. "For the record, he thinks he's here because you're having a break*down* prompted by your break*up*. But, cutie . . ."

My nickname was back. We would be okay, at least for now. "Yes?"

He wiped my eyes with his thumbs, then kissed my forehead lightly. "Tell him. Right away."

. . .

"You're awfully quiet," Paul said, examining me from the other side of the kitchen island. Shiloh left right after we emerged from the bedroom, claiming he was meeting a friend on the other side of the island. "Are you still upset I didn't tell you I was coming?"

"No, no. It's just that I'm starving," I twittered as I stuck my head in the fridge, as though I had not just done sick things to a can of pasta. "You know how I get when I'm hungry." Bypassing a container of sliced papaya and a container of yogurt, I located the jug of pineapple juice. Then I reached into the cupboard for the bottle of rum I had purchased the day before.

Paul watched me as I put the alcohol on the counter. "Rum, huh? I've been trying to get you to imbibe since you were twelve. If I knew it was as easy as dropping you on a tropical island, I would have done that years ago."

"An island, and a failed marriage," I said as I poured two glasses, topping both with pineapple juice. I slid one of the glasses to him, avoiding his eyes.

Paul took a demure sip of the drink, sputtered a little, and put it back on the counter. "You're aware that alcohol isn't food, right? And I won't even mention that the gap between your thighs worries me. Skinny isn't a good look for you, Libbers."

I glanced down at my legs and realized that for the first time since fourth grade, I could see between them. "If you say so. Anyway, how's work?"

"Work, shmerk. It eats my life, and I secretly love and loathe every minute of it, so no change there. On to more important things: how are *you*?"

I took an enormous swig of my drink and ignored his question. "Why didn't Charlie and the boys come with you? It would have been nice to see them."

"Charlie's filming. And I can't take care of Toby and Max without him, especially not on a trip that involves flying. Besides, I thought it would be good for you and me to have to spend some quality time together."

"Because you were worried I'm cracking up," I said. My face was starting to feel hot, and I could feel my pulse quickening.

"Because I *love* you, you ninny," Paul said. "Now why aren't you happier to see me?"

"I am."

"But . . . ," he supplied. When I said nothing, he came around to the other side of the kitchen island and stood next to me, as though we both intended to look at the beach together. "Libs, what is it? Did you find out Tom was sleeping with someone already? Is Jackass suing you for quitting? Has Shiloh made you a member of some bizarre cult I need to know about?"

I managed a small laugh. "No, no, and no."

"Well, then? Come on. While you would certainly be justified to be this blue over your breakup, I'm sensing that there's something else going on."

You know what they say about hindsight. It was moronic of me to think I could conceal the truth from the very person who made the transition from zygote to fully formed human being beside me in the womb. Yet even with Paul in front of me, sensing my deception like a dog smells fear, I was considering whether I *really* had to tell him. Wouldn't he be best protected if I continued concealing my big awful thing?

"Um, it's just that . . ."

"Cripes, Libs. Are you trying to give me a coronary?" Paul's hands were on his hips, and his brow was furrowed; I could only imagine that if I were one of his minions, he'd have already tossed me out of the room.

Still I couldn't say it. "Let's go down to the beach," I told him.

Glasses in hand, we walked to the shore. It was late afternoon, and the sun sagged beneath the clouds. The shore was all but deserted, and we stood at the water's edge, letting the waves lap at our feet.

"You're right. This isn't just about Tom. I'm sick, Paul."

My brother spun around toward me, but I didn't meet his eye. "Like, in the head?"

"I'm not joking."

"Libs, please don't say what I think you're about to say."

"Okay. I don't have cancer."

Paul inhaled. "No, you do not."

I kicked at the sand. "I'm sorry to say that I most certainly do."

"And when were you going to tell me this?"

"You know. Shortly after I died."

He threw his still-full glass into the ocean. "Dammit, Libby. *Dammit.* No wonder you've been so dodgy lately."

"Sorry," I said lamely.

He didn't say anything for a solid two minutes. When he finally looked at me again, the pain etched on his face made me wish that rather than cancer, I'd been diagnosed with a fast-acting, flesh-eating bacteria that would swallow me on the spot. "What kind?"

"You've never heard of it."

He reached into his pocket for his phone. "Spell it," he said.

"Don't look it up right now," I pleaded, thinking about the images I had found online. But I spelled it for him anyway, and stood there, cheeks burning, while he stared at the small screen in his hand.

He took a deep breath and stuck his phone back in his pants pocket. "Okay. We can deal with this. I have a client at Mount Sinai, and he'll know the best oncologists in the city. Or there's the Mayo Clinic or Fred Hutchinson in Seattle. We can—"

"No," I said.

"What do you mean, no?"

"Just . . . no."

He looked as though he wanted to shake me. "Sorry, Libby, but this isn't a choice you get to make."

"Um, yes, yes, it is. It's my life."

"Do you hear yourself right now? You sound like a crazy person."

"I shouldn't have told you."

"You *are* a crazy person, and it's Tom's fault," he said, as much to himself as to me. "You just suffered a major trauma."

"Two traumas," I corrected. "And it's not Tom's fault. He did me a favor. Otherwise, I would have died never knowing the truth." Even as I said this, I found myself wishing the exact opposite were true. Yes, I had Paul; but as much as I loved and relied on my brother, it was not the same as having my husband—my purported *life partner*—by my side when I needed him most. Tom had buoyed me. Really, he was probably the single reason I had stayed so optimistic all those years. His love was like a constantly streaming subconscious message that said, "See, Libby? Even though your mother died, things can and do work out for you." Now my life raft had thrown me overboard and taken off in the opposite direction. Despite what I'd said to Paul, it would have been easier—so much easier—to leave the world without ever learning Tom's truth.

I had begun crying, and in an instant, Paul was at my side, soothing me. "We can get through this, Libs. We *will* get through this."

I carried on for a moment. Then I rubbed my eyes and looked at him. "I wasn't kidding, Paul. I'm not going to get treatment."

He took a step back and glared at me, at once ferocious. "Christ on a cracker, Libs! How selfish can you possibly be?"

"Don't you think I'm allowed one selfish moment?"

"A moment, yes! An eternity? That's some bullshit! You know that?" Now he was crying.

"Please stop that," I said, even as salty tears ran into my mouth.

"I'm going to cry! Get over it!" he yelled. Then he began glancing around.

"What are you doing?" I asked, as if I didn't already know he was searching for an escape route.

"Leaving," he muttered.

"*Leaving?* What do you mean, leaving? You don't even have any place to go."

He'd already begun walking. "It's called a hotel," he called over his shoulder.

"And how are you going to get there?" I yelled, hands on my hips.

"With my two feet!"

*But Paul* never *left*, I thought as I watched him speed walk in the opposite direction.

"Paul!" I cried. "Come on! . . . Come back!"

He stopped and turned around, and for a split second, I thought he would change his mind. Then he hollered, "I'm going to give you a day to think about how incredibly stupid your little plan is. At that point, you and I will get on a plane and fly back to New York together."

I shook my head. "I'm not going anywhere."

"Fine." He turned back around and began walking toward the road.

"Paul! *Paul!*" I yelled, but he was already gone.

# TWENTY-FIVE

I thought about calling Shiloh, but felt too dejected to have yet another conversation with someone who didn't understand my stance on treatment. Instead, I took my horse pill of an antibiotic and proceeded to drink most of the remaining rum. When it became evident that no amount of alcohol was going to soothe the ache in my heart, I swallowed a sleeping pill and got into bed, still fully dressed.

I woke to the sound of pounding. It was dark out, and the glowing red numerals of the alarm clock informed me it was 5:43 in the morning.

*Paul.*

I bounded out of bed.

He stood at the door, still wearing the now-wrinkled button-down and thin wool pants he'd arrived in yesterday. His eyes were bloodshot, and his dark curls went every which way.

"You look about as hot as I feel right now," I remarked.

He walked past me into the kitchen and flipped on the lights. "As bad as you feel, as a person with newfound knowledge of his sister's cancer, I guarantee I'm feeling even more rotten."

"Only one of us is dying," I said, joining him in the kitchen.

He eyed me from the other side of the counter. "That's inaccurate."

"And how's that?"

"You can't die, Libby. You're all I have left."

"That's not true. What about Charlie? The boys?"

He leaned forward, putting his elbows on the counter, and rubbed his eyes. Then he looked up at me. "You're all of I have left of *Mom*. And don't tell me I have Dad, too, because you know it's not the same."

"Oh."

"So now that you see where I'm coming from, I have to ask again: Why would you do this?"

I wasn't sure how to respond, so I asked Paul to come with me into my bedroom. After locating *Y tu mama*, I grabbed my laptop off the dresser and climbed on the bed, motioning for Paul to sit next to me. I put my laptop between us and slid the disc into the computer.

"See?" I said after we'd finished the movie. "Now do you understand?"

Paul pushed himself up and turned so we were facing each other. "What I see, dear sister, is a woman in crisis who has managed to confuse real life with Spanish-language cinema. I mean, I understand your initial impulse to leave Chicago behind. I've heard the first couple weeks after a person is diagnosed can be surreal—that you don't feel like yourself. But you're not Luisa, Libby."

"No," I agreed. "I'm not. But I have a reason for all of this."

"And what would that be?" he scoffed.

"Before Mom died, she asked me to take care of you," I told him.

He and I both smiled at the ridiculousness of our mother's request. "She did?"

"Absurd, I know," I told him. "Mom dying is the single worst thing that ever happened to me. Even all these years later, I feel like there's a big hole carved out of me. When the doctor told me that I had this terrible cancer, all I could think about was how I was going to put you and Dad through that again. I don't want to draw it out and make you suffer longer than necessary."

"Oh, Libs," he said. "I'm sorry."

I took his hand, so like my own—it was one of the few physical characteristics we shared. I examined his long, squared-off fingers, then turned his hand over. He, too, had a long lifeline running across his palm. "No, I'm sorry," I said. "I shouldn't have kept you in the dark. But you've seemed so happy lately, and I didn't want to spoil it."

"I *am* happy lately. Life with Charlie and the boys is better than I could have expected. But keeping your pain from me is the exact opposite of taking care of me." He pursed his lips. "I mean, who else is going to tell you you're looking at this all wrong? Feel free to correct me here, but you don't even know what stage your cancer is yet."

I thought about what Dr. Sanders had told me, and the studies I'd read online. "I'm pretty sure the two stages of my cancer are diagnosis and dying."

"But you don't know that for sure."

"No."

"Exactly. So, come on then. Let's see it."

"See what?" I said, already lifting my shirt so he could look at the battlefield that was my stomach.

He regarded the wound for a few seconds, then pulled my shirt back down and looked at me. "You're going to be okay."

I snorted. "Paul Ross, human MRI."

He waved off my skepticism. "Now's not a good time for you to die. It's as simple as that."

"I'm sorry that my disease comes at an inconvenient time for you."

"I didn't say it was inconvenient. It's implausible."

"*Now* who's Pollyanna?"

"Stop it, Libs. Just—all I'm asking is that you consider doing this for me, okay?"

"Treatment?"

"Yes. Wherever you want. New York, Chicago, Puerto Rico—it doesn't matter. With any doctor or hospital you want. I'll cover anything your insurance doesn't."

After my unceremonious exit from work, I was fairly certain I no longer had insurance, which was why I had paid for the doctor's visit in Vieques with my debit card. I thought it was best not to mention this to Paul for the time being. "You sound like Shiloh," I told him.

"He's not so bad."

I thought for a few minutes. Then I said, "I planned to be here for a month, and I want to stick to that. I still have to finalize the apartment sale. Then—and not a second sooner—I will see a doctor and reconsider my options. Okay?"

Paul managed a small smile. "And come spend time with Charlie, the boys, and me?"

"This is assuming I'm not in the hospital."

"Perfect." He hugged me. "Spoiler alert!"

"What is it?" I asked warily.

"Everything's going to be fine, Libby," he said, hugging me again. "I just know it."

"Right," I said. "Just fine." I hated to lie to my brother yet again, but there he was, sliding down my old rainbow, and I didn't have it in me to push him off.

Paul was not one for *good enough*. No, he preferred to change his banking passwords by the week, triple-check his zipper after leaving the bathroom, and grill a steak past the point at which a person could expect to bite into it without accidentally dislodging a dental crown—just in case. So I was not surprised when he continued to press me about my illness despite my telling him I would consider my options. "You have to tell Dad, you know," he shouted. We were sitting at the bow of a gleaming white boat that Shiloh had chartered so the three of us could take a day trip to Culebra, one of the small islands we had seen flying in.

"I know," I yelled. The wind was high and the ocean spray splattered against our faces, making it hard to hold a conversation. Not that this was of any consequence to Paul.

"Soon!" he yelled. "Preferably in person."

"I know," I said, not bothering to raise my voice this time.

The boat slapped against a large wave, and I hugged my life preserver tight to my torso, dubious about its ability to do its eponymous duty. The boat hit the surf again, and I put my hand on a metal safety rail to steady myself, then yanked it back when I realized how silly I was being. Cancer or shark bite, what did it matter? Death was death.

*Of course, it wasn't*, I admitted to myself as I watched Shiloh chat animatedly with the boat's captain. The whole idea behind this lark was to avoid a sudden and surprising end, to retain some semblance of control as the big hole in the sky closed in on me. But as diagnosis day slipped farther into the past, it seemed as if I were aiming less for a graceful exit and more for a lurching reentry.

Paul was having reentry thoughts of his own. His questioning resumed as soon as we'd docked in the shallow water off one of Culebra's beaches. "Have you started thinking about what you'll do after treatment?" he asked as we trudged through the glittering sand behind Shiloh, who was searching for a shady spot where we could sit and have lunch.

I squinted at him from behind my sunglasses. "What do you mean?"

"You have a chance to start over. I'm not saying you have to come to New York, though I think it would be smart. But either way, you could do something different. Even without a recommendation from Jackie, you've got a great résumé and you're brilliant, if I do say so myself. You choose an industry, I'll make a call to a contact, and you'll have a job the next day. You would make a great producer or event planner. Hell, become a feline behavior consultant if you're so inclined. You can do anything you want. Anything! How exciting is that?"

I supposed it was exciting in the abstract. As it pertained to my actual life, the idea of starting over made me want to go spear fishing for my own eyeballs. "Maybe," I said.

"Libby, will you give me a hand?" Shiloh asked as he attempted to spread a thin cotton blanket under a tree.

I gave him a grateful look, then grabbed a corner of the blanket to pull it smooth. Paul took it from my hand. "Here, let me," he said.

"I'm not an invalid, you know," I said, placing one of my sandals on the blanket's edge to help secure it.

He raised an eyebrow. "I didn't say you were. I just want you to take it easy."

I sat down on the blanket and took out a bottle of sparkling water from the picnic basket Shiloh had packed. "I'm in the middle of the Caribbean with some of my favorite people, and there's not a thing in the world that I have to do right now. If this isn't taking it easy, then I don't know what is."

Paul pressed on. "Naturally, everything depends on where you go for treatment. I did a little research last night."

"Of course you did."

He was sweating even more than I was, and he pulled off his polo, then carefully folded it and placed it in the canvas tote he had brought. "And if our roles were reversed, would you just sit there and do nothing?"

"No."

"*Ding ding ding!* We have a neural connection!"

I snatched a plastic knife from the picnic basket we'd packed. "Shall I use this on you?"

He ignored me. "The Mayo Clinic is doing a second-phase clinical trial that sounds really promising. And there's a doctor at Columbia who has written several papers on T-cell lymphomas."

"One thing at a time," Shiloh said, putting an arm around me.

Paul frowned at him, and I could see his wheels turning, taking in how this practical stranger was being protective of his sister.

Paul must have decided Shiloh's angle was a good one, because after a minute he said, "You're right. One thing at a time."

After lunch we took a trio of kayaks out. The sea was still, and Shiloh and Paul easily paddled several hundred yards out, but I lingered near the shore. I had agreed to treatment, yet couldn't envision it; when I tried to picture myself propped up in a pastel pleather recliner, the steady drip of an IV unloading into my veins, it was my mother's face, not my own, that stared back at me.

I shook my head, then looked down at the sea, trying to encourage my mind's eye to envision some positive aspect of my post-Vieques existence, but the glassy green water held no inspiration. The fact that I could not visualize the alleged next phase of my life felt like further proof that Paul's reasoning was wishful thinking.

I wasn't sure how long I had been floating there when Paul circled back around. "Have you spoken to Tom about your health?" he asked as the nose of his kayak gently bumped the side of my own.

"No," I said, watching a school of silvery minnows pass between us, then disappear into darker depths.

"Do you plan to?"

"No. But if you want to invite him to my funeral, I guess you can. I would prefer that you seat him at the back."

Paul grimaced. "I really wish you'd stop talking like that."

"Sorry."

His kayak began drifting backward, and he lifted his oar and latched it to the side of my boat, linking us together. "Do you miss him?"

I shook my head. "Not at all."

*I don't*, I told myself, but this was not even remotely true. I missed the way Tom pulled me into him at night, our bodies curved against each other like Russian nesting dolls. I missed how he would tuck a stray curl behind my ear while he was in the middle of talking to me. I missed the feeling of belonging to him, and believing that he, too, belonged to me.

"You'll love again," said Paul.

"Maybe," I said, looking over my shoulder at Shiloh, who was paddling in the distance.

"Is it weird?" Paul asked. "Being with someone else so soon? Not that I think it's a bad thing, but . . . you two seem awfully cozy. I hope it doesn't make things harder for you."

"It won't."

He gave me a look.

"What?"

"Careful, Libs," he said, looking again at Shiloh. "I like the guy, but he's not worth your life."

"Trust me, he would be the first to agree with you. Despite his 'one thing at a time' shtick, he's constantly on me about getting out of here and going to see a specialist."

"Huh," said Paul, in a way that said he was unconvinced. "Anyway, enough about Shiloh. The only person we need to focus on right now, Libs, is you."

On the boat ride back, Shiloh put his arm gently around my waist, and I laid my head on his shoulder, which is how we remained until we arrived at the marina in Vieques. *Maybe Shiloh is clouding my vision,* I thought. Maybe I should never have gone to dinner with him; then I wouldn't have fallen for him, and Paul couldn't have contacted him to find me, and I would've had more time to plan my final days without interference. This was all possible, but as the boat bumped up against the dock, dislodging my torso from Shiloh's, I felt oddly grateful that it hadn't worked out any other way.

# TWENTY-SIX

"Sing to me, Libby Lou."

"What song, Mama?"

"*Our* song, Libby," she said, attempting to smile as she recited her well-rehearsed line. There was only one option. But Paul and I always asked, and on that day, as ever, she responded, "You Are My Sunshine.'"

She had about a week to live, but I didn't know it at the time. She had been in and out of consciousness for days. When she was awake, she mostly warbled nonsense. But when she was lucid, I snatched up that fool's gold like it would buy me forever, assuring myself that she was going to pull through. I put my hand over hers and sang as though time was a suggestion, and the end a choice.

*You are* my *sunshine, Mama,* I thought as I watched her eyes flutter beneath pale lavender lids. As long as I could remember, she'd sung the song to Paul and me before bed. After cancer robbed her of her strength, dictating that she could no longer live at home, let alone sing at our bedroom doors at night, Paul and I sang our version to her instead. "Please don't take my sunshine away" became "More and more every day"; the verses about waking up and finding the love gone were omitted entirely. If my mother noticed our feeble attempts to lighten the tune, she didn't mention it. She just asked us to sing it one more time.

After she passed, I swore I would never sing that song again. It was a ruse: death and doom swaddled in a lullaby. As an adult, I once fled my cousin's daughter's nursery after coming upon a teddy bear playing the tune. Some toy maker had sewn the music box into the beady-eyed animal, undoubtedly aware that the child who received the bear would one day learn the song her toy played was about losing the best person you ever had.

But darn if it wasn't the first thing that popped into my head the morning Paul was set to return to New York. I hummed a few bars before I realized what I was doing, then turned on the radio to drown my internal melody with the bright, clangy sounds of salsa.

Pointless. The song still ringing in my ears, I drove to Paul's hotel. He was standing in the lobby, phone in one hand, luggage in the other. He immediately dropped both to embrace me.

He kept hugging me. And hugging me. "Are you already medicated?" I laughed.

"Little bit. But mostly I just don't want to leave you. Are you sure you won't come with me now?"

"You know I can't," I said, pulling back. "But we'll be together soon."

"We haven't made definite plans, though," he said as we got into the Jeep.

"Not definite, but what more is there beyond flying my butt to New York?"

"You have, what, six days to buy a plane ticket? You might want to hop on that."

"Who says I haven't already?"

He raised an eyebrow, and I laughed. "Okay, okay. Maybe I haven't exactly been forward-thinking about this whole thing, but I'll buy a ticket later today. By tomorrow at the absolute latest."

"Be a peach and let me take care of it. My assistant can get it done in five minutes flat. And while we're on the subject, why don't you come to New York first, and figure the rest out once you get there?"

"Yes, I'm just dying to arrive in New York in the dead of winter."

"Enough with the death puns already."

"Too much?"

"Always."

I steered the Jeep into the ferry parking lot. "I'll take care of the ticket. Don't worry."

"You'd better." He glanced at the ferry, which was just pulling into the dock, then turned to me. "As much as I'm itching to get back to Charlie and the boys, I wish I could stay here."

"I know," I said, opening the car door. "But you don't want to miss the boat. There isn't another one for five hours."

Paul sighed. "Then let's do this."

We said good-bye roughly eighty-two times, each tearier than the last. After Paul boarded the boat, he leaned over the rail. "Libby!" he called. "I love you the most!"

I blew him a kiss, then waved until the ferry was a speck on the horizon. All the while, that stupid song floated through my head.

*Please don't take my sunshine away.*

When I returned to the beach house, Shiloh was waiting for me on the steps. He had called the night before to see if he could stay with me for a few days, rather than at the company's studio, and I'd happily agreed.

I eyed the large suitcase that was next to him on the cement stairs. "I had no idea you owned that much clothing."

He winked. "I packed an extra pair of underwear."

"Aw, you shouldn't have."

"Anything for you. And I brought my telescope."

"All that just to spy on the neighbors?"

"You would catch a lot more action in San Juan. But the stargazing's far better here, and the moon is beginning to wane again."

We dropped his bag off inside, then drove to the west side of the island to explore a small park he'd told me about. At the park, we came across a good dozen horses grazing: gangly things, all muscles and ribs, making their way from one cluster of long grass to another. After the horses broke through my panic attack on the beach, I could not help but regard them as a sign of something good—although what good this time, I couldn't say. Afterward, we opted to have dinner at the beach house. As Shiloh grilled fish and onions for the tacos he was making, he told me about his childhood. His father had moved their family from Puerto Rico to the States again and again, always returning to the island within a year or two. It was the catalyst, he said, for his mother filing for divorce. Shiloh didn't like constantly relocating, but he loved flying back and forth. He was hooked from his very first flight, he told me, and never considered being anything but a pilot. "Do you remember when we were in the plane, how you said you loved being away from the rest of the world?" he asked. I nodded. "When I'm in the air, I feel completely free. The average person hates takeoff. I live for those few minutes, when I hit the clouds and all my troubles are below me."

He kept talking long after he put his spatula down, and throughout dinner I found myself staring at him, interjecting little more than the occasional question as I listened. How quickly I'd written him off at the airport; how easily I'd convinced myself that I was in it for nothing more than pure pleasure. But here before me was a good man. It struck me that I had yet to hear him say a negative word about another person. Even if he was describing a terrible action, like his father's inability to care for his family in the way that they needed, he spoke in terms of the event, rather than blaming the person. I loved people like this, and encountered so very few.

As the sun began to set, we went outside to set up the telescope. While Shiloh positioned the tripod in the garden, he asked me about my mother. I didn't usually like discussing her. There was the pity factor: *Poor Libby, motherless at just ten years old.* The larger issue was that there are no words to adequately describe what it is to lose the person who matters most to you. Though I'd had decades to ponder it, it still did not make sense. How can a person be with you one moment, and then one terrible moment later, just be—gone? Forever? Tom's answer was always the same: "Your mother's not *gone*, Libby. You'll see her again one day." I clung to this belief, even as I cursed its complete and utter inability to offer real comfort. I did not want to hear it, even from my own husband. Nor did I want to hear about God having a plan, or all things happening for a reason, or any other number of Hallmark sentiments that pinged against my heart like pebbles on a thin windowpane.

I told Shiloh all of this. It had been years since I last said more than a few words about her to anyone other than Paul or my father, and I spoke haltingly, unsure of how to explain my loneliness. "I'm sure this sounds all kinds of stupid," I said when I had finished.

He kissed me lightly. "It doesn't, not to me. Johnny, a kid I grew up with in San Juan, died when we were in our late teens. It was a freak thing—he had an undetected heart problem and collapsed in the middle of a soccer game. Believe me, I know it's not the same as losing a parent. But even now, I have a hard time wrapping my mind around the fact that I'll never have another conversation with him. We came up together and stayed friends even after my family kept moving back and forth. He'll never get to see the person I am as an adult. I'll never get to find out who he would have become."

I nodded. It's permanence that distinguishes grief from other emotional pain. The unfixable nature of never—that's what makes it so terrible to bear. Was Paul right? Did I owe it to him to try to delay *never* as long as I could, at any cost?

Shiloh adjusted the telescope dial, then motioned for me to look through the viewfinder.

"Can you see?"

Slowly, the cloudy clusters above us revealed themselves as countless individual beacons of light. "Wow. Yes."

"Excellent."

"You sound like such a dude sometimes," I teased.

"I *am* a dude, cutie. You can't grow up on a beach without getting sand in the cracks of your brain. So, do you recognize any constellations?"

I squinted. "Does the little dipper count?"

"Sure. But you can do better." He took the telescope from me and redirected it. "Now look through it. Stare right in the middle, and you should be able to see Cassiopeia. Any other time of the year and you'd struggle to see her, but she burns bright all through November. Look for two *L*s, connected on the diagonal. Around her are some of the youngest stars in the galaxy. Pretty amazing, right?"

"Aha!" I said. But as soon as I spotted the constellation, a reddish twinkling light to the far left caught my attention. "Are the red-looking ones planets or something?"

"No, they're stars, too. You probably spotted a red giant. They're older and closer to the end of their lives, so they don't burn as hot, which changes their color."

"So the closer a star is to death, the more beautiful it becomes."

He laughed. "If you like red. I guess you could argue that time makes a lot of things more attractive."

"Not Tom."

"Maybe it doesn't look good yet. But look at how well you're doing. Give yourself time, Libby."

*Time is a luxury I don't have,* I thought as I stuck my head under the telescope, watching a star flicker. It could have been combusting that very moment, or maybe it had blown up centuries before and the evidence had not yet reached the Earth. Eye still to the lens, I asked Shiloh if he thought there was an afterlife.

"Well, I'm culturally Catholic, so I should probably say yes. But mostly I think worrying about it is pointless."

"So you don't believe in heaven."

"I didn't say that. I mean, sure, it sounds cozy, but who knows? Most people don't really care about heaven. I think they worry about being relevant to other living people, even after they're dead. But one day there won't be anyone left who fits that bill. One day this planet will combust, and we'll all turn into star stuff. Cleopatra? Abe Lincoln? Adam and Eve? Relevant to no one."

"Well, *that's* optimistic."

"It is, kind of. It takes guts to stop fretting about the unknown and concentrate on the present moment. That's what matters, anyway."

"And what if your present moment sucks? And you can't even imagine what the future looks like, let alone fix your hope on that?"

His breath was hot on my neck. "But does it? You're dealing with some ugly stuff, Libby. But does right now, this very moment, suck?"

I leaned in, my skin tight with anticipation as his lips grazed my flesh. "No," I whispered.

"Then enjoy it," he whispered back.

# TWENTY-SEVEN

The apartment. I'd nearly forgotten all about it. With several thousand dollars' worth of commission hanging in the balance, Raj, bless his heart, had not.

"Time to make it official, Libby. You still planning on coming back to Chicago?"

I was sitting in the side garden. Not far from my feet, a couple of inky black birds were fighting over a few crumbs that had crumbled from the baguette I was gnawing on. "That is a very good question, Raj," I said, my mouth still full. Despite my promises to Paul, I hadn't purchased a ticket to New York. But with just days left in Vieques, it was time to do so. I finished chewing. "For the time being, let's go with no."

"Can you change your plans?" he asked. "The way your mortgage agreement is worded, either you or Tom needs to show up to the closing."

There went my New York flight. I stood up from the bench, sending the birds flying in opposite directions. "Fabulous."

"And unless he dies between now and then, I'm going to need his signature on everything. You guys *are* legal co-owners. Let me know where I can find him, and I'll send him the papers myself."

I sighed. This wasn't going to go over well with Tom. "Won't be a problem, Raj."

On the one hand, I could make what was left of my life a whole lot easier by faking Tom's signature, which I could practically do in my sleep. On the other . . . I didn't really want to make my karmic load any heavier by deceiving Tom about the sale. I decided to consult Milagros.

"Do you believe in revenge?" I asked her.

We were walking down the side of road. Given my run-in with the yellow truck, I wasn't thrilled to be on foot on a skinny stretch of grass alongside an almost equally narrow swath of asphalt, but Milagros said she had exhausted her beach vocabulary and it was time to teach me something different before I left.

"*La venganza?*" she said. "*Como un* payback?"

I replied with my new favorite phrase: "*Más o menos.*" More or less. "Like, when your husband cheated on you, didn't you want to stick it to him?"

She looked at me through narrowed eyes. "How could I stick him when he was sticking someone else?"

I giggled.

"Listen," she said, "the universe takes care of that. Look at my husband—poor bastard drowned."

I thought it was her one true love who had drowned, but perhaps he and the cheater were one and the same. Anyway, I'd come to see that Milagros's past was a parable; taking any of her stories as a literal interpretation meant you would miss the point.

"Don't bunch your panties up about *la venganza*. Especially if we're talking about your husband."

"Ex."

"That's what I said." She laughed.

I told her about the apartment—how I was concerned that Tom wouldn't sign the papers, and I was considering forging his signature.

"*Y?*" she said. "There's something else."

I had to tell her; I should have weeks before. "I have cancer," I said quietly, bracing myself for a slew of questions.

But Milagros just nodded. "Your ex doesn't know."

"No."

"*Ay.*" She bit her bottom lip and kept walking. "I'm sorry to hear about your health, *mija*," she said after a while. "But give him a chance to make the right choice about the apartment."

I thought about house hunting with Tom all those years ago. I had wanted to buy a split-level apartment in a limestone building in Logan Square. Tom argued that its turn-of-the-last-century quirks—a small kitchen, bedroom closets constructed in corners, the narrow staircase connecting the first floor to the garden level—would make it hard to resell; and besides, it was too far from downtown. This was all probably true, but it felt like a *home* to me, and I had loved it. Then we went to see the apartment we ultimately bought, which was located on the border of Bucktown and Wicker Park. Though I couldn't deny that it had lovely light and a layout ideal for entertaining, it seemed sterile. Tom argued that it was simply because the building was new construction. What's more, it was mere blocks from Jess and O'Reilly's place, and in a rapidly appreciating, if overgentrifying, neighborhood that was close to almost everything. I did not relent because of these points, but because Tom was in love with it and I was in love with him, and I wanted him to be happy. It was quite possible that he would not willingly part with that happiness.

"Even if giving him the choice may leave me in a bad situation?" I asked Milagros.

"*Sí*. Otherwise, you are just as bad as him. Now where were we?"

"You were teaching me the word for—" A four-wheeler whizzed by and I jumped back, pulling Milagros with me. She stumbled, then leaned into me, sending us both tumbling to the ground.

"—cars," I said as a searing pain shot through my stomach.

Milagros rolled off me and pushed herself up. "New phrase: *cuidado con el carro*. Be careful of the car!"

"I'm sorry, Milagros. Better careful than crippled?" I said sheepishly, and stood up.

"Tell that to my hip," she said, accepting my outstretched hand. "Now come on. We're not done with your lesson."

I called Tom shortly after we returned. "I'm giving you the chance to make the right choice."

"Um, hi," he said. "Surprised to hear from you."

"Don't be. I'm calling because I've accepted an offer on the apartment. I need you to sign the paperwork."

"You don't mean that."

I hopped off the counter and opened the fridge. Unless I wanted to attempt to survive on eggs and guava juice, it was time to restock. "I assure you that I do, Tom. I really do."

"Libby, don't take this the wrong way, but I really do think you should see someone. My therapist said this would be as hard for you as it is for me. Maybe harder."

"Did he? How interesting," I said, shutting the fridge.

"She," he corrected.

"Well, *she* is right. This is hard for me. There's a lot of stuff going on, and I'm in no mood to explain it to you."

"Like you losing your job?" he asked. "I'm guessing Jackie didn't sign off on a monthlong vacation."

I moved on to the cupboard, whose contents were as dismal as the fridge's. "I did not *lose* my job, Tom. I quit."

"Come on."

"I'm serious."

He was silent for a moment. "So you're selling the apartment because you need cash?"

"Actually, I was planning on donating the money from the sale to charity." If I really did go through with treatment, I would soon require my own charitable fund. But now wasn't the time to divulge this.

"What?" He sounded panicked. "All of it?"

I would have to go out for food, I realized, and slipped on my sandals. "The down payment was never yours. It was never mine, either. It belonged to my mother. And you know I paid for the bulk of the mortgage myself."

"I suppose that's true, but sheesh, Libby, don't you think you should have run your plans past me, given that it's my home, too? I know I hurt you, and I wish to God I hadn't. But you can't just act like we haven't spent the past eighteen years together."

I didn't respond.

"I wish you would have at least let me stay at the apartment while you went off gallivanting in the Caribbean," he added.

*Gallivanting.* How very droll were the workings of his mind. "Tom, I'm sure you don't believe me, but I *am* sorry. Getting out of Chicago seemed like my only option. But you're an intelligent person. You're gainfully employed. I'm sure you can figure it out from here," I said as I grabbed my keys from the hook near the door.

"Can I?" He was not being sarcastic. "We've always done everything together. I miss you."

Maybe that was why Tom had been making preposterous comments about wanting our marriage to work. We really had done everything together, and he didn't know how to figure out what to do without me. I sort of wanted to help him, if only out of habit.

"Tom, I miss the 'you' who didn't break my heart," I said as I locked the front door behind me. "I'll have the papers sent to O'Reilly's. Please keep an eye out for them."

"I'm not signing. I think you're making a rash decision, and it's because of me. I can't let you do this while you're in a state of shock."

If only he knew, I thought as I climbed into the Jeep. "There is no 'letting me,' Tom. Let go," I told him. "Tell Jess that I said hello, and that I'm doing fine."

He didn't hang up, and neither did I. "Will I ever see you again?" he asked after a while.

"I don't know." Unlike the apartment sale, a legal divorce would probably require face time with Tom. The sting of his betrayal was wearing off, though, and it was not unfeasible that I would find it in myself to fully forgive him before we were in the same room again.

"I'm sorry, Libby," he said. "I didn't mean to ruin your life."

The Jeep faced the sea; through the windshield, I watched white-topped waves crest over a thin strip of sand. "Tom, I'm sure you probably won't believe me, or even understand what I mean by this, but you didn't ruin my life." I started the engine. "The truth is, you gave it back to me."

# TWENTY-EIGHT

I bought two one-way tickets: one from San Juan to Chicago, where I would spend a week settling the apartment sale; another from Chicago to New York, where, if all went according to Paul's plan, I would immediately offer my services as a human guinea pig.

"I don't want to do this," I told Shiloh, who was sitting next to me in a tiny café that offered Internet access.

"By 'this,' do you mean treatment? Or leaving Puerto Rico?"

"Both," I said, and clicked the Purchase button for the first fare.

"What do you have to lose?"

Through the window, palm trees danced in the breeze. "Paradise," I said. Thinking of the many things that would soon be foisted upon me—medication, attention, sympathy—I added, "Control."

Shiloh drained the contents of his espresso cup. "Control's an illusion. You know that."

"Do I?" I said, staring at the Buy Now icon that would enable me to fly from one cold, overpopulated city to another. I clicked it, then turned away from the computer screen. "I mean, I'm not trying to broker world peace here, but I would like to think I have some say over what happens to my brief and newly eventful life."

"If you say so, cutie." He got up from his seat and stood behind me, gently running his fingers through my hair. I leaned my head back, wishing there were a way to bottle the relaxed feeling running through my body. "My offer stands. I would be happy to come with you for a few months."

"You have a life here, wackadoo."

"Right. My glamorous bachelor pad. My drinking buddies. My family—oh wait. My closest relative lives hours from my apartment."

"But you just got cleared to fly again," I protested. "You've been itching to get back in the air."

"And I plan to." He kissed me lightly. "Besides, you know I don't operate like that. I like to do what I want, and what I want is to be with you a little longer."

I was flattered, but it still seemed like an unviable option. "What happens if you and I don't do so well when we're farther from the equator, and you discover you just wasted several months of your life with the wrong woman?"

He untangled his fingers from my curls and sat down. "Are we talking about me here, or you? Personally, I don't care very much about everything working out perfectly, but I'm not going to *not* take a chance because of all the what-ifs involved."

I couldn't come up with a single sarcastic response. Instead, I leaned toward him and kissed him. "I'm going to miss you terribly."

"I'll miss you, too. But you already know that." He kissed me again, then said, "What about after treatment? What then?"

What *did* happen then? I stared vacantly as my brain cells fired past one another. Suddenly, I was not sitting in a coffee shop in the Caribbean with a man I was fairly certain I loved, but instead walking the cold, wet streets of New York, staring into the faces of a million strangers. I was filling out an endless string of job applications for positions I did not actually want, which would be summarily dismissed by human resources professionals or computerized screening programs that deduced I had not used the correct power verbs in combinations demonstrating my unbridled talent and ambition. I was on a string of progressively bad dates in a city where eligible men under age fifty were rarer than the ivory-billed woodpecker, and single women far younger, prettier, and less damaged than me swarmed like ants. In the future I had managed to conjure up, I was alive, which was more than I'd been able to say about my previous forecasts. Even so, I was adrift and alone.

"Aren't I supposed to be enjoying the present moment?" I asked Shiloh.

"Touché. In this case, it seems like a good time to start at least contemplating what might make you happy."

I gave him what I hoped was a sunny smile. "Let me think about it."

And I did. The next few days were filled with more *cafecitos y mallorcas*, more strolls on the beach and excursions through untamed parks. A last Spanish lesson with Milagros, which began with travel-related terminology and devolved into the two of us drinking our faces off as she tried to teach me various ways to insult a drunkard. And most of the time, I tried to ponder what it was, exactly, that I might want if I did survive this disease.

It used to be that what I really wanted was a child of my own. Even more than I had yearned to be Tom Miller's wife, I had always wanted to be a mother, preferably to a daughter named Charlotte, after my own mother (though a son would have made me equally happy, provided he didn't mind being called Charlotte).

But it didn't happen for Tom and me, even after years of trying and tests. When the doctor suggested in vitro fertilization—which my insurance did not cover and which cost as much as all of our fancy furniture combined—Tom hemmed and hawed about the expense, and when I said we should try to adopt, he balked, citing the gut-wrenching uncertainty of the adoption process, and said we should just let it go.

And I agreed, even though it was a lie against my soul.

It was not so much that the longing had gone away, but that in light of my marriage and health woes, having a child seemed sort of selfish, if not entirely beside the point.

But the night before I was scheduled to fly to Chicago, when Shiloh again inquired about what I really wanted, I did not pretend to be excited about a sparkling new career, or a shining outlook on life, or even the possibility of returning to Puerto Rico. Instead, I confessed that if, by some miracle I lived and was given the bonus gift of decent health, it was a safe guess that a child would again preoccupy my wishes.

"A child?" Shiloh said with surprise.

When I held Toby and Max, the heft of their chunky bodies and the silky down of their skin triggered a visceral, even greedy reaction: I wanted to gobble them up, somehow consume all that goodness. To live long enough to have my own child, to experience her first day of kindergarten, her high school graduation, maybe even the birth of *her* child—well, short of my mother's resurrection, I could not think of a single thing that would be better. "I get it if that freaks you out," I told Shiloh.

A hint of moonlight shone on his face. "Who said I don't want kids, Libby? Just because I don't have them doesn't mean I wouldn't like to be a father."

We'd been lying on a blanket on the beach, looking up at the stars. I sat up and shook the sand out of my hair. "I'm not trying to start a fight."

"This isn't a fight; it's a tough thing to talk about. There's a difference."

I sighed and lay back again. "Sorry, it's a touchy subject for me."

"It's okay. It's touchy for me, too. If you had asked, I would have told you that I would love to have at least one child. A girl, if I had my choice."

"I always wanted a girl, too," I admitted. "I'd call her Charlotte."

He nodded. "For your mother. What about Charlotte Patrícia? That's a nice name."

"I love it," I confessed.

"And I love you."

I stared at him, half expecting him to say he was joking. When I saw that he was smiling, my chest flooded with warmth. "Wow."

"I get it if that freaks you out," he teased. Then he grew serious. "Really, Libby. I know it's early, but that's what I'm feeling, and I don't really believe in holding good stuff back."

"I'm not freaked out," I said, and it was true. "That was lovely. Thank you."

Yet it was impossible to not think of the first time Tom said he loved me. It had been early for him, too—just months after we began dating. "You're wonderful, Libby," he whispered to me, just after he had leaned over the gearshift of his old hooptie and kissed me goodnight. "I'm in love with you. No—it's not just that." He touched my cheek. "I love you." I was so astounded that I couldn't respond, but in my head I was thinking: *I love you, too, Tom Miller. I have loved you since the day I laid eyes on you, and I will love you forever and beyond.*

What I felt for Shiloh was different from that, and maybe that's why I continued to let myself indulge in it. Because in spite of the whirlwind way we'd come together, and the instant attraction I had toward him, I didn't have the same crazy, intense feeling that I'd had for Tom. Instead, my affection felt calm and right and . . . like something that just was.

After we made love that night, I lay in Shiloh's arms, bereft yet content. Through the open window, lapping waves competed with nothing but the sound of his heartbeat in my ear. The breeze was cool against my cheek, but the heat of our skin warmed us beneath the thin duvet. His leg still slung over mine, Shiloh began to snore. After a minute or so, he roused and turned toward me. "Night, cutie. Love you."

"I love you, too," I said.

# TWENTY-NINE

I rose just as the sun began to peek over the horizon. Shiloh was facedown on the bed, fast asleep. The sight of his bare back was still a minor shock. I knew Tom's every freckle and facial expression, exactly where to touch him—just below his left shoulder blade—to make him dissolve into laughter. I had no idea whether Shiloh was ticklish, and while he had freckles, I couldn't say with certainty where a single spot was located.

I would never learn.

I tried to push this idea into a cobwebbed corner of my mind as I quietly opened the back door. Still in the T-shirt and underwear I'd slept in, I walked out to the empty beach and went directly into the sea. It was cold—far colder already than when I'd arrived—but it was my last chance to feel the Caribbean on my skin, so I waded in anyway. The waves rose past my knees to my waist, enveloping the incision that throbbed but no longer stung, and finally covering my chest, so that my T-shirt bubbled and floated around me like a jellyfish. As I bobbed in place, staring out at the beach and the house from the sea, I considered how easy it would be to let myself be carried off by the tide.

The thought no longer tempted me. Not even a little.

The fear had not subsided. I did not feel like a brave woman warrior ready to take on the literal fight of my life. But I no longer welcomed the idea of being in command of my own death.

When I returned, Shiloh was making coffee. "You ready for today?" he called from the espresso machine.

I finished toweling off, then walked into the kitchen and kissed him. "Not even a little."

"As much as I want you to stay . . ."

"Yeah." I accepted the coffee cup he handed me and took a sip. "I know."

"Libby. Don't—" He stopped abruptly.

"Don't what?"

He shook his head: *nothing.*

"Don't what?" I pressed.

"Please don't change your mind about treatment," he said quietly.

I cocked my head, thinking of how I'd been unable to channel my inner Ophelia in the sea not ten minutes before. "Now why would I do that?"

"I don't know, actually. But I just worry . . . you haven't talked about it once since Paul left."

"I'm going to deal with it when I get to Chicago." *Or New York,* I thought; at this point, it wouldn't much matter either way.

Shiloh put his arms around my waist and pulled me close to him, burying his face in my hair. "You promise?"

The word sat heavy on my tongue. I swallowed hard, then let it roll out. "Promise."

. . .

After the sheets had been stripped and the surfaces had been wiped clean and I'd made one last walk around the beach house, Shiloh and I locked the door behind us.

Milagros was waiting in the courtyard. *"Mija,"* she said, her arms outstretched.

I hugged her tight, even though it made my stomach hurt a little.

"Old Milly will be here when you're ready to come back to Vieques," she told me.

I attempted a laugh, knowing that if I did see her again, it would likely be at a location several light-years north of Puerto Rico.

She misunderstood my halfhearted response. *"Verdad,"* she insisted. "I may be wrinkled, but I'm healthy as an old thoroughbred."

"Oh, I know you are," I assured her. "Believe me, I know."

She put her hands on her hips. "Where do you go from here, Libby?"

"First Chicago, then to New York, to be with my brother."

"And what will you do after you're done with the doctors?"

"I'm going to put one foot in front of the next, take each day as it comes, and try not to focus on Tom or my diagnosis. Beyond that, I have no idea."

She stared past me for a second, then met my eyes again. "Smart girl. Don't look back too much, you know? You're not going that way."

My voice caught. *"Gracias,* Milagros."

She took my hand and squeezed it. "I'll miss you. But"—she released my hand and flipped it over, then stuck her index finger in the center—"something here tells me we'll meet again in a happy place."

I peered down at my palm. "Really?"

Her eyes twinkled. "You tell me, *mija.*"

. . .

We returned the Jeep and took a shuttle to the ferry. Fingers entwined, we said little on the boat ride over, and even less on the drive to the airport. When we got there, Shiloh was able to use his pilot's badge to go through security with me. I was collected—stoic, even—until we reached the gate. The agent had begun the boarding process, and I took one look at the line of passengers lined up for the jet bridge and fell into Shiloh's arms.

"I can't believe this is it."

"Neither can I. Libby . . ." He was laughing and crying; we were both on the verge of crumpling. "You made me feel something that I didn't even know it was possible to feel."

*Me, too,* I thought. *Me, too.*

It took everything in me not to suggest we reunite when he visited his mother in New York, or propose that I return to Puerto Rico after treatment. Unkeepable pledges and pacts would cheapen what we had shared.

Instead, I put my hands around his neck and kissed him long and hard. Then I told him I would love him as long as I lived, because it was the truth.

"I meant what I said," he told me, reaching into his pocket.

My stomach made a beeline for my bladder as I watched him pull out a small, unwrapped box.

He took one look at me and began to crack up. "Don't freak! It's not a ring."

I managed a small laugh. "Thanks, I think."

He put the box in my hand and told me not to open it until I was in the air. I said I wouldn't.

The agent called for all passengers to board. Shiloh and I looked at each other: this was it. I kissed him one last time, trying to memorize what it was to have this with another person.

"Good-bye, Libby," he said into my ear.

"Good-bye, Shiloh."

I boarded the plane just before the doors to the jetway closed. Averting my eyes from the curious gazes of the people seated near me, I hunkered down in my seat, wiped my tears, and stared out the window. As the plane lifted into the sky, I shook the box lightly. The clunk-clunk-clunk of metal on cardboard confirmed it contained jewelry.

There's something uniquely unnerving about accepting a gift from a person you love. Tom's gifts were unfailingly practical: a fitness-tracking bracelet for my birthday, a planner and pen for Christmas. He knew exactly what I needed, to the point where it was almost like having my own personal shopper. Every once in a while, though, I would peek under the lid of a gift box and wish that instead of a pair of fleece gloves, I would find, say, a sexy bra set.

So as the plane lifted into the clouds, it was with no small amount of trepidation that I peeked beneath the lid of the box Shiloh had given me.

Nestled on a cotton pillow was a thumbprint-size star charm made of rose gold, dangling from a delicate chain. Shiloh had tucked a small slip of paper beneath the cotton.

> *Libby,*
> *Thank you for the past month. It was one of the brightest of my life.*
> *Shiloh*

The charm, which I rubbed between my fingers like a worry stone, was perfect. Shiloh's note: perfect. Our affair and my vacation were, in the most roundabout way, absolutely perfect.

And now it was all over.

# THIRTY

Chicago greeted me at the jet bridge with a gust of frozen air. I collected my bags from luggage claim, then zombie walked to the L train on the other side of the airport. Sitting on a hard bucket seat, I watched the train rise from beneath the ground until it was above the city. As leafless trees and buildings streamed past in a gray blur, I told myself, *This is a mistake.* I'd never been one for second-guessing, but then again, I'd never before been kicked in the teeth by cancer only to be sucker punched by my husband. Why had I come back to a place that was a massive symbol of all that had been, and perhaps still was, wrong with my life?

But a promise was a promise, and I'd made the same one to both Shiloh and Paul. So after I got off the train and let myself into my echoing, ice-cold apartment, I dialed Dr. Sanders's office. When I gave the receptionist my name, she told me to hold. A few minutes later, Dr. Sanders came on the line.

"I wasn't expecting to speak with you," I said.

"I'm between appointments," he said, as though this explained everything. "Elizabeth—"

"I believe we established that I go by Libby."

"Libby," he said, "have you sought medical care since, um, our last visit?"

I finished gnawing on a hangnail before answering. "Not really. That's kind of why I'm calling. I'd like to find out what my options are."

He exhaled. "I'm relieved to hear that. I'd like you to start by meeting with the team here. You'll need a scan, blood tests, then an appointment with oncology . . ." He droned on like this for a while.

"Okay," I said when he'd finally stopped talking. "When?"

"Really?" He sounded surprised, disappointed even, like he'd been geared up to make more of a case for himself. "I can get you in for testing as early as tomorrow."

It was my turn to sound surprised. "Really?"

"Yes. I don't want you to wait a second longer. I've been chatting with a chief oncologist here, and there's a clinical trial that you may be a candidate for—well, I'm getting ahead of myself. We'll talk more when you come in. Stay on the phone and Kelly will arrange everything for tomorrow and beyond for you. Eliz—Libby, I'm so glad you called."

Tomorrow was as good a day as any. Of course, I wasn't planning to get treatment in Chicago, but I would explain that when I saw him.

Though it was only five p.m., I was exhausted and had already texted both Paul and Shiloh to let them know I'd arrived. There was nothing of any importance to do. I slowly lowered myself off the counter and went to the bedroom, where I stripped down and slid between the icy sheets. I fell asleep almost instantly, and woke several hours later, feverish and beaded with sweat. Disoriented, I reached beside me, expecting Shiloh to be there, or maybe Tom, only to realize I was on my own. My heart sank. I closed my eyes and waited for unconsciousness to set in.

.   .   .

The next morning, swaddled in the warmest clothes I hadn't sold, donated, or shipped off to Paul's, I walked the few brisk blocks to the L. The Blue Line took me to the Loop, where I transferred to the Red Line.

"This is Chicago. Clark and Division is next," said an electronic voice as I reached my stop. Passengers rushed past me toward the train's double doors, but I couldn't seem to unstick my feet from the laminate floor.

Ding-dong went the alert.

"Doors closing," said the voice overhead.

But I just stood there, as motionless as Lot's salt-pillar wife, until the train began to move again.

I rode the Red Line until the last stop, then turned around and took the opposite path home. I could have gone to my appointments late or rebooked the first one that I missed, but I didn't.

"Don't change your mind about treatment," Shiloh had said. He must have known that when push came to shove, I couldn't even bring myself to step inside a doctor's office. That deep down, I was too afraid.

When I returned to the apartment, I called Jess, making the decision just an instant before I pressed the Call button.

"Are you free?" I asked before she could greet me.

"You're back?!"

"Sadly, yes. Wanna get a drink?"

"Christ, Libby. It's not even eleven o'clock in the morning. Are you feeling okay?"

*Not really,* I thought. "We can meet at noon if it would make you more comfortable."

"Now is good."

"Great. Café De Luca. See you there."

De Luca was halfway between Jess's apartment and my own; we'd spent many hours there over the years. She was perched at the bar when I walked in, but immediately hopped off her stool to greet me. "Libby, you look . . ." She regarded me with what can best be described as suspicion. "Skinny," she concluded. "Slightly disheveled, but so damn tiny! And you're *tan*! I'm jealous."

I smiled; I was happier to see her than I had expected to be. "Guess extramarital sex agrees with me."

Jess's mouth popped open.

I laughed. "Sorry, did I say that out loud?"

"Tell me everything," she said, dragging me back to the bar, where she ordered us a round of champagne.

I asked her how she'd been, but she waved my question off, eager for me to recount my trip. Her mouth was still hanging open when I finished. "I can't believe you left your Latin lover behind!"

"Shiloh," I said.

"Sorry, Shiloh. Does Tom know?"

"Of course not."

"Probably for the best." She tugged on one of the numerous thin, crystal-studded leather bracelets roped around her wrist. "He talks about you nonstop. He really wants to see you, Libby."

I took a sip of champagne. "I'm sure he does."

"Really, Libby. I'm being serious."

"Whose side are you on, Jess?"

"Yours. Obviously," she said, with a hint of exasperation. "It's just that this is hard for Michael and me, too," she said. "I don't agree with what Tom did, but he's like a brother to Michael. You know that."

I drained my glass, then stared at the couple of air bubbles remaining on its sides. "Please don't tell me about hard. I have cancer."

"That is not funny."

"No, it's not," I agreed. "Not even a tiny bit."

Jess stared at me. "Are you for real?"

"For a limited time only, my dear."

Her eyes welled with tears. "Oh, God, Libby. I am so sorry. What happened? When did you find out?"

I gave her the quick-and-dirty version. "So, that's why I've been running around like I've had a partial lobotomy," I concluded.

She shook her head. "Why didn't you tell me earlier?"

"I don't know. It just seemed like too much at the time."

"What can I do to help, Libby? I'll do whatever you need. Do you want me to talk to Tom for you?"

"Thanks, Jess. That means a lot to me. I know it's a lot to ask, but would you mind not saying anything to him? I'm not ready for him to know. I'm not sure I ever will be."

Jess must have been taking it easy on her beloved Botox injections, because the line in her forehead deepened at least half a centimeter. "You're not going to tell him? Even after everything, he *is* your husband."

I sighed. "Was, Jess. Tom *was* my husband. I'm not exactly brimming with self-knowledge right now, but I know enough to say with certainty that I don't want him involved with anything relating to my health status. So would you mind helping me with this one thing?"

She nodded.

"Thank you." I slid off my seat and gave her an enormous hug.

"Are you *hugging* me right now, Libby Miller?"

"I might be, but don't get too used to it."

"Why's that?"

"I'm going to New York for a while."

"For treatment?"

"Something like that."

She laughed and planted a kiss on my cheek. "Come back sooner this time, okay? And when I call you, pick up the phone."

I smiled. "I'll do my best."

.   .   .

As I was falling asleep that night, a strange sensation overcame me. I was awake, but my body was paralyzed; it was almost as though I were encased in glass, unable to move—not even to open my eyes. My chest was heavy, my breathing labored, and panic set in. *The cancer's spreading,* I thought to myself. It had been more than a month since diagnosis, and I had already been fairly sure malignant cells were swimming through my body, leaving a trail of destruction in their wake. I did not need one of Dr. Sanders's fancy tests to tell me time was running out.

Then a peaceful feeling passed over me. I could have been dreaming, but it felt as though there was a cool, steady hand stroking my forehead.

As quick as it came on, the paralysis was gone. I sat straight up and reached for my phone on the bedside table, knowing what had to be done next.

# THIRTY-ONE

I signed the real estate papers early, and had a notary sign a letter stating that Raj had the power to make any outstanding decisions on my behalf. Either Tom or I had to be present for the closing, but I was hopeful that Jess, newly aware of my predicament, would somehow be able to convince Tom to attend. The apartment sale would net nearly twice the amount I'd inherited from my mother's life insurance.

It was a lot of money, at least to me. And yet the entire sum could be erased with one medical treatment, and it could turn out that said medical treatment did not make a lick of difference in my survival. I hated to even think about it.

I called Paul on the way home from Raj's office. "Well?" he said.

"Well, what?" I said, knowing precisely what he meant.

"Have you called your doctor yet?"

"He's not *my* doctor, and yes, I did call him."

"So what did he say about treatment?"

"He said you and I should go to Detroit together."

"No, he did not."

"Okay, he didn't exactly say that. But since you've gotten over your fear of flying—"

"Gotten *over*? More like developed urinary incontinence and a consortium of ulcers."

"Even so, you got on a plane. Twice, in fact. So . . . would you consider coming with me to visit Mom's grave? It's been years."

He was quiet for a minute. "It has been a long time," he conceded. "I'm not exactly itching to join you, but you knew when you called that I wouldn't say no."

This was true. "It'll be good for you," I told him. "For us."

"What would be good for *us* would be for *you* to get your butt in treatment. As in yesterday. Detroit can wait until you're done."

"It can't, and I'm going either way. Before a single needle touches my body. It would mean a lot if you came with me."

"What happened to the lovely and compliant sister who was under my sway not one whole week ago?"

"She's still here, Paul. Mostly. And she needs you."

"You're the worst, Libs. The absolute worst. Call me tonight so we can coordinate flights."

I sighed with relief. In spite of my threats, there was no way I was doing this without him.

Two days later, I touched down in Detroit, where Paul was waiting for me at the rental-car desk. As he embraced me, he said, "Sweet, sweet Libs. Have you slept since we last spoke?"

"I wouldn't be so quick to judge, chunks," I said, attempting—and failing—to find extra flesh on his side to pinch. "What are you up to now, seven percent body fat?"

He took my suitcase from me. "Don't try to change the subject."

"All I've been doing is sleeping," I said, thinking of the twelve hours I logged the night before. "It's like I'm falling into a coma at an incredibly slow speed."

"And what does your doctor say about that?" he asked as we walked through a set of automatic doors to the parking lot where our car was waiting.

I shrugged.

Paul stopped in the middle of the walkway connecting the airport to the parking lot and stared at me.

"Move before you get run over," I said as a small red car sped at us.

Still staring, he didn't budge. "You're really starting to freak me out. Don't you think exhaustion is something to talk to the doctor about, given the circumstances?"

The red car honked at us, long and loud. Paul glared at its driver before moving. "It's getting ridiculous," he huffed as he pulled our bags behind him. "I'm basically waiting for you to tell me that you've tapped into *The Secret* and aren't doing chemo because you plan to manifest your own good health from the goodness of the universe."

"That would require far more optimism than I have at my disposal right now, Paulypoo," I said, calling him the nickname I used to piss him off when we were kids.

"Just know that Paulypoo is not above having you committed, dear sis," he said without so much as a hint of humor.

We checked into a generic hotel in a beige suburb not far from the airport. Paul only reserved one room because, as he told me, "I knew you wouldn't want to be alone," which was accurate. After settling in and freshening up, we drove into Detroit to a barbecue place Paul's coworker had recommended.

The food was good, I guess; I didn't much feel like eating.

Rather than continuing to prod me about my health, Paul found a fresh wound to poke at.

"You haven't spoken to Shiloh once since you got back to the mainland, have you?"

"And what makes you say that?"

He extended his hand. "Hi, I'm your twin brother. Have we met?"

I didn't shake it. "Perhaps we should dine in silence. You can scan my mind while I try to remember that deep in that dark heart of yours, you really do love me."

"I'm surprised you fell so hard," he said, ignoring my snark. "I really thought it was just a fling."

"It *was* just a fling," I said. Then I added morosely, "Unfortunately, I love him."

"I know you do, you hopeless sap. I've gotta give it to you: I was almost convinced you would stay in Puerto Rico for him. He's a nice guy, but I'm glad you didn't."

"Yeah." I reached for the star around my neck.

"Ooh, shiny!" Paul said, noticing the necklace for the first time. "From him?"

"Yeah."

He smiled wistfully. "It doesn't have to be over, you know."

"I know," I said, though in truth, I knew no such thing.

Paul got up and moved his chair to the side of the table closest to me, then put a hand on my back. "It doesn't have to be over," he repeated. "Treatment won't last forever."

"It's meant to be over. We barely know each other, and I have to focus on getting better."

He squeezed my shoulder lightly. "That's the Libby I know and love. Are you feeling better about Tom?"

"Tom who?"

"I take it you still haven't told him."

"Never will."

"I'm not going to tell you what to do, but he'll find out at some point. You might want to be the one to deliver the message."

I pointed my fork at him. "I've delivered all of the messages I have for Tom."

"You don't feel bad for him? Just a little?"

As I moved the chicken on my plate around in small circles, I thought of an evening earlier in the year, probably no more than a few weeks before I first discovered the lump in my stomach. I'd taken a long shower, slathered my limbs with lotion, and draped myself in a short silk robe. I went to our bedroom, where Tom was lying on the bed. A book was propped on his stomach and he was staring blankly at the wall opposite the bed. He didn't see me at first, so I stood in the doorway, admiring the perfect slope of his nose, the flat plane of his torso, and the way his long lashes stood out in the lamplight. *How incredibly lucky I am,* I thought. As familiar as my husband was, the very sight of him still made my skin prickle with pleasure. And I told myself, as I had so many other times, that God had given me him to right the loss of my mother.

On this particular evening, I'd crawled next to him and curled up in the crook of his arm. I ran my foot up and down his leg. As I was about to reach into his boxer shorts, he kissed the top of my head. "Love you, Libby," he said. Then he picked up his book and began to read again.

Yet again, I used my optimism eraser to rub out all signs of doubt that night. I shouldn't be offended. So he wasn't in the mood at that particular moment. So what? He was a great husband, and when we did have sex, it was pretty good. I couldn't expect perfection, now could I?

"No, I don't feel bad for him," I told Paul. "Frankly, I wish that it had been him diagnosed with cancer. I wish he'd died." My voice was rising, and I knew the people next to us were trying not to stare; they probably assumed Paul and I were a couple quarreling. So be it. "Then I could have gone on believing that I had been loved fully and completely. Now I know that he wasn't capable of loving me all the way, not in the way that I needed." I sucked in my breath sharply.

Paul looked at me tenderly. "You're right. You shouldn't feel bad for him."

"Thank you," I said quietly. "Maybe one day I'll get over him. I'd certainly like to. Right now I just wish he'd sign the fricking apartment papers."

"Oh, he will," he said, then took a sip of his wine. "If I have to hire a henchman to hold the pen in his hand and scribble his signature, he'll sign it."

"I like that you didn't volunteer to do the dirty work yourself."

Paul smiled. "It appears your violent streak is genetic."

We paid the bill and returned to the hotel. While Paul called Charlie and the boys, I took out my contacts, scrubbed my face, and split Tom's last sleeping pill in two, half of which I gave to Paul after he hung up the phone.

He popped the pill in his mouth and swallowed it without water. "Tomorrow," he said.

The stiff mattress groaned beneath my weight as I climbed into my bed. "Tomorrow," I repeated, and pulled a pillow over my head.

Of course we'd chosen the coldest day in November to visit the cemetery. I woke shivering, and a hot shower, a cup of coffee, and the thick sweater I put on made not a lick of difference. When we got in the car, I turned the heat on high and pointed the hot-air vents at my body.

"Don't bother. It's your nerves," Paul said from beside me. "I shake like a wet chihuahua when I have to give bad news to a major client."

"You, nervous? I don't believe it."

"Sock it away, because you won't hear me admit it again."

"I'm not nervous. Just . . ."

"Apprehensive," Paul supplied.

"That," I said. That and so many other confusing, unnameable emotions. My teeth were still clanking against one another like cheap china when we pulled into the cemetery. The iron gate and small sign had not changed, nor had the evergreens circling the perimeter. Yet, as I got out of the car, the field of graves before us appeared so much smaller than when I'd last visited.

Paul reached for my hand, and together we walked down the winding path through the center of the cemetery. I'd always thought of cemeteries as eerie, but on that morning I saw what some part of me already knew when I made my father drive out to my mother's grave so many times: they were a place of comfort, too. I wasn't sure why I'd been so set on ending up in an urn, but as we walked through the graveyard that day, I decided I would request that whatever was left of me be buried. Maybe even near my mother.

My breath caught as we came upon her grave site. Paul released my hand and knelt before the headstone, running his fingers over the etching in the granite.

I let him be alone for a few minutes, then walked over and sat next to him, cross-legged on the frozen grass in front of the large stone. I closed my eyes and began to speak to my mother in my mind—more like a prayer than an actual conversation, knowing that if she was listening, she would piece together the fragmented bits. I told her everything: about Tom, about Vieques and Milagros and Shiloh, and about my diagnosis. I told her I loved her and wished she were there. Then I opened my eyes and looked at the headstone again.

*Charlotte Ross—1954–1989—Beloved Wife and Mother*

Beloved wife and mother: true, yet wretchedly insufficient.

Sometimes, when I was feeling especially blue, I would imagine what it would have been like if I'd been a different age when my mother died. At ten, I was old enough to understand the terrible thing that had happened to us, but too young to have soaked up so many of the details that I, as an adult, longed to know about her and her life. Now the little I did remember was fading with time. My mother's hair, for example, was straight and chestnut brown, her eyes the same dark hazel as Paul's. But what about her laugh? Was it the jingle of loose change I heard in my head, or was that something I'd imagined? Was she as fun loving and unfailingly kind as I recalled, or was that a fairy tale of my own creation? What had she thought of Paul and me? What did she dream for our futures—and her own? I would never know.

I would never know.

As that reality again set in, I put my head to the ground and cried for my family and all that we had lost. Beside me, Paul saw my shoulders shaking, took me in his arms, and cried with me, reminding me again that I was not alone.

That evening, I stared at the drab landscape print hung in our hotel room, thinking about Shiloh. I wanted to call him, to tell him about my day, but I worried that one call would lead to a cascade of correspondence that would make me question whether I should have asked him to come with me to Chicago, or if I should have stayed there and tried to get treatment in Puerto Rico, or—or, or, or. So many possibilities, and not a single one was right. I switched off the lamp and pulled the covers up to my neck.

Paul was sitting on the other bed, his face lit by the glow of his laptop. "I should have saved the last sleeping pill," I told him. "Do you have any?"

"Nope."

"Don't they give you downers with your uppers?"

He finished typing, then turned to me. "I'm off the junk."

"Really?"

"Yep. I haven't touched a stimulant since a few months before the boys were born."

"Hard to believe your energy owes nothing to a pharmacy."

"Can't argue with my God-given gifts." He shut his laptop, switched off the lamp, and got in bed with me. "Will it help if I lie here?"

I closed my eyes. "Yeah. Thanks."

"Libs?" he said after a few minutes. "Remember when we were little?"

I opened my eyes, even though the hotel's blackout shades had obscured all light, save the red digits of the alarm clock. "You mean how you used to trick me into doing things?" I said. "Like allowing you to lower me out of a second-story window using nothing but a sheet and your nonexistent manpower?"

We both laughed as we recalled how shocked my father had been to answer the front door and discover me standing there barefoot in the middle of a February snowstorm, clutching the bruised arm I'd landed on. "As I was *going* to say," Paul said, kicking me under the covers, "remember how you hated sleeping alone, so I convinced Dad to get me bunk beds? I think you were sixteen before you slept in your own room again."

I grunted. "I was fourteen."

"Sure you were. Hey, Libs?"

"Yeah?"

He paused. "I should have told you this in Vieques, but Mom said the same thing to me that she said to you. She asked me to take care of you."

I blinked. "Really?"

"Yes. Right around the same time, too."

"Do you think she knew she was going to die?"

"Yes."

"Think she was afraid to leave us?"

"Since I can't think of anything worse than leaving Toby and Max, I have to believe she was terrified. She knew we had each other, though." He flipped onto his stomach. After a minute, he added, "I hope she knew we would be okay."

I did, too. But as I lay next to my brother, it occurred to me that even more than that, I wished that my mother, like so many stars in the sky, were still in transit. That some part of her, somewhere, was able to see that Paul and I were still here, making our way.

# THIRTY-TWO

Paul and I had stopped to get coffee on our way to the airport when Jess called. "Tom won't do it, Libby," she said, all panicky. "I tried everything. Michael even found him a cheap sublet so he would feel like he had a place to call his own. But he refuses." She sucked in, then exhaled loudly; she was probably smoking on her back porch. "Let me tell him about you being sick. I won't even say 'cancer'; I swear."

"Not a chance, Jess," I said, recalling Tom's concern over the cancer center's calls; he would figure it out immediately. "I really appreciate you trying for me, but this isn't yours to fix. I'll figure something out. Just, please—do not tell Tom. Don't even *hint* that anything is wrong with me."

I hung up and turned to Paul, who was still watching me from his seat near the window. "Sorry, *hermano*," I said with a grimace. "Looks like I'm heading back to Chicago today."

"If this is about the apartment, I will buy the damn thing from you, okay?"

"Wow, baller. Who knew you had that kind of cash?"

He flicked a coffee stirrer at me. It hit my chest and bounced back onto the table. "Who knew *you* had the kind of cash to change your plane ticket at the last minute yet again? Seriously, Libs. I don't work this hard just to stick change in the bank. I'll get you your own little hamlet in the Jersey 'burbs if you don't want to be in Manhattan. Just come with me, okay? Toby and Max are itching to see you. Come home with me."

"I will. I promise," I said in what I hoped was my most convincing tone of voice. "I have to do one thing first."

"Blah blah blah," Paul said, opening and closing his hand like a puppet. "All I hear is one excuse after another. I understand going to see Mom, but anything else that needs to be done can wait until after the doctor."

I shrugged apologetically. "You and I are going to have to agree to disagree on that one."

"Guess so," he said, standing up. He grabbed his coffee. "Let's go. One of us has a plane to catch."

Shiloh called while I was waiting to board yet another flight to Chicago. Which meant Paul had contacted him. But Shiloh's voice lacked the anger Paul's still contained when he said good-bye to me at the gate a few hours earlier. "Hey, you," he said softly. "How are you?"

"Hey, yourself," I said, feeling as if I were going to cry. "Okay, I guess."

"Really?"

"Sure." I was leaning against a column near a terminal, and people were rushing past me to the various flights that would let them get on with their various lives. Not a single person gave me a second glance. "I went to visit my mom's grave."

"I heard that. How did it go?"

"Okay, I guess. It was hard to be there. But I'm glad I did it."

A bird twittered in the background, and I wondered whether Shiloh was sitting on his balcony, or maybe even on the beach. "Why haven't you been to see the doctor yet, Libby?" he asked. "You promised you would go."

"I was going to. Really, I was. But then I got to the train stop and . . . I don't know. I just couldn't make myself get off the train."

"Libby."

"Shiloh," I deadpanned.

"Libby," he said again, "I'm being serious. If you'd taken someone with you, that wouldn't have happened. You would have gone to the doctor's office and learned more about your options, and signed up for testing and treatment. Quit trying to go this alone."

"You did," I protested. "Carla left you before you were even done with treatment."

"Yeah, she did. But my mom and sister were there to support me."

I almost said, "How lovely for you." Instead, I said, "Having my mom help me isn't an option."

"That's a sucky reality, Libby, and you know I feel terrible about it," he said. "But you have Paul, and his partner, and your nephews. You have your dad, who would probably jump at the opportunity to be a bigger part of your life. Your friend Jess? She'd be there for you in a heartbeat. You know that. And you have me."

A lump formed in my throat. When he put it like that, I had to admit how stupid I was, trying to be a cowgirl about the whole thing.

"You owe it to yourself to at least make an effort," Shiloh said. "And if you can't do it for yourself, do it for your mom. You know it's what she would have wanted."

*Don't go it alone*, I told myself as I marched down West Wacker, the wind whipping at my face and making my eyes tear. I tucked my head closer to my body and pressed on another block, until I came upon the building where I had once spent more time than my own home.

"You'll need to sign in, ma'am," said the security guard as I walked up to the reception desk. She did a double take. "Libby, is that you?"

"Hey, Georgie," I said, smiling at the woman who had greeted me most mornings for the better part of a decade.

"Girl, I barely recognized you! Tell me those are not jeans," she said, giving my legs a long, skeptical look.

Now I laughed. "No need to dress up when I'm not punching a clock these days. I am here to see Jackie, though. Did she come in this morning?"

"Like a hurricane," Georgie snorted. "You sure you want to see that bag of angry on a day like today?"

"No, but I need to."

"Want me to call up for you?"

I shook my head. "I'll explain it to her assistant when I get up there."

"Oh, my. If you think Jackie has an assistant, you've lost your damn mind. She's been through at least four, not a one lasting more than a few days." Georgie looked at me questioningly. "You here to try to get your job back?"

"Not quite."

She put her hand on her forehead. "Praise the Lord. I miss seeing your mug, Libby, but you don't need that in your life."

The click-clack of a keyboard was audible from the other side of Jackie's door, but when I knocked, she didn't answer. I knocked again; still no response. So I let myself in. "I'm in the middle of something," she yelled without turning her head away from her oversize computer monitor.

"Jackie?" I said quietly.

"I'm in—" She stopped abruptly. "Libby, is that your sorry ass? If you're here to ask for your job back, you're out of luck. At best, I'll hire you back as a low-level secretary, but there's no way in hell you're getting your title back after the mess you left behind."

"I don't need a job," I said. "Well, maybe I do, but not right now. I'm sick, Jackie."

"In the head!" she barked. "Why else would you leave a ridiculously high-paying job you were completely underqualified for? And don't tell me you got a better offer, because a hobo wouldn't work with you looking like that."

I looked down. My black down jacket did make me look a bit like a charred marshmallow, and my wrinkled jeans were only half covered by the leather boots Jess had coaxed me to buy. It was entirely possible that after battling the lake-effect snow, my makeup was now sliding down my face. "You don't like my makeover?" I said, tilting my head. "I thought it was a lot cuter than the chains and shackles you had me wearing every day."

"Good God, woman! It's like your personality got a makeover. What happened to the not-so-little woman I hired, who couldn't even say boo to the sandwich delivery guy?"

"Focus, Jackie," I said. "I'm here because I need health insurance, and I need it yesterday."

"You're pregnant!" she said, her voice dripping with accusation. Jackie was childless by choice, and because I had never shared my fertility struggles with her, she assumed I was as well. Other than my unflagging competence, it was perhaps the only thing she'd ever liked about me.

I crossed my arms. "No, sadly, I am not pregnant. I have this unfortunate chronic condition called cancer. Perhaps you've heard of it?"

"Right, and a Ugandan prince is waiting to sweep me off my feet after I wire you each twenty thousand dollars."

"Jackie."

She stood up and walked around the desk to where I was standing. Then she slowly looked me up and down, and apparently decided I wasn't trying to run a scam on her. "Christ, that was not the news I needed today. Is that why you flipped out on me?"

"I flipped out on you because I asked you for a tiny bit of time off, and you flipped out on *me*," I said. "Now, stay on point. I didn't sign up for COBRA on time, and the other insurance policies I've looked into have deductibles that, frankly, I'd have to sell a kidney to afford. For all I know, my kidneys are cancer corroded, too, so that's probably not even an option."

"So what do you want me to do about it?"

"I don't want you to do anything. I *need* you to tell HR that there was an error in the date of my termination so I can still sign up for COBRA coverage. I need to be officially working for you five days longer than I actually was," I said.

She stared at me for a minute. "Okay."

"Okay?"

"Did I stutter?"

"No, it's just—" It was just that I hadn't expected that response, at least not right away. "Thank you."

"Despite what you may think, I'm not a bad person, Libby. I know you put in a lot of good years for me. You shouldn't have quit like you did, but I'm not going to let you rot of cancer."

"Thanks . . . I think."

"You're welcome." She uncrossed her arms and went back to her desk. "I'll e-mail human resources now, before I forget." She peered over her monitors. "Please wipe that worried look off your face. If anyone can beat cancer, it's you."

Normally this sentiment would have sent me into an internal rage, but I felt I should take it as Jackie had intended it. "I hope you're right."

Her eyes narrowed. "Repeat after me, Libby: 'I plan to.'"

I didn't like where this conversation was heading. "If you think I can *will* my way into beating cancer—"

"Let me finish, you deaf dairy queen. Do you think I, as a not particularly attractive woman in a male-dominated field, managed to make it to the top of a publicly traded company by *hoping* I was right?" She preempted my response. "No! No, I did not! I operated as though I would succeed; obstacles be damned. There's always a reason why things might not work out. Millions of them. The more you focus on those reasons, the easier it will be to get in your own damn way. So do yourself a favor, mm-kay? Put your rose-colored glasses back on, and leave them on. Because while I applaud your newfound attitude, you're going to need a lot more than that to get you through whatever's coming your way next."

I was almost too stunned to speak. "Thanks, Jackie."

She waved me away. "Go on. I've got work to do, and from the sound of it, you've got stacks of paperwork to file."

"Right. Well, thanks again," I said, and turned to walk away.

"Door's open if you ever want to come back to work for the best boss you'll ever have," she called after me.

I stopped and looked over my shoulder. To my surprise, Jackie was smiling. I smiled back. "See you around, Jackie."

# THIRTY-THREE

Sleeping pills were no longer of interest to me. I needed some of Paul's old uppers and an IV drip of coffee, as the only thing my body seemed capable of was rest. As such, I almost slept through the apartment closing.

"Didn't you get my message?" Raj said as I dashed through the front door of the office where I had been instructed to meet him.

"Message? What message?" I wiped what was either saliva or melting snow from the corner of my mouth, then hiked up my pants, which were threatening to reveal the set of pancakes my butt had become.

He looked at me with concern. "Don't worry about it. You're here now. Though I should probably tell you—"

"Tom's here," I said as the door in front of me swung open, offering a glimpse of my husband sitting at a long wooden table. A rush of emotion came over me, but it wasn't exactly anger. Thankfully, it wasn't affection, either. It was more like . . . disappointment. I would not be able to avoid seeing him again, after all.

". . . Tom's here," Raj said. He clasped his hands together. "I trust this won't change your intentions about today's sale."

I ignored Raj and charged into the conference room. "Jeebus, Tom," I said, like God wouldn't notice his only begotten son's name if I fudged a few letters. "All that hollering and you show up anyway? I could have been sleeping right now." I narrowed my eyes at him, as another distinct possibility surfaced in my mind. "Please don't tell me you showed up so you could try to block the sale."

Not waiting for his response, I turned and extended my hand to the petite woman sitting a few seats down from Tom, who was watching me with interest. "Hi, I'm Libby Ross Miller. Don't worry; I still plan to sell my apartment to you, even if it requires hurting my soon-to-be ex-husband in order to do so."

The woman laughed nervously and slowly offered me her hand. "Great."

Tom cleared his throat. "Libby, I'm not here to block the sale."

"So what then, Tom? You thought it would be fun to remind me you still exist?" I plopped into the chair that was directly across from where he was sitting. "I almost managed to forget, but it's nothing a little electric shock therapy can't fix." *Or chemo,* I thought, recalling how at the end of her life, my mother had struggled to remember even major details, like how old Paul and I were.

"Libs, come on," Tom said. "I thought we were doing better."

I raised my eyebrows. "Doing better would have been you agreeing to come here, rather than pulling this surprise crap."

Raj rapped his knuckles on the table. "Listen, you're both here now, so let's get this over with. I'm going to go grab the title agent and the other Realtor. I'll be right back."

As Raj rushed out the door, I stared at Tom, who stared at the table, while the woman—who now knew she was buying a home haunted by the ghosts of two people who may or may not have once loved each other—was furiously texting on her phone, probably asking her friends and family whether she should back out.

Raj returned with two polished, professional-looking women, and the three of them sat down at the table like ducks in a row. They began shuffling and passing papers, instructing us to sign here, then there, and over there, again and again until I thought my hand would fall off. The fluorescent lights gave everything a halo effect, and as I was staring at the white light around Raj's head, I began to wobble in my chair.

Before I knew what was happening, Tom was at my side. "Libby," he whispered. "Are you okay? You don't look so hot."

"Too close, Tom," I mumbled, wondering if this was a slow-motion panic attack or if I was simply going to faint again.

Tom looked up at Raj and the two other women. "Can we take five?" he asked, not waiting for them to respond. "Come on, let's get some water," he said, holding me by the arm and leading me back into the building's lobby. He sat me on a bench, then walked over to a watercooler. He returned with a Dixie cup full of water, which he handed me. "Did you eat breakfast?" I accepted the cup.

"Not really," I said. Come to think of it, I hadn't eaten dinner, either; the cancer diet had pretty much sapped my interest in any sustenance that wasn't forty proof or higher.

Tom jogged over to the receptionist and quickly returned with a granola bar, which I ate in less than a minute, washing it down with another cup of water that Tom provided.

"Feel better?" he asked, almost eagerly, after I'd finished.

"Yeah. Thanks."

"Good. I know this has been really hard on you, and I hate to see you showing up here, all . . ." His eyes washed over me. "You look frail, Libby, and so tired. Even though I know you don't want me to, I'm worried about you."

How could I not soften, when he was being so kind and attentive? But his tenderness hurt, too, because it was just one more reminder of what we'd lost.

"Yeah, you're not alone there," I told him. "But let's get through the rest of the rigmarole. Then we'll talk. All right?"

He looked so elated that I instantly regretted making the offer. "I'd love that."

Half an hour later, I was homeless. I had six hours to remove my remaining items from the apartment, though Natalie, the woman I sold the place to, agreed to let me leave the bed behind.

"I have the car. Do you want to head to the neighborhood?" Tom asked after we'd said good-bye to Raj. "We could go to De Luca or something."

I shook my head; hanging out at a place we once frequented as a couple sounded about as smart as setting up camp at a nuclear plant. "There's a diner around the corner. Why don't we just go there?"

"Sure," he said agreeably. He seemed so cheerful that I almost missed the combative Tom who had tried to stop me on the way to the airport a month ago.

The diner smelled of day-old coffee and bacon grease. I knew Tom was thinking of how the odor would permeate his pressed button-down and that he would change the minute he got home.

"So," he said nervously.

"So," I said. I looked at him—*really* looked at him for the first time that day. His skin was as unblemished and unlined as it had always been; not a hair on his head was out of place. Yet his eyes were dull, ringed with purple, and his clothes seemed to hang from his frame.

"How are you feeling?" he asked as the waitress tried to hand us menus. I waved them away, and asked for coffee, toast, and a side order of bacon for good measure. Tom ordered tea and a bagel.

"Oh, you know. Fabulous." In fact, I was deflated, like my body had sprung an oxygen leak. But my stomach wasn't hurting, and I no longer felt as though I were going to fall in a heap on the floor, which was about as good as I could hope for. "I fell in love with someone," I blurted.

Tom blinked, attempting to process what I'd just said. "What? Seriously?"

"Seriously."

"When? Was it that guy you used to work with?"

I let out a strange little laugh. "Ty? Oh, no. It's someone you've never met. His name is Shiloh. I met him in Puerto Rico."

"Wow. That's . . . that's wonderful."

"Really."

"I mean it. You deserve to be happy."

"Sounds like you've been talking to your therapist."

"O'Reilly, actually. He and Jess said it's not right. Me trying to hold on to you."

"They're not stupid."

"No, they're not. I mean it, Libby. I am sorry. Really, really sorry."

Here was where I told him it was okay. Where I asked myself, *What would Charlotte Ross do?* and promptly forgave him. Except I couldn't.

"I didn't know, Tom," I said.

"What—what do you mean?"

"When I came home that day, I was upset about something else. I had no idea about you being gay. Would you even have told me if you hadn't thought I already knew?"

He looked down at his hands. "Um. I don't know." He lifted his head and met my eye. "I hope so. That's why I went into therapy. But no, I wouldn't have told you that day. What were you going to tell me, when you came home upset?"

"It doesn't matter now," I said, fighting the urge to run out of the diner, possibly into oncoming traffic. Yet I did not want to have to speak about this with him ever again. "Were you—are you—in love with O'Reilly?" I asked.

God help me, Tom actually laughed. "*O'Reilly?* I mean, I love the guy, but no. No and no."

"Who, then?"

The waitress came back with our food. I thanked her without looking away from Tom.

"I had a few crushes here and there. But that's not what this is about. I just . . . couldn't keep lying to you. You know?"

I responded with silence.

"I'm sorry, Libby," he said. "I tried to tell you, but . . ."

I took a sip of my coffee, scorching my tongue on the too-hot liquid. I swallowed anyway. "Oh yeah? And when did you try to tell me, Tom?"

This time he didn't hesitate. "After you brought up adoption, and I said I didn't want to do it. I told you I had something else I wanted to talk to you about. And you kept saying you couldn't handle one more thing. That if I wasn't going to give you good news, you didn't want to hear it."

I gasped.

He looked at me sadly. "You honestly don't remember."

I told him I didn't remember it like *that*. But as I stood there digging small holes into my palm with my nails, it came back to me. He *had* tried to sit me down. He said there were other things we needed to sort through before trying—again—to have a child. I had become angry—belligerent even, because I thought he was trying to divert my attention from the real issue. When, really, I'd been the one doing the diverting.

I took another sip of coffee, then asked Tom if there were other times when he'd tried to tell me.

He coughed awkwardly. "I pried a little. Remember in college, I told you my friend Luke was bisexual? You told me you could never be with someone who liked men, even a little."

My face grew hot. While I didn't remember Luke, I could imagine myself saying something like that.

"I told myself I would work harder to be the man you wanted me to be," Tom said. "I read all those psychology books, and I looked for information online about, um, staying straight, and I tried to focus on studying and getting a good job. I've always been crazy about you, Libby, and I wanted to make you happy. You're the most fun, wonderful person I've ever met. It just . . ."

"Isn't enough," I said.

Tom had known me most of my life; it was little surprise he understood what I was not saying as well. "It's not your fault, Libby. It wasn't up to you to give me permission to tell you. I didn't want to hurt you, but I was lazy, too. Life was so good for us. It was so easy being half of the couple that looked like they had it all together."

"We had that in common," I admitted. In many ways, our so-called ideal marriage had been the foundation of my adult life. I would never admit this to my father, but after my mother died, our three-person family never felt whole again. What I'd seen in Tom was not just a person whom I was deeply attracted to, but also a steady man with whom I could build a new family. Even after our two-person team did not expand as I'd hoped it would, we were nonetheless a unit: Libby-and-Tom, happily married, content in our shared existence. And I had been so intent on maintaining that foundation that I was unwilling to see the cracks forming beneath my very feet.

"My therapist says that part of my need to have things seem perfect stems from having a childhood where everything was pretty much the exact opposite," said Tom.

I bit into my bacon, considering Tom's father's drunken tantrums and flying fists; his mother's disheveled appearance and nonexistent housecleaning skills, which were her own silent form of retaliation.

"I understand now why you—" I knew he was about to say "stabbed me," but he stopped short. "Why you were so upset, and why you left Chicago. Though I'm sure it's little comfort to you, I hate myself."

I sighed and met his eyes, which were full of pain. Tom's battle to forgive himself—to learn to love himself again, if he ever had at all—was going to be far more difficult than any struggle I would endure as a result of our separation. I had my own issues to work through. But as far as our relationship was concerned, I had already gone over the hill, while Tom was at the bottom, trying to figure out how to begin his climb.

"Please don't hate yourself," I said. "*I* don't hate you." It was hard to, with him sitting in front of me, reminding me that he was a real live human being whom I'd loved for so long it was hard to remember a time when that had not been the case. I wanted to tell him that we might be friends again one day. But I had a very strong feeling we wouldn't be seeing much of each other in the future. So I simply said, "Just give yourself time, and some grace, okay? It'll work out."

He dabbed at his eyes with a stiff paper napkin. Then he exhaled. "I feel like you just gave me a gift."

"You're welcome."

His plate was untouched, his teacup still full. "Are you going to be okay, Tom?" I asked.

"Shouldn't I be asking that about you?" he said, and for a moment, I wondered if he suspected the truth about me. But then he said, "What about you, Libby? The apartment's gone now, and you're not working for Jackie anymore. What will you do next?"

"I'm going to start a foundation for children who've lost a parent to cancer," I said. My lie to Ty and Shea aside, I had not truly considered this until it came tumbling out of my trap, but the moment I heard myself say it, I knew there was no going back. However long I still had to live would have to be long enough to get the charity started.

Tom smiled. "That's wonderful. That's exactly what your mother would have wanted for you."

"Yeah. It is," I said quietly. Then I stood. "Would you mind getting the bill? It's time for me to go."

"Of course," he said. "Libby?"

"Yes?"

"I'd like it if we could stay in touch."

I smiled wistfully, even as my eyes filled with tears. "I wish we could, but to tell you the truth, I'm not so sure I can handle that."

Tom was right in front of me, so close I could touch him. But it now seemed we were on opposite sides of a rapidly expanding pond. It would not be long before that pond was a lake, and the lake, an ocean, and we would never again see each other from our respective shores. I would miss him.

He nodded. "I understand. Good-bye, Libby. I love you."

I looked at him, one last time. "Good-bye, Tom."

# THIRTY-FOUR

The wind rattled the windows and howled through the cracks in the back door. I had an hour or two to kill before I was required to legally vacate the apartment, but even with a winter storm brewing, there was no point hanging around a place that was no longer my home. Besides, there was something I needed to do. I packed my suitcase, made sure the counters and floors weren't too filthy, and dropped my keys on the counter. Then I walked to Damen, where I hailed a cab.

As the driver began speeding east, I pulled my phone out of my bag and typed in a number.

"Can you hear me?" I said into the phone.

"Yes," said Shiloh.

"Good. Thank you for doing this."

"You don't have to thank me. Thank *you*."

"Let's not dog pile the gratitude, okay?"

"Aye, aye, captain. You nervous?"

I wiped the foggy window with the edge of my palm. Through the clear spot in the glass, cars whizzed past, their drivers seemingly unfazed by the fast-falling snow. "I feel not unlike my plane is about to nosedive into the ocean."

Shiloh laughed. "Deep breaths, Libby. Deep breaths. You can do this."

I breathed in deeply, which kind of hurt. Then out. And in again.

"Good," he said, like he was coaching me through Lamaze. "You're doing great. Remember, get it over with so you can move forward."

"Forward," I said.

"Forward," he repeated. "Now, did I tell you about my first day back to work?"

Shiloh jabbered on for the next ten minutes, until the cab pulled up to a covered service drive. "Well, I'm here," I told him.

"Sure you don't want me to stay on the phone a little longer?"

"No, but I promise I'll call you if I freak out. And I'll let you know as soon as I'm done, okay?"

"Cutie, I'm proud of you. I love you."

"Love you, too."

I walked through the double doors, took yet another deep breath, and marched up to the reception window. "I'm here to see Dr. Sanders," I announced.

The receptionist looked confused. "He's in clinic on the other side of the building."

"Do you expect him back at some point?"

"Yes, though I have no idea when. Do you have an appointment with him?"

"No, but I can wait." I leaned through the window toward her. "I'm Libby Miller. The patient who wasn't going to get treatment. I missed my appointment with Dr. Sanders last week."

Her mouth morphed into a soft *O*. "I see. Let me page him. Please have a seat."

A long, stale hour passed. People came in and out of the waiting room, presumably to see other doctors in Dr. Sanders's practice. I tried not to look at them too closely, knowing I would inevitably attempt to tea-leaf my own health based on their appearances, even though it was statistically improbable that a single one of them had the same type of cancer I did, if they even had cancer at all. I struggled to stay awake as another hour went by. But I was determined to wait it out, mostly because there was no guarantee I'd be able to convince myself to return.

I was nodding off when I felt someone sit beside me on the sofa where I'd been stationed. I looked over sleepily, and there was Dr. Sanders, dressed in pale blue scrubs. I sat up quickly and he smiled, then clasped my hands in his own. I resisted the urge to yank them back.

"I can't tell you how happy I am to see you here," he said, leaning in so close that I could see the broken capillaries swimming up and down the side of his nose.

"Try me," I said.

He laughed. "Will you come with me?"

I agreed, though my bravado had been replaced by the sensation that I had showed up to my own surprise party after it was over. When we reached his office, he motioned for me to sit in the same chair where he'd barely managed to deliver bad news the first time around. This time he didn't go behind his desk. Instead he pulled another armchair across from me, just below a section of wall decorated with scripted diplomas, and sat down. Crossing one long leg over another, he regarded me for a moment. "Well, Libby, you're the first patient who has ever disappeared on me, but my colleagues say it's not unheard-of."

I stared at him.

"No one wants to hear they have cancer. There is absolutely no way to prepare for it. And in your case . . ." He shifted. "Let me put it this way. I lost my father to lung cancer when I was eighteen, after watching him fight with it for nearly five years. Those were years he should have been going to baseball games with me, helping me choose a college. But he was either in the hospital or wasting away in his recliner, smoking and watching TV and waiting to die. I remember you saying that you lost your own mother to cancer. I know the trauma of watching a parent succumb to a terrible disease. I assume that is why you didn't want to continue your medical care."

"Sort of," I said. "And I'm sorry. About your father, I mean."

He folded his hands together. "Thank you. I'm sorry for your loss as well. It doesn't have to be like that for you, though. Do you understand what I'm saying?"

"Not really," I confessed.

"We've come a long way since my father was in treatment, and since your mother was, too. I'm not promising you that you can be cured, but you *can* fight this. And you should. Can you agree to take it one day at a time? We need to find out whether the cancer has spread, and if so, how far. Then we can tailor a treatment plan to your needs. As you know, this form of cancer is rare, but as I mentioned before, I've been researching your options, and you may be eligible for a clinical trial. I'd love for us to begin this process right away so you have the best possible chance of getting better."

"So . . . here's the thing," I said. "I'm not planning to stay in Chicago. In fact, as of today, I no longer even have a home."

"Is this a financial issue? Our social work department can help you navigate insurance and assist you with housing issues."

"No, no, it's not like that. It's just that . . . I'm kind of going through a divorce, and Chicago is the last place I want to be."

"How terrible for you." He sounded sincere, and my throat caught. "Thank you."

"Of course. Do you have plans to go to a specific city?"

"My brother and his family are in Manhattan. It's not exactly my favorite place, but . . ."

He nodded. "I'd be concerned if you said you were heading to rural Kansas, but New York is a good place to seek treatment. Our cancer care center has a close relationship with Sloan Kettering. You'd be in good hands if you chose to go there, and I could help you make the transition."

"What am I up against, exactly? The last time I was here," I said, gesturing around his office, "you said six months."

Dr. Sanders was staring at the space just above my head, which did not feel like a good sign. "I shouldn't have said that."

"But it's not untrue," I said, heat rising in my chest. "Don't sugarcoat it. I was basically ready to die a while ago, so nothing you say now is going to shock me."

"As I said, this cancer is so rare . . ."

I resisted the urge to pull a move from the Paul Miller playbook and start opening and closing my hand like a puppet. Sensing my exasperation, he looked me in the eye and said, "What I am trying to say is that until you go through more thorough testing, I cannot give you a real answer. That's exactly why I never should have said that in the first place. I made a mistake, and for that, I am truly sorry." He put his hands on his knees and leaned forward. "What I can tell you, Libby, is that you're going to have to be strong. And I know you have it in you."

I stood up and adjusted the shoulder strap on my bag. "I am well aware that I'm strong enough."

"Please sit down," Dr. Sanders said.

I looked at him, then at the door. Then I sat back down on the edge of the chair. "I know I can be strong," I said, more quietly this time. "It's just that I don't want to." I had been strong before—stronger than I would ever need to be now, because truth be told, my mother's life meant far more to me than my own. And it had not changed a damn thing.

"You have a choice—"

I cut him off. "If you tell me to choose life, I will murder you in your sleep."

He held his hands up. "I was going to say something along those lines, but I'll refrain."

"Good choice."

We sat in silence: Dr. Sanders, staring in my direction; me, staring out the window at the frozen white waves lining the lakeshore.

"Okay," I said after a few minutes.

"Okay?" Dr. Sanders said with surprise. It's true that he had no reason to believe me, considering the last time I said that very thing, I followed up with a no-show.

"Yes. If you can help me get into a good hospital in New York right away, then I'm ready to do this."

He stood up. And he walked over to me and held his hand out. "I'd be happy to, Libby. Thank you."

I reached out and let him help me stand. "Thank *you*, Dr. Sanders," I said. His bedside manner was not going to win him any awards, but his persistence may have bought me a little extra time.

# THIRTY-FIVE

After leaving Dr. Sanders's office, I got into another cab, this one heading to the airport. As I stared out the window, I didn't think about treatment, or Tom, or anything concrete, really. I just kept seeing my father's face in my mind. And the longer he lingered there, the more ashamed I became. Mental break or no mental break, I should have told him weeks ago, before my silence took shape as a lie. And so, in a not-so-quiet corner of O'Hare, I finally called him.

Naturally, my father assumed my mewling (which began before he even answered the line) was on account of Tom. And then I had to correct him with three words he had undoubtedly prayed he would never have to hear again:

*I have cancer.*

Let's be honest: it was awful, and that was my fault. My father cried, and I cried some more. When we got through the worst of it, he asked questions I could not answer, and I had to explain why I couldn't answer them, which made me feel not unlike someone who had run over a basket of puppies.

"What can I do to help you through this, Libby Lou?" he asked, and even though I'd just calmed down, a strangled sound escaped my mouth. I thought of my father wiping my mother's brow with a cool washcloth as she lay lifelessly in bed. He had already been through enough, which is what I told him.

"Nonsense," he said. "It's not your job to shield me. Being your father means seeing you through this and anything else you need help with. That is the single most important thing to me in this world. Let me at least do that for you."

"I'm sorry," I said, for what was probably the thirteenth time.

"The only thing you should be sorry about is apologizing again."

"So I probably shouldn't apologize for that."

"Don't even think about it." He laughed. Then I heard him sigh deeply. "So this is why you took off to Puerto Rico."

"Yeah."

I could almost see him nodding. "That does make some sense."

I sniffed. "Try explaining that to Paul."

"Well, your brother's not wrong for wanting you to get help immediately."

"I know."

"So, kiddo, tell me something good. How was the trip?"

"It was wonderful," I said without hesitation. I told him about the beach house, and Milagros, and even a little about Shiloh, minus the heady affair and brush with death parts.

"You see the horses?" he asked.

"Yes. And the phosphorescent bay. You were right—it was amazing. A once-in-a-lifetime experience." I felt a pang of regret for not snapping more than a few pictures. "Dad, how long were you and Mom there?"

He said it had been a week, maybe ten days; he couldn't recall. "I do remember one thing well. Hang on a second. I'm going to e-mail you something."

I switched modes on my phone. After a moment, an e-mail from my father popped up in my in-box. I opened it, and centimeter-by-centimeter, a scanned photo of my mother appeared on the screen.

She was standing on the beach in a yellow bathing suit, the swell of her belly outlined against the sea. Her hands were overflowing with shells and she was laughing.

"I found it while I was cleaning out some boxes in the attic a few weeks ago. I meant to send it to you last week," my father explained.

"It's incredible, Dad. Thank you. I didn't realize you and Mom went to Vieques while she was pregnant with us."

"She was maybe four or five months along, though everyone thought she was about to give birth at any moment. She was so tiny, and there were two of you in there."

"Thank you," I repeated. "I can't tell you how much the picture means to me."

"I'm glad you like it. You remind me so much of your mama, kiddo."

A lump formed in my throat. I hadn't heard anyone refer to her as "mama" in years. "It's Paul who looks like her," I said.

"True, but who do you think you get your sunny outlook from? You're just like her that way."

I shook my head, thinking of how similar Paul and I had been for the first decade of our lives. It was only after our mother got sick that he'd become so cynical, and I'd begun denying the existence of any and all bad things. "I wasn't really like that until everything happened," I said.

"Not true, kiddo. Not true at all. That's how you came out of the womb. Paul was colicky, but you? You just lay there cooing. We used to joke that you were singing to Paul to calm him down."

"So I didn't . . ." I wasn't sure how to say it. "I didn't get all weird and chipper because of Mom's cancer?"

"Oh, gosh, no. Not at all. Do you not remember much of your childhood before that? I suppose that's normal. That grief counselor I used to see once told me that many of your memories would be formed around that one awful year. But there was—" My father blew his nose into a tissue and continued. "There is so much more to our family. We had great times together. And you and your mom staying positive throughout the not-great times was one of the few things that kept me going. I just don't think I could have handled it if she hadn't believed, deep down, that everything was going to be okay."

"But she died," I said softly.

"Yes, she did. You know what they say: no one makes it out of life alive. But she was still right."

"I don't understand."

"Libby, you and Paul are happy, functioning people who have lived, and loved, and made the world a little bit better by being in it. That was your mama's exact definition of *okay*."

I could feel the sobs coming on. "Thanks, Dad. I needed to hear that."

"You're so welcome, Libby Lou. I love you."

Afterward, I went to the bathroom and cried in a stall for a while, then splashed my face with cold water. I was turning from the sink when I almost ran into a girl—she couldn't have been more than eight or nine—who was attempting to walk while reading a well-worn copy of *Little House in the Big Woods*. She looked up at me and scowled, but I smiled down at her anyway, because my mother had loved that book. I hadn't adored it the way she did, but I never told her that, because I was happy just to sit with her and take turns reading aloud. In fact, there was little I now recalled about *Little House*, save the main character, Laura, and her family, and the occasional cameo from a bear or panther in their woods.

But as I returned to my gate, I realized there *was* something I could remember. At the very end of the book, Laura tells herself, *This is now,* and feels happy because the *now* could not be forgotten as it was happening. "Isn't that wonderful?" my mother said to me after she finished reading it. Her arm was around me, and she squeezed me tight. "This is now, Libby Lou. And it's all ours."

It was a night like any other, except the flood of bad memories from the following years had not washed it away. And though it was no longer *now*, it was still ours.

People were crowding around the boarding area, jostling one another to speak with the gate agent or get in line. I was less than eager to sandwich myself between them and take another flight. Especially *this* flight, which would herald an unknown and undoubtedly difficult period.

Yet as I stood and began slowly wheeling my suitcase to the gate, I had a deep, restful feeling of relief—a feeling I had not had since long before the double dose of news that started it all. My conversation with my father had not been an epiphany so much as a reframing. Life is devastating, if only in its limited run; but it's incredibly good, too. And in spite of my circumstances, I could not deny that I was ready for more.

"New York LaGuardia, now boarding zone one," said a voice over the loudspeaker.

I took a deep breath and got on the plane.

# EPILOGUE

Something Shiloh taught me is that to see the night sky clearly, you can't overfocus; it's the stars outside of your direct vision that come in brightest. So it goes with life's triumphs and troubles. Though it would be several months after my departure that I could fully recognize this, my stay in Vieques gave me the distance to see my situation for what it was. And even with illness and separation, what it was, was incredibly good, simply by virtue of its existence.

I wasn't eligible for a clinical trial after all, but as my new oncologist, Dr. Kapur, explained, this was because though the cancer had spread in my abdomen, it had not metastasized to other areas, rendering my case blessedly straightforward. I began a chemo cocktail that could be taken at home: pills that had me in the bathroom for hours while my stomach tried to secede from my body; and a topical cream that caused my skin to blister, making my Puerto Rican sunburns seem like spa treatments. But because the medication was administered in cycles, with recovery breaks, there were calm weeks when I wasn't weak or nauseous, and I could almost forget that longevity and I were on tenuous terms.

Paul and Charlie had generously converted the garden floor of their brownstone into an apartment for me. Despite their hospitality,

I found the city in winter to be overwhelming. Even a simple trip to the deli or post office required battling the elements, say nothing of the foot traffic. I preferred to stare out the high egress windows of my safe, warm nook, watching people stream up and down Eighty-Eighth Street at all hours of the day.

Yet, just as I had settled into a routine in Vieques, I began to adapt to New York, and as the cold gave way to temperate air and budding leaves, my days took on a comfortable rhythm. When I didn't have a doctor's appointment, I would read the paper, then walk in Central Park before heading home for lunch and a nap. Afternoons were often spent with Toby and Max. The three of us would make cookies and read books, or if I was up for it, go on outings (which required the twins to help me navigate the streets and subways like the urban experts they already were). A few times a week I spoke with Shiloh, sometimes for a few minutes, other times for hours on end. On occasion we discussed the possibility of him visiting me in New York. Yet with my health status up in the air and with him happily flying again, I was hesitant to make concrete plans.

I was lonely at times, but not alone. I would often be doing something benign—say, standing at the stove, watching the boys while I stirred a pot of chili or pushed chicken about in a pan—and find myself overcome with pure gratitude.

And there was much to be grateful for. The tumor, which was really a Pollock-esque splattering of cells beneath my navel, began to shrink. To celebrate, Paul—who had not said as much, but had clearly scaled back significantly at work since I'd moved in with him—took a day off and went to the zoo with me and the twins. It was chilly for late April, and as we walked back to the house, I tucked my head down to minimize the wind's sting. As such, when I reached the brownstone, the first thing I saw were a pair of feet on the bottom stair. Actual feet! What kind of nutter wore sandals in such weather?

"Cutie," said a voice, and when I realized that the voice belonged to the man I loved, I squealed, then kissed him like a crazy person.

"I know this was unexpected," Shiloh said when I'd finished mauling him.

"You have no idea how happy I am to see you," I said. "Never leave me again."

"Technically, you left—" he began, but I kissed him again before he had a chance to finish.

Five months later we were married on the beach in San Juan. It was a mild September evening, and the Caribbean was calm and blue. Milagros came in from Vieques for the ceremony, and our families flew in, as did Jess and O'Reilly. Tom was not invited, but he sent his blessing, and even better, a case of champagne.

Shiloh wore a pale linen suit, a yellow shirt, and an enormous grin. I wore a wreath of orchids in my hair, which had thinned but not fallen out, and had somehow straightened, too, fulfilling one of my lifelong wishes. I decided against ivory—who were we kidding?—and opted for a flowing yellow dress that Jess helped me choose. She claimed the dress was the wardrobe challenge of the century because whatever we chose had to be flattering while still accommodating my bloated abdomen.

Yes, two months after Shiloh moved into the garden apartment with me, one of the battery of tests I regularly took revealed a set of suspicious, rapidly proliferating masses. The good news was, they would only grow for a set period of time before expelling themselves. It turned out that I wasn't infertile, after all, and Shiloh had gifted me with twin girls.

Dr. Kapur and his team fretted over the pregnancy. The babies could potentially be harmed from lingering chemo in my system, and I would have to discontinue treatment until after I gave birth.

Happily, the initial chemo had been successful enough that I showed no significant change in tumor activity during my pregnancy.

Shiloh and I hoped to eventually return to Puerto Rico, but in the meantime, he found a good job at a small regional airport in New Jersey. His commute and shifts were long, and I was all but immobile by the second half of my pregnancy, but I used the downtime to establish the Charlotte C. Ross Foundation. Our first donor: one Lily Broderick-Oshira, whose mother had been gracious enough to mentor me during the first few months of the foundation's existence.

On an unseasonably warm day in early February, a little over a year after I left Vieques, I brought two new lives into the world: Isabel Milagros, who emerged with fair skin and a full head of light curls; and Charlotte Patrícia, who has Shiloh's caramel skin, and is otherwise the spitting image of Paul as a baby. Both girls are healthy, preternaturally calm, and a source of joy that I can never adequately put into words.

I am again undergoing chemo, and though I have not kicked cancer's proverbial ass, and may be miles and a dream from remission, I believe in my heart that I will live long enough to help my daughters find their way in the world. And if I am wrong about that, well—tell it to someone else, because I don't want to know.

It's often said that cancer forever changes you. Maybe so. I'd like to think that it didn't change me so much as give me clarity about the woman I am, and my role in this mess of a world. After my diagnosis, I vowed to do something meaningful, and the foundation certainly fit the bill.

Yet I've come to understand that the way I will truly honor my mother's memory is not with a big act, but through my daily choices: to be compassionate with myself, even when my will is weak and my body fails me; to give myself freely to those I love, even when it means my heart may be broken; and to live fully and completely while I have the chance—just as my mother did.

# AUTHOR'S NOTE

Cancer has directly impacted so many of my loved ones, friends, and colleagues. Because of this, I did not take writing a novel about cancer lightly and deliberately chose to give my protagonist, Libby, a very rare form of the disease. Although I consulted medical literature and physicians about subcutaneous panniculitis-like T-cell lymphoma, Libby's experience is still very much a fictionalized account, and should not be used for reference purposes.

# ACKNOWLEDGMENTS

A million thanks to my intrepid agent, Elisabeth Weed, for believing in me and championing this novel.

Danielle Marshall and the team at Amazon, thank you for your enthusiasm and support; it has been a breath of fresh air working with you. Tiffany Yates Martin, this story owes so much to you. Thank you for your wise and witty editorial guidance.

My endless gratitude to Shannon Callahan for reading many early versions of *Life*, and for cheering me on every step of the way. Likewise, Sara Reistad-Long, Pam Sullivan, Janette Sunadhar, and Darci Swisher, your support means the world to me.

Thank you, Lizarribar, Masini, and Pagán families, for sharing your Puerto Rico with me.

JP, Indira, and Xavier Pagán, you give me a reason to write.

And to my sister Laurel Lambert: I love you the most—but don't feel bad, because I couldn't have written this novel without you.

# ABOUT THE AUTHOR

*Photo © Joni Strickfaden 2015*

Camille Pagán's work has appeared in dozens of publications and websites, including *Forbes*, *Glamour*, *Men's Health*, *Parade*, *O: The Oprah Magazine*, *Real Simple*, WebMD, and *Women's Health*. She lives in the Midwest with her husband and two children.